RISE
OF
ANCIENTS

RISE

OF
ANCIENTS

ALLEN REBOT

atmosphere press

This book would not have been possible without the following people:

My gorgeous wife, Michelle, for your encouragement and helping me see the light, even during my darkest of times.

My loving parents, without your support and your nightmares, this may have been a completely different book.

My friends Jimmy and Eric, for being my backboard and first editors.

My editor, Shaun Duke, for your tremendous effort in helping turn this dream into a reality. I could not have asked a better person to discuss this book with over drinks.

My other friends, family, coworkers, and any other unfortunate souls that allowed me to not only talk about my ideas but continue to associate with me afterward.

Thank you all!

TABLE OF CONTENTS

A hot sun beat down on a silent, rolling countryside. Toasted-tipped grass slipped through a boy's fingers as he ran through the golden field behind a rustic cottage. A new day dawned. Bugs leapt from their places of rest to avoid the giggling giant. Stopping in an opening, he spun around and crouched to the ground. From the grass emerged a small lizard that excitedly leapt into the boy's hands without hesitation. With pure delight, he brought the small lizard up to his face. As if sensing his joy, the lizard looked up at the boy's smile and flicked its tongue.

I

DISCOVERY

"The shipment arrived last night!" Running through the lab, Melissa beamed with excitement. "We haven't seen anything like this in years. Today feels like Christmas!"

Jeremy watched as his over-energetic coworker gathered her papers. "You know we've done this before, right?" He was too tired to share in the excitement, but he still enjoyed watching Melissa. How could he not? Every movement she made was like a dance.

Bracelet charms acquired on their recent vacation jingled on her wrist as she moved gracefully about the room. Her light brown hair bounced with each step. As luscious hazel eyes locked onto his, a puppy-love smile spread across Jeremy's face. He was nearly old enough to be her father, but that barely kept them off each other. He ran his fingers through his thick, silver-streaked hair and went back to his work.

"But this one is nearly as ancient as you," Melissa teased. "I can treat this like our thorough examination last night."

Jeremy could feel his heart start to race as the night replayed through his mind. His life had been mundane before Melissa. Weeks, glazed over with excruciatingly similar projects, moved along a seemingly endless lazy conveyor belt.

Even the Friday after-work ritual of ordering the same dark ale at the same bar down the street had lost its gleam. Her playfulness made him feel twenty years younger.

"Go prep the room, and I'll be right in there."

"Yes, sir." With a wink, Melissa strutted off into the next room. In the center of the room, on a lowered table surrounded by red lights and standing cameras, lay a stone sarcophagus. Her eyes slipped over the intricate etchings and painted images that adorned its sides. In the nine years that she'd worked for Regenifact, she'd never come across a relic such as this. Instead of proclaiming great deeds and blessings, this individual came with the image of Osiris; the caretakers of this individual went against tradition. Scenes of death wrapped around the stone container. Painted beneath the feet was an image of Anubis and his scales. Tipping the scales and holding a feather high was the head of a jackal. She grabbed a loose camera off a nearby table and started to take pictures of each scene on the sarcophagus.

"Any idea who this could be?" she shouted toward the door.

Jeremy looked up from his work and walked over. "No idea. Based on where this was found, he had to be someone important, though." Curious, he eyed the golden face on the sarcophagus. "The file we got with this says that it was found in a tomb discovered outside of Cairo. Everything was cleared out years ago, but scans picked up a second chamber behind the main one. After they busted the wall down, the only thing in the room was this thing here." He nodded toward the sarcophagus.

"It doesn't make sense," Melissa muttered. "Why would they put so much effort into this sarcophagus but leave so little for him to take into the afterlife? Who was this guy?" Placing down the camera, she eyed the lid. "I know we should wait for the others, but I'm itching to get this thing open now."

"We need to wait for the rest of the team to get here. Just because we opened up the lab doesn't mean we can start opening up the artifact." Jeremy chuckled and wrapped his arms around Melissa. "In a few hours, they'll get here, and we can do that. Until then, let's hold off."

She gave him an annoyed look. "Fine. But the second they're here, we're cracking open this piñata." She leaned her head back to rest against his shoulder.

Jeremy tilted her face and kissed her softly. They both smiled and looked back at the artifact before them. Enjoying the sensation of Melissa's fingers gently running along his arms, he studied the sarcophagus. This was an odd piece, but something different was bound to resurface eventually. Sifting over the etchings, he tried to make sense of the story upon the stone. The smile left his face. "Those shouldn't be there."

Confused, Melissa looked at him. "What do you mean?"

"This was found in Cairo. The only thing on this should be Egyptian art and hieroglyphics. But there's another language on here." He let go of Melissa and took a step back from the table. "It looks like ..." His pupils carved out the characters. "Greek. What the hell is Greek doing on here?" Looking back up at the golden face, he studied its features to make sure he understood what he was seeing. "The design is definitely Egyptian, but the etching that runs along the rim is ancient Greek."

Melissa walked to the next side of the table. "There are etchings here as well, but not Greek. It's Latin."

Jeremy rushed to her side. "Was this thing dragged through the ancient world before being sealed in that tomb?" He continued to circle the table. "Hebrew." Then he came to a stop at the final side. Repeatedly drawing a line by pressing and running his thumbnail along his index finger, Jeremy shook his head. "I've seen ancient writing from across the globe. I've never seen this before." He grabbed Melissa's camera off the table and snapped pictures of each side, with close-ups of each flowing character from the unidentified language. "I'll be in the library."

Melissa fought the urge to follow as Jeremy left the room. She grabbed her notebook and eyed the symbols. If her understanding of the written languages was correct, there was no way they could be one continuous message. The three languages she recognized were placed in a way that meant none of them could be read in an order based on the direction in which they were read. They had to be individual messages. She jotted down each line of characters into the notebook, tore out the page, and shoved it into her pocket.

The inscriptions could wait. The desire to open up the lid bordered on madness. She had to know what was inside. She looked around the room until her eyes locked on to a closet. Mischievously trotting up to the plain wooden door, she opened it and maliciously smiled at the occupant. Inside was a mobile lift used to move heavy objects around the building. Compared to earning her Ph.D., how much harder could operating this machine be?

Despite her light frame, the weighty-looking machine moved effortlessly across the floor on hidden wheels. Positioning the machine next to the sarcophagus, she looked about until she found a control panel. She pushed up the left-most lever, and the giant arm atop the machine whirred to life. The dangling hooks, connected by adjustable straps, loudly clinked together with every jerky movement she awkwardly enacted.

Positioning the arm over the sarcophagus, she toyed with the controls until she realized that none of them had anything to do with opening up the four fingers of the device. Physically moving the four fingers at the end of the arm and attaching the hooks to the edges of the sarcophagus, she pulled on the adjustable straps until they were tight. Satisfied with the security of the hooks, Melissa went back to manning the controls.

After what seemed like an eternity, the lid was finally off. What would have taken an entire team had been accomplished by one exceptionally brilliant girl with the use of the mechanical lift. Many a time, she'd scraped up her hands trying to get these weighty coffins open. While not much faster, the lift had saved her from the blisters and aching muscles.

With a sense of accomplishment, she abandoned the controls and turned toward the sarcophagus. The hard part was over. Now the fun could begin. She looked down into the stone box and scrunched her face in confusion. Normally, a wooden coffin would encase a mummy, but sitting snug in its stone bed was a metal box. It looked almost like it was made of stainless steel. Even so, this type of metal wasn't even possible until the last hundred years.

She put on gloves and ran her hand along the top. Marring the metal box were numerous cuts, dents, and scuffs. In contrast, the stone sarcophagus in which it sat was perfectly smooth. Feeling something odd, she stopped at the center. Curious, she lifted her hand. Spanning two inches across, this cut was longer than the others. Clicking on a flashlight, Melissa peered into it. It didn't look too deep. Whatever had cut into the box, luckily, hadn't gone through completely.

Muffled noises swept in from somewhere down the hallway. If it was Jeremy seeking more for his research, he would see what she was up to and be furious that she was risking damaging the artifact by tampering with it. Fearing repercussions and missing out on the juicy parts, Melissa did the unthinkable. Acting quickly, she ran her fingers around the edge of the lid. *Were those hinges?* Melissa thought to herself as her fingers slid over partially covered contraptions. Lacking the time to do proper research on the anomalies, she ran around to the other side of the table. She dug her fingers under the edge of the lid and lifted it up slowly.

Before she could see under the lid, something ice cold grabbed her wrist and pulled her arm into the box. She tried to scream, but a hand wrapped around her neck and cut the sound short. With nowhere to go, her screams remained trapped in her throat.

Forced up from beneath, the lid swung open and hit the stone wall of the sarcophagus with a bang, sending particles of stone into the air. Slowly, a figure rose from the sarcophagus. As its legs extended fully, it lifted her from the ground. While jerking to free her left arm, she clung to the attacker's wrist with her free hand for support. Melissa's eyes widened in terror.

Sanity-stripped eyes bore into Melissa's skull as the figure growled in a language she couldn't recognize. Cinching its brow, the figure surveyed the room while taking in quick, deep breaths. It returned its gaze back to Melissa, and she could see twin reflections of her silently struggling within them.

Releasing her left arm, mouthless snakes slithered against her right temple and into the safety of her hair. Stricken with fear, she couldn't bring herself to fight back. Like a tidal wave, visions of her life came crashing down onto the forefront of her mind. Memories most dear collided with others long forgotten; mixed among them were clear images of another life.

Approaching footsteps at the door caused the figure's hand to pull away from Melissa's skull. Barely able to breathe, Melissa struggled to utter the name of the bloodied, forsaken man—a being she had somehow known her entire life. Expelled by emotions from the visions, a single tear ran down her cheek. His mouth formed into a grim smile, and he once again locked eyes with her.

"Thank you, Melissa," he spoke in a cold, gravelly voice.

With a sickening crunch, the man crushed her throat. Pain

radiated up the back of her skull and down over her shoulders. Any thoughts she had about her new memories were flushed out by the overwhelming agony. The door to the room opened just as Melissa was released and fell to the floor.

"I was able to translate three of the—" Jeremy stopped in shock as he saw Melissa holding her throat on the floor. His eyes darted to the figure still standing in the sarcophagus. Looking down upon him was a man dressed in tattered ancient clothing, a man whose hair was black as night. Gazing into Jeremy's soul were bluish-gray eyes the color of a decaying corpse. Under the filth that covered that sickly white body, Jeremy saw fresh wounds.

Jeremy ran to Melissa and dropped to his knees beside her. Scooping her up with trembling arms, he cradled his love. Tears formed in his eyes as hers rolled back. Preoccupied with his dying light, he barely noticed the heavy thud beside him. Seemingly amused, the attacker mumbled something under his breath. Jeremy's dams burst forth, and tears streamed down his cheeks as he held Melissa's body to his. The last thing he saw was the face of his murdered love twitch before the room went black.

Jeremy regained consciousness sometime later, groaning as he turned over and sat up. His head screamed with pain. Were the events that transpired part of his imagination, or were they reality? Did a man who was trapped in a sarcophagus for centuries without food or water just stand up? It wasn't possible. Shakily, he tried to get up, using a nearby table for support. He looked around the room, but his blurry vision concealed the room in a haze. In a corner, he made out the shape of a person.

"Melissa?" Sorely, Jeremy rubbed his aching head. After what just happened, she'd surely want to go home and rest—

although the police would need to be contacted first.

The shape turned toward him. Long hair draping off its head swayed with each injured movement. After not being able to wake him, Melissa must have tried to call for help. Even with the strain she was put under, she should have said something by now.

"Melissa, are you ok?"

The shape limped in Jeremy's direction. His eyes, still adjusting, slowly brought clarity to his vision. He smiled and moved toward her, still leaning on the table. Finally, his eyes came into focus, and he noticed that Melissa's face was a sickly shade of blue. Relief turned to fear. Jeremy took a step back as Melissa reached for him, causing her charms to clink together around her wrist. He tried to run, but his body still hadn't regained its sense of balance, and he fell to the floor.

Her hands were already on him as he scrambled to get back up. She spun him around and crawled on top of him just as a spider does its paralyzed prey. Hours earlier, this would have been accompanied by her caressing touch and the sound of her moans. Now, the only sounds heard were his screams as her teeth sunk into his flesh.

Only a week before, beneath the dancing leaves of the oak tree overlooking the fields of wheat, he saw the small green lizard sitting on an exposed root. Despite the ruckus of the boy's playing, it didn't run in fear like the squawking bird that had been next to it only moments before. With a scrunched face, the boy walked over and sat down beside it.

After a moment of observation, he leaned in and whispered in his softest voice, "Hello."

The lizard gently shook itself and slowly turned toward the sound of his voice.

II

CARDBOARD WALLS

29 hours after Regenifact.

Halfway across town in a cramped office cubicle sat Matt Ontoradugh. Brushing tickling strands of unkempt onyx hair off his forehead, the groggy worker swore to himself as a small box popped up on his screen to once more mock him. He dragged his cursor until the pixelated arrow loomed over the magic button and half-heartedly clicked it to cast away last week's meeting reminder—the fourth time that day.

Five months ago, Matt was living the upper-middle-class dream. Comfortable home, hot shot job, and a gorgeous gal wearing his ring. Captain of his very own Man O' War, he was untouchable.

Without warning, disaster pierced his hull. Seemingly endless blissful years of marriage fell apart like logs lashed with cotton candy rope in the rain. Leaving only her ghost behind, his wife, Maddison, boarded another man's boat. Cloaked in decadent silk and virgin wool spun by Clotho herself, the interloping captain drowned Matt in his lavish shadow.

Matt's unanswered prayers fermented into vengeful daydreams to burn down the bastard's empire. The King might possess his tinted-glass tower of gold, but Matt had his own jewel. Frozen in time and tucked into his wallet, Maddison's heart-melting smile paid for his voyage to a better world each night.

Just a few weeks later, another domino fell. Refusing to keep mopping up the melancholy-drenched man's puddles, Matt's job escorted him from its premises. Like a depressed dragon, he began hoarding empty bottles and grew scales beneath his eyes to match.

He continued along a downward spiral, a coin in a funnel waiting for the moment the final drop would come. Then three weeks ago, Matt's dormant phone shook to life, breaking the cycle. On the other end, waving the flag of friendship, was a secretary from the office of home wrecking. Empty, oil-stained paper bags crunched beneath his feet as he stood up from the couch. This was his moment to scrape together some dignity and shove the offer right back into the man's smug face. Unfortunately, dignity was out of his budget.

Sitting atop Matt's obnoxiously fake wooden desk, wrapped in cheap aluminum foil that consistently failed to contain grease, was his breakfast. Chock-full of questionable ingredients, it barely passed as an edible burrito. Wishing he had woken up to one of his earlier alarms, he thought about the decent breakfast he could have made at home. Instead, $4.95 went down the drain for this garbage. Biting into it, he could feel the artificial meat caressing his teeth. He sent it down the hatch anyway and turned toward the office cube across from him.

Crammed into tight jeans and a stretched-out purple polo shirt sat Kevin Straus. Preferring to keep his curly brown hair cut short, the man's head resembled a ripe kiwi. An unpolished silver chain necklace hid under his shirt, only visible by a small strand poking out from above his collar. Despite saying that he had never worked out a day in his life, Kevin was built like a professional football player.

Feeling jealous and a bit angry at Kevin, Matt looked down at his own stomach. Seeing a dark grease spot from the burrito, he looked around for a napkin. "Not again," he groaned to himself. Digging through a pile of paperwork on his desk, he found a hidden napkin and used it to dab away the grease.

How could Matt stay mad at Kevin, though? His coworker was funny and always helped him out with work. Although Kevin had been here for five years, he'd never moved up despite the pleas of his love-struck supervisors.

Normally, Matt's athletic coworker was in a lively mood, but today was different. He'd never imagined the joyful giant of the office could get so tense.

Tired of sipping on a lukewarm cocktail of boredom and loneliness, Matt saw a small window of opportunity to garnish his glass. Not wanting to come off as the office slob, Matt shuffled in his chair as he attempted to tuck in his shirt. Everyone else seemed to have friends at work, so why shouldn't he? Gathering up his nerves in a single deep breath, he leaned over in his seat, causing a corner of his shirt to come untucked.

"Computer acting up again?"

Kevin sighed and shook his head. "I wish. Heard something that brought back memories. Happens every once in a while. I'll be fine after a few days."

Matt faced Kevin, wondering if the man had been through a war. Kevin was surely built like a soldier. "Something happen that you want to talk about?" A few moments passed, and Matt realized his question was going to go unanswered. He took a deep breath and sighed. "Did you hear about the most recent find in Egypt?" Now, he smirked like a politician. "People online are trying to get someone to grind up the mummy and make it into a drink."

Kevin shot a glare at Matt.

Matt raised his hands in defense. "Didn't mean to piss you off. Jeez." He turned his chair around and went back to work.

"Everything alright over here?" Walking toward them was their supervisor, Candace. Her high-heeled shoes clicked against the gray office tile.

Matt nodded. "Just saying good morning to Kevin."

Candace stopped next to Kevin's cube and leaned against it seductively. *Accidentally* pulling on her red blouse, her pink-lace bra peaked out. "There's someone here for you in the lobby. Needs you to sign off for something. Once you're back up, maybe you could show me your package for a little *hands-on* inspection?"

Kevin, unfazed by Candace's display, looked her in the eye. "Did they say which courier they were from?"

Candace chuckled. "If they did, I didn't notice. Sorry," she said in a ditzy manner.

Kevin closed his eyes and sighed. "Thanks for letting me know, Candace. I'll be right back." He stood up and, walking past Candace toward the lobby, swore under his breath. "Alone," he snarled after catching the cougar's eye. The grown woman audibly pouted.

Matt couldn't imagine how Kevin put up with her. Candace might be in her forties, but she acted like a careless sorority girl. With how openly she flirted, he was surprised that her husband hadn't filed for divorce yet.

Matt watched as Candace tailed Kevin to the end of the aisle and then turned to go back to her office. It was too early for this. Snatching the burrito off his desk, Matt raised it to his lips. Fumes from the putrid eggs and over-seasoned sausage infiltrating his nostrils locked his teeth together. Fearing the phantom taste of vomit on his tongue, Matt leaned back in his chair and chucked the burrito into the trash with a satisfying thud.

Matt could feel his stomach grumble. There was no way he could make it until his lunch break. He needed to get something edible soon. He peaked up over the thin cubicle wall.

Candace wouldn't dare make another move on Kevin for at least another hour. Who would even notice if he left for a bit? Lowering himself back into his seat, he looked at Kevin's empty chair. *Kevin could really use a distraction,* Matt thought to himself, *and it wouldn't hurt to indulge every once in a while* ... Matt suddenly had an idea. When Kevin returned a few minutes later, he stood up. "I'm heading out to a coffee shop. Care to join me?"

Kevin walked into his cube with a package roughly the size and shape of a small thermos. Placing the package into a drawer, he didn't even look up to respond. "I have a lot of work to get through."

Matt pushed farther with a smirk. "It has incredible do-nuts. Some are even filled with *bacon.*"

Kevin smiled and snapped his head toward Matt. "That's all you needed to say. Who's driving?"

Matt dangled his keys in front of him while smiling like a maniac. "I've got us. You are going to love this place!" Like children about to sneak a cookie from off the counter, the two men looked around to make sure the coast was clear. Kevin closed the drawer and followed Matt to the elevator. When they reached the ground floor, they waved to the elderly attendant at the front desk and slipped out the front door before the retired cop could question them.

At the back of the lot sat the last good thing in Matt's life: his trusty sedan. Blue paint chipped near the bottom revealed the previous coat of sun-kissed pear underneath. Beeping twice, the car unlocked, and they jumped in. Moments later, they were out of the parking lot and on their way.

Glimmering facades of modern towers fought for dominance of the sky. Scattered like jewels in the sand were ageless architectural works of art with smooth stone skin, decorative turrets, and mob-related rumors. An overgrowth of large rectangular weeds of metal and paper grew wherever land or space could be bought. Devilishly smiling children held up sloppy burgers on the most recently constructed metallic weed, which now blocked Matt's view of his favorite building.

Kevin watched sign after sign go by. "So, you've been at the job for three weeks now. What do you think of it?"

Matt looked at Kevin. "It's not as bad as I thought it would be. The work itself is pretty manageable most of the time. A little boring at times, but next to no stress. The only stress really comes from Candace. She can be, well, annoying. Otherwise, the job is good."

Kevin nodded. "I might be wrong, but when you started, it looked like you hated the boss. If eyes were actual daggers, you'd be on the five-o-clock news by now. Over the last two weeks, though, you seem to have warmed up to him. Did something happen between you two?"

Matt cracked his neck and ran fingers through his hair. "I used to be married. Then Thomas came into my wife's life. She had him over a few times and said he was *just* a friend. Apparently, they were more than that, and she left me for him." He warily eyed a drunk walking in the street who looked in his direction as they passed. "Guilt must have eaten him up enough over the last few months, so he offered me a job."

Spotting the shop, Matt pulled into a parking space and turned off the car. "You'd think I'd hate the guy after doing what he did, but he's been so damn helpful. Hard not to like him."

Kevin sat with wide eyes, regretting having said anything. "How about we go grab those coffees?" Kevin gave Matt an awkward smile and a nod. "My treat." He got out of the car and looked up at the storefront, chuckling. "Really? The Koffee Kraken?"

Matt locked the car and rolled his eyes. "Trust me. It sounds dumb, but this place is amazing. My friend Stacey works here, and sometimes she hooks me up. A good batch of donuts was made today. So, give it a chance."

Kevin snickered and walked toward the door. "Gotcha, but don't blame me if I start *Kraken* jokes." He opened the door to the shop and stood aside so Matt could go by.

As the door closed, the aroma of baked perfection swept over them. Light pink walls were adorned with pictures of roasting coffee beans and whimsical scenes involving donuts. Past the small circular tables and chairs rested a glass case filled with fluffy pastries. Line after line of decadent donuts sat patiently on trays, proudly presenting their names on small paper signs in colorful ink. The very mention of their spirited names could transform even the hardest of souls into an excited child.

At the very center of the top rack was the siren to their hunger: chocolate donuts filled with bits of bacon, wrapped in bacon, then sealed with chocolate. No sooner had their eyes laid upon the donuts than they were in a box and ready to be eaten. Snatching the box and their drinks off the counter, they walked over to a table by the window.

The donuts were just as good as Matt claimed them to be. Kevin bit into a chocolaty donut filled with bacon bits and was carried away to a land of bliss.

Matt triumphantly took a sip of his coffee. "Told you it was good."

Kevin swallowed. "Never doubting you again." Then he plunged another donut into his mouth.

Matt, savoring his own coffee, looked out the window to take in what the city had to offer. Noticing yellow tape across the street, his dark-roasted vacation ended. "Stacey! What's going on across the street?"

A blond-haired woman walked out from behind the counter over to Matt's side and followed his gaze to the police cars. "No idea. The cops showed up and hauled two people away. One apparently bit a cop, but they were able to get the guy off and into a squad car. The bite must have been bad 'cause they put him in an ambulance and rushed him off."

Studying the scene laid out before him, Matt crossed his arms and shook his head. "I wonder what they found that caused them to turn on each other." The rest of the group looked at him, puzzled. "That place was just on the news last night. The thing they found in Egypt was sent there for study."

Kevin's eyes widened.

"Tried talking with Kevin here about it earlier. Stayed up late last night just looking up articles online. I've heard of ar-cheologists and other scientists fighting before, but never to this extent."

Kevin looked up, with sprinkles and bacon bits covering his face. "I'll be right back. Stay here. I'm gonna run over there for a second to see what's going on." He wiped his face with his sleeve and then walked out of the shop toward the squad cars.

Crossing the street, Kevin jumped onto the curb and looked around. Not a single police officer in sight. He casually strolled past the first cruiser, carefully eyeing the contents of the car. In the second car, he spotted a clipboard. He looked down at his watch, using the corners of his vision to check if the coast was still clear. Satisfied by the lack of law enforcement, he walked closer and studied the clipboard.

Scribbled on the yellow paper clipped to the board were the usual notes. He kept reading. What caught his attention was the witness report. A woman mentioned that she and a few visiting co-workers walked in at around 7 AM. An archae-ologist that had come in earlier immediately attacked the group. Unable to reason with the attacker, the group fled. One member was bitten in the attack and lost consciousness not long after they escaped; they were revived by the first officers on the scene but needed to be restrained after they attacked the officers.

Worry spread across Kevin's face. After a minute, he looked toward the building ahead, now surrounded by yellow tape. Whatever consequences his next move would bring, he knew it needed to be done.

Ducking under the tape, he approached the building. If he turned back now, and if he was lucky, his life would stay the way it was. He had become used to the mundane. Years ago, he would have rather suffered a painful death, but now he enjoyed the simplicity of a routine and the quiet days the office offered.

His hand hovered over the doorknob. If his worst fears had come true, it wouldn't matter if he walked away or entered. No, he needed to put his fears aside. His suspicion would either be confirmed or dissolved.

He cracked his neck and shoulders and readied himself. Time to go in. He turned the handle and entered the building.

Matt and Stacey watched as Kevin slipped into Regenifact.

"Ah shit," Matt said, wiping the crumbs from his shirt. "If he does anything stupid, I might get dragged with him and be in a worse mess than I am already." He stood up, thanked Stacey, and ran out the door.

No cars were coming, so he bolted across the street. Realizing that running would look suspicious, he changed to a brisk walking pace. "No, no, no, no." He ducked under the tape and slipped into the building, quietly closing the door behind him.

Spanning the length of the building was a small windowless lobby where a few chairs loitered beneath framed pictures of archaeological digs. Light poured into the room from a lit hallway to the right. He needed to find Kevin and get them both out of there before someone noticed them.

"Kevin. Kevin, where are you?" Matt whispered as loud as he could. Holding his breath, he listened intently. Ignorant to the order, his heart sped onward. He focused his attention on the hall, and his stomach tightened at the thought of needing to traverse farther into the facility. Feeling the scorn of his halted lungs, Matt sucked in a much-needed breath. Startled by a shuffling sound to his left, he nearly tripped over a chair. Emerging from the shadows, a menacing figure armed with a rod quickly closed in on him. Stricken with fear, he cowered behind his own arms and let out a shrill cry.

Sensing hesitation from the attacker, Matt peaked out from behind his curled fist. Pressing a finger against his own lips, Kevin shushed Matt. Panting, Matt nervously smiled at Kevin. Mentally adding "stealthy" to the growing list of his coworker's traits gave Matt just enough time to relax his arms.

"What the hell are you doing?" Matt's eyes darted to the metal bar. One of the ends was capped with rubber padding, while the end closest to him ended in a jagged edge. "And where did you get that?"

Kevin's shoulders relaxed. "You didn't need to follow me." He shook his head. "If you came in any faster, you wouldn't be standing right now." The last comment bought him a glare from Matt. "This'll be quick. You can go wait outside or come with me. Either way, try to stay quiet." Kevin held up a hand to shush his anxious coworker. "We can talk about this once we're both outside again."

With that, Kevin walked past him toward the lit hallway. Matt's eyes followed and then leapt to the door, his body suddenly flush with heat. Swallowing hard, he pushed through the fire with a frustrated groan and quietly caught up with Kevin.

Pressed up against the wall next to the hall entrance, Kevin looked like a spy out of a cheesy 1980s movie. Holding a finger to his lips, Kevin carefully peeked around the corner, then made a "come here" motion before slipping into the hall.

Down the corridor the duo went. Pictures of ancient artifacts and ruins bathed in the light of a setting sun lined the walls. Approaching the first door, Kevin peered through a thin window at eye level. Despite the lack of light within the room, nothing seemed out of the ordinary. Satisfied, he mentally checked the room off a list and continued down the hall.

After a few more darkened rooms, they finally came across one that was lit. Kevin looked in to find what looked like a small library. Surrounded by bookshelves, a lonely table sat in the center of the room, covered by messy piles of papers. Seeing nothing particularly striking or out of place inside, Kevin carried on with his search of the facility. The stiffness in Kevin's jaw seemed to ease with each step.

After passing a few more darkness-filled rooms, they came to a set of double doors at the end of the hall on the left. Light shone through the small windows on the doors. Kevin peered into the room. Desks and metal shelving filled the L-shaped room. Slowly, he opened the door and stepped inside. Matt shuffled in and closed the door behind them.

Feeling safe to talk, Kevin nudged Matt. "Take a look around the room. If you see anything strange, let me know."

Matt nodded and walked toward the closest desk. Hastily scribbled notes and open books were scattered everywhere. Wearing only their bathing suits and their smiles, a picture of a family sat propped up against a cup filled with pens. Matt scratched at his overheating skin, hoping Kevin had a good reason for them to be here. At any moment, the police could barge in and either arrest or shoot them. He moved on to the next desk.

Kevin's search of the room was equally as fruitless. Nothing of interest could be found: papers on Egyptian ruins, a temple found in Mexico, and coins from the colonies. When he turned a corner, the room opened up, and he was relieved to only see more of the same desks and shelves. At the very back of the room, a pair of windowless doors were shut. A small plaque hung above the door with "LABORATORY" written on it in stiff white lettering. He put his ear to the door. After a moment, satisfied by the lack of movement heard within, he opened it.

Across the room, Matt continued his search. The next desk looked the same as the last: messy papers and a few photos of smiling people. A clipboard filled with erratic scribbling caught his eye. It was hard to read, but it seemed like something out of the ordinary. He picked it up and walked up to Kevin, who was standing in a doorway. His eyes hardly left the pages.

"Kevin, you're going to want to see this. One of the researchers found something inter—"

Sprawled in front of them, surrounded by a pool of congealed blood, were the remains of a mutilated corpse. Chunks of torn flesh, broken bones, and blood painted the floor. A bloodied skull lay a few yards away from the body next to a fallen light. Patches of graying hair still clung to the bone.

Towering above the horror like an idol to the gore was an open sarcophagus resting on a low table. Matt immediately felt his stomach churn and vomited profusely onto the wall behind him. He should've just stayed at the Koffee Kraken.

Kevin tightened his grip on the metal bar as shock turned to anger. "We need to get back to the office." Turning away from the nightmarish scene, he pounded his shoes toward the exit.

Using the sleeve of his shirt, Matt wiped his mouth. "What the hell do you mean 'we need to get back'?" Matt shouted. He ripped the pages from the clipboard and shoved them into his back pocket.

"There's something there that I need to get." Kevin

grunted as he shoved the door open.

Matt tossed the clipboard aside and jogged to catch up with him. "We just saw a body that was messed up beyond belief, and you want to go back to the office to grab what? A gun you keep under the desk?" He was losing the ability to talk between breaths. Fear now showed on his face, and his voice rose to a shout. "You snuck into a crime scene, and the shit we saw back there barely phased you. What's going on?"

Losing his patience, Kevin stopped suddenly and faced Matt. Placing both hands on the man's shoulders, he looked into Matt's eyes. "Right now, you need to trust me. I'll explain later."

After a moment, Matt sighed and hesitantly nodded.

"Alright. We need to get to your car and head back," Kevin said. With that, his hands left Matt's shoulders, and he continued on down the hall.

The rest of the walk through the building was silent. Emerging into the cool autumn air almost made what they just saw feel like a distant memory. The world was calm. Customers still sat in the Koffee Kraken, enjoying hot coffee and pastries fit for gods. Leaves rustled on the ground in the soft breeze, only to be whisked away in the other direction by a passing car. The two men looked at each other and made their way across the street and back to the sedan. With haste in mind, they hopped in and sped off to the office.

The highway was a terrible idea. They had left Regenifact nearly half an hour ago, and they probably could walk back to the blood-soaked building within fifteen minutes. Matt craned his neck to try and see past the vehicle in front of him. Groaning, he slumped back into his seat.

"The highway is never this bad. We should have been back by now."

Kevin tapped the metal bar against the floor with uneasiness. The sound of a siren was faint in the distance, but quickly became a blaring wail as an ambulance passed them on the shoulder. The sound faded again as the vehicle sped out of sight.

Of course there was an accident, Matt thought to himself as he closed his eyes in acceptance of the situation.

Tapping his foot against the stained car floor, Kevin looked over his shoulder and then back at the floor. "Drive on the shoulder." Amidst the silence, his foot tapped harder. "Now."

Matt looked at him with scrunched brows.

"We might be in this line all day. If we get pulled over, I'll take care of it," said Kevin. Matt prayed they wouldn't. Kevin continued, "There's an off-ramp about a quarter of a mile up. Just take it, and we'll get back by taking normal roads.

Matt bit his lip and looked around to see if a police car was nearby. His quick search quelled his nerves just enough to give the bold idea a try, and he slowly moved his car from the lane to the shoulder.

Within minutes, they were off the highway. They passed street after street, only hitting a single red light over the course of a mile.

Matt remembered the papers in his back pocket and took them out. *Just random notes,* he thought to himself as he flipped through the pages.

Each page was a breakdown of different characters. At the top of one page, underlined twice, was "Hebrew," on another "Greek," and then "Latin." The fifth page of characters was crowned by a question mark. Matt was startled by a car honking behind him and realized the light had turned green. He pressed the gas pedal and sped onward.

Now with his interest piqued in the notes, he flipped to the final page. Unable to look down for long enough to read, he slowly made out that the characters from each page were written in a line, one after the other, with English translations written below. All had been translated except for the mystery characters.

Matt looked around him. Not a single light in front of him for a short time and no cars beside him. He looked down at the notes. Each line read slightly differently. At the very bottom of the page was a message circled in red ink that drew in not only his attention but also his neck:

All engravings on the sarcophagus are warnings.

Enclosed within is immortal destruction. Enclosed within is Hades, the god of death.

Matt mouthed these words to himself and cinched his brow more and more with each repeat. What did it mean that Hades was enclosed? Slipping the notes back into his pocket, he wet his lips and looked up at Kevin only to see the front of a gray pickup truck as it crashed into them.

Enthralled by the miniature reptile, the child spent every free moment he could in its company. After a tiring and lengthy race from the prior day, the lizard not only managed to keep up but also took the lead just as the child reached the finish line, earning it the esteemed name of Zip. Not feeling particularly ready to lose another race so soon, the child had a different idea of how they could play today.

Using sticks, leaves, and rocks, he created an obstacle course fit for the finest of competitors. Filled with harrowing leaps and swinging twigs of death, the child believed he surely had his friend beat. However, each challenge within his miniature course, no matter how daunting, Zip completed with ease.

In the distance, he could hear his mother calling out for him. Dinner was ready, and his hunger, previously tucked away in the back of his mind, suddenly matched the level of his excitement. He placed his new friend back on the root where it had been found. Using a finger, he gently petted the lizard and said goodbye.

III

REBIRTH

As the doors closed behind him, the music of screaming filled his ears. Too long had he been trapped in that tomb. For nearly two thousand years, he had been conscious and bound by living rigor mortis, with only the darkness and piercing silence as his companions. The moments before that suffocating darkness played endlessly through his head, taunting him with his failure. With his release, Hades' rage had been renewed.

He looked to his right and down a long hall lit with hanging balls of fireless light. This world had changed. He closed his eyes and searched through Melissa's hazy memories until he found what he needed. Etched into his mind, as if he had wandered these hallways countless times, was the layout of Regenifact. Following the memory, he made his way to the exit.

With each step, he noticed more and more the aches of his body and the wounds of his flesh. He pushed down the pain and replaced it with his hatred. He had two thousand years to rest; now was the time to move. Soon, the exit would be in his sight.

Emerging from the building, he was greeted by a breeze and the cool night air. Before him lay a river of black lined with more fireless lights held high on poles. Searching Melissa's memories, the things before him were given names. The black river was solid and called a *street*, while the light sources were contraptions of electricity, metal, and glass. He allowed her memories to fade into the back of his mind as he was brought up to date. How far this world had come.

A rustling noise to his left jolted his entire body into a defensive position. Leaves scraped along the ground and drifted past his feet. He slowly relaxed his arms. Farther down the street, he noticed a large man walking in his direction. The man would do nicely. He walked toward the man with a slight hobble.

Oblivious to the world, the man stared down at a flashing object, emotionlessly reading something off of it. Hades approached and drew his fist, punching the man's temple hard enough to cause him to drop his phone.

"What the—"was all the man muttered before he was pushed into a dark alley. When he looked over at his attacker, the man stumbled over his words: "W—whatever you want. It's y—yours." He removed his watch and shakily offered it.

Knocking the unwanted sacrifice from the man's hands, Hades looked him in the eyes. "I have no need for your wrist ornament, but you do have something I want." He grabbed the man's throat and held him against the brick. The man clawed at Hades' hand. He could feel it, hear it, pulsing through the man's veins: rich, delicious life. Within Hades, *Essence*, the energy that comprised the dark realm of the *Void*, flowed through him.

Reaching out with his *Essence*, he took hold of all that delicious blood and called it forth. The man's eyes turned a dark red as vessels burst within them. Blood flowed from his eyes and crawled down Hades' arm like liquid snakes. The man's screams soon turned to gargles as blood began pouring from his mouth. Small streams of blood also snaked their way around Hades' body, finding homes in cuts and scrapes, causing them to heal. With each second, the man's skin became increasingly pale.

Soon, the man's hands fell to his sides, and he lost consciousness. The heart, having nothing to push, collapsed and shriveled along with the rest of his flesh. As the last of the blood entered Hades' body, his wounds sealed completely. Satisfied, he cast the husk of the man deeper into the alley.

Taking in deep breaths of the chilled morning air, Hades felt renewed. Yet despite his drinking, weakness still plagued him. He thought back to Melissa's corpse when he had reanimated it. It walked like a child without mind or direction. Hades looked at his hands. What had they done to him? He had once led armies of the dead that were as agile and cunning as the living, yet he now struggled to effectively control a single corpse.

With more blood, maybe his power would return. Success had been stolen from him during his last attempt. Fickle was the gift of freedom. Even with this hindrance, he would not waste this second chance. The ritual must be completed. In his current state, what would once only have taken a few hundred bodies to complete would now require nearly one million.

He needed to find more humans to drain, and the surrounding area was too quiet. Suddenly, a blinding light disrupted his thoughts. A deep growling sound approached, rapidly coming closer and closer. Hades braced for a fight with the attacking mystery beast. But unconcerned with him, the beast whooshed past.

Blinded no longer, Hades observed the fleeing challenger. A strange metal box containing a woman—a van—rumbled off into the distance until it could no longer be heard.

Relieved and partially amused, Hades unclenched his fists. The simplistic ants that he had once loomed over had mastered the use of metals. Quieting the voice in his mind, Hades focused on his mission. *Humans tend to congregate,* he thought to himself. *Where one goes, there are likely to be more.* He turned in the direction of the strange contraption and started walking.

His search did not take long. Along the buildings and in alleyways, humans slept in their raggedy clothes. Often, they were alone, but at times, they lay in small groups. No matter their numbers or attempts at resistance, they only added to a growing trail of withered bodies. With increasing frustration, he soon realized that no matter how many he drained, his *Essence* would not strengthen. He stared into the eyes of a new husk in his grasp. Its face was distorted into a fusion of fear and pain.

He remembered that same pained look marring the face of the one he loved as she lay dying in his arms. Emotion rushed over him as the memories flooded back. Even after two thousand years, the wound was still fresh.

In a fit of rage, he gripped the head of the husk and smashed it into a nearby wall. The entire skull caved in. Bits of skin and bone littered the ground at his feet. No longer finding satisfaction in its destruction, he flung the remains to the side. He closed his eyes and pushed down the memory, slowly feeling his body relax.

A scraping sound jerked him from his short meditation. Dodging to the side, he narrowly avoided the bite of a thrusting knife. Not allowing his attacker the time to recover, he sent a strong elbow into the assailant's chest, causing them to stagger backward. Hades turned his neck just enough to give a sideways glare at the bold human.

Clutching his chest with one hand and brandishing a knife in the other stood a man whose clothes had become brown with filth. His unkempt hair was just long enough to cover his eyes. Through gritted teeth, the man screamed, "What the hell did you do to him?"

Hades looked down at the corpse and back to the dead man's avenger with a smirk. "I gave him a purpose." The raggedy man adjusted his footing and grip on the knife. "Just as I have a purpose for you," snarled Hades.

"Like hell you do!" The man charged Hades and lunged with the knife.

Deflecting the first strike, Hades was taken aback by the man's strength. Each consecutive blow was stronger and faster than the last. The man scored a shallow slash on Hades' arm. Taken away by the man's skill, he lost his footing and stumbled over the shriveled corpse, allowing the assailant to create a deep gash in his side.

Judging by the man's clothes, Hades had assumed this would be an easy fight. That assumption had cost him and would not be made again. He quickly recovered and formed a defensive stance. The fight had gone on for too long.

The man lunged again with the knife only to find himself grappled by Hades, lifted overhead, and flung to the ground. With a heavy thud, the man hit the dusty cement. Dazed, the man could hardly react in time before Hades ripped the knife from his hand and swiftly plunged it into his chest. A red stain quickly soaked through the man's dirty clothes. His remaining breath escaped his lips as his eyes rolled into the back of his head.

Slowly standing with a hand covering his wounded side, Hades looked down at his kill. Conducting another blood regeneration would be needed soon, but enough time had been wasted. He was sure the others would have kept eyes on him somehow and would confront him at any moment. This human's ferociousness, however, should not go to waste.

Reaching out his hand toward the assailant's corpse, he focused his *Essence* outward. Like invisible tendrils, his *Essence* extended from his fingers and wrapped around the corpse. Hades could feel the muscle and bone as if it were his own, and as he pulled his fingers back, the corpse lifted from its slumber. The fallen assailant's body twitched, unholy life returning to its flesh. Slowly, the corpse rose and looked toward Hades with empty eyes.

Lowering his arm, Hades observed his created nihanim. Just like the one created in the lab, the reanimated corpse before him looked weak. The blood regenerations were done in vain; his power had not been restored. An untrained Death-Touched, he knew, could have raised a better nihanim than this.

The glint of metal shone from the dead man's neck, catching Hades' attention. As he wondered what it was and wished his creation would relinquish it, the dead man's hand rose to its neck and awkwardly grasped the object of Hades' interest. With a metallic snap, it extended its arm and revealed a necklace.

Hades took the snapped necklace and eyed the small metal plate hanging from it. Engraved into it was the name "Andrew Harking." A slight smile formed on his face as he realized that mentally transferring orders still worked—albeit simple orders. He pushed past the reanimated corpse, pulling the knife from its chest with him. Lifeless eyes followed Hades, and then like a lost child, Andrew followed.

Annoyed by the sound of scraping feet behind him, Hades looked over his shoulder and eyed his creation. "Be useful and take the street to the right. Kill anyone you come across. Turn as many as you can."

These words echoed in Andrew's empty mind. The meaning of them lay behind a dense fog. Before the puzzle could be deciphered, the nihanim felt the pull of Hades' *Essence* and changed directions. It slowly made its way around the building and continued down the sidewalk away from its master.

Anything that moved gnawed at Andrew's attention—from the rustling of leaves to the distant squawking of horns. Cars seemed to be the only potential victims crossing his path. No matter how he tried to catch them, the cars simply honked and swerved around him. Every attempt was fruitless.

With a rush of energy, he lunged toward another passing car. With a loud bang, he connected with the speeding vehicle and flew through the air, landing hard on the pavement. His body rolled until he came to a face-down stop.

Grit pierced his skin. Flesh from his knees and the left side of his face had been scraped away. Despite this, numbness was the only thing Andrew felt aside from the drive to stand up and carry out Hades' order. The sound of a car door opening jolted his body.

Putting his weight on both hands, Andrew began to raise himself from the ground. With a sickening snap, his right arm gave away, and his face slammed onto the ground. Without skipping a beat, Andrew placed his left hand down and tried to push himself up once more. Suddenly, he felt himself being pulled to his feet.

Gaining his footing, Andrew turned toward the source of the help.

Meeting his gaze was the concerned face of a tall, blond-haired boy in jeans, a brown button-up shirt, and a matching brown hat. "Oh my god. Dude, why the hell did you do that? Are you ok?"

Andrew answered the question with a plowing fist to the boy's chest. The boy stumbled backward, coughing, and then quickly turned to escape to his car. Determined to not let this one get away, Andrew lunged forward, grabbing hold of the boy's collar. With his unsupported weight, he brought both of them to the ground.

Screaming, Andrew's prey elbowed and kicked in vain. With a grip still on the collar, the nihanim climbed onto the boy's back and moved his left hand to the boy's neck. Now crying, his prey begged for mercy, repeatedly apologizing for hitting him with his car. Andrew dug his fingers into the sides of the boy's throat, drawing blood.

Wisps of *Essence* entered the boy's bleeding neck through Andrew's fingers. A less-than-human scream escaped Andrew's lips as he began to smash the boy's head against the cement. Specks of red soon turned into a pool of blood as his victim lost consciousness. Deeper his fingers went into the boy's neck until they broke through his flesh.

A large force knocked Andrew away and pinned him to the ground, causing his dug-in fingers to rip open the boy's throat. Holding him to the ground was a large, muscular man in a black uniform. The morning light glinted off a metal badge on his chest.

Andrew lashed out, but the more he tried to attack this new opponent, the tighter the hold on him became. The man removed handcuffs from his belt and slapped them onto an exposed wrist.

Andrew, now lying on his stomach, felt his broken arm being pulled behind him. Then a scream erupted above his ear, and when he looked up, he saw the boy, whose shirt was now stained with blood beneath the gaping hole in his throat, biting into the man's right shoulder. The man punched the boy with his left arm and turned to defend himself. Andrew, no longer pinned down, turned onto his side and dug his teeth into the victim's leg.

The man's screams fell onto the deaf ears of a city just waking from slumber. Andrew and the boy tore into juicy flesh, blood covering their faces. The sound of their feeding soon replaced the sound of whimpers. The man's final breath was only the beginning as *Essence* took hold of him.

Five blocks away, turning every damned soul that crossed his path, Hades felt the subtle growth of his army. Like weaponized generators, each new nihanim amplified his power and brought him closer to his earlier strength. He could feel them all, every single nihanim shambling about. A block away, a store owner was being torn apart atop a conveyor belt. Three blocks away, a human was backed into a corner in an alley. Half a mile away, one nihanim made it onto a bus.

Hades was able to mentally direct and give basic orders, but he was nowhere near his full ability. Whatever the others had done to him had caused his abilities to regress a considerable amount.

Closing his eyes, he listened to the world through his nihanem. Screams of fear and anger blended together. The humans of this era are weak. Attempts at resistance were sparse. Most seemed to run or cower in fear. At least the runners allowed him to test the limits of the corpses he controlled.

His hatred for humanity was an inferno that demanded blood. Within that flame, he would incinerate those that placed him in his prison. This world would crumble under his fist.

The *God of Death* had returned.

No sooner had the last of the soup been slurped from the wooden bowl than he had asked to be excused from the table. His eagerness to go back outside earned him a sly grin from his father. Flying through the door, he raced across the field toward the oak tree. His new friend had most likely run off for the day, but maybe, just maybe, they would still be there and able to play again.

It was nearly night, and he had to be back indoors before it was dark. Going around the tree, the exposed root came into sight. To his relief, resting atop it was Zip. He lowered his hand, resting it on the root. As if excited to be in the presence of a friend, the lizard quickly scampered forward and crawled into the child's hand. United once again, warmth filled the boy's chest. He looked back at the cottage. His parents would never let him bring the lizard inside.

With a sigh, he looked down at his scaly friend. "If you're going to stick around, you need a home of your own."

The lizard crawled up his arm and rested on his shoulder. Using a stick, he dug out a small area in the dirt. Gathering pebbles and torn grass, he went to work, constructing walls and even a small comfy bed for his friend. It was the perfect home. Grabbing sticks and leaves, he topped the cozy den off with a sturdy roof.

"There. That should keep you safe and warm," he proclaimed proudly. Using his hand as a ramp, Zip crawled down his arm and slipped into its tiny new home.

IV

NEW REALITY

Matt awoke to the sound of breaking glass.

"Matt, are you ok?" said a muffled voice.

He looked toward the source but was unable to focus his eyes. His seatbelt clicked, and his head slammed into the roof of the car. Hands took hold of him and pulled him through the window. Jagged edges of broken glass clawed at his clothing.

"Can you stand?" The voice was less muffled now and sounded more like Kevin.

Matt nodded, despite the soreness that coursed through his body. With some help from Kevin, he was quickly back on his feet. Pressing his palm against the cool metal of the car, he attempted to regain his sense of balance.

"Stay here. I need to check on the others."

Before Matt could protest, Kevin had already left his side, leaving him alone with his tinnitus. Feeling less like a water-bed, the black asphalt provided increasingly better support. Attempting to stabilize himself further, Matt gazed at the ground beneath him. Barely noticeable and blending almost perfectly with its surroundings, a single ant proudly toted a bright green section of leaf. Bumping into Matt's shoe, the bug altered its course and traveled alongside his rubber sole.

Nearby, the squeal of an unoiled truck door opening could be heard.

Hearing Kevin swearing loudly pulled Matt away from the entertainment. Looking in Kevin's direction, Matt realized that his vision still had some recovering to do. While distance was a bit shot for the moment, he could clearly see one of his car's filthy tires enjoying sunlight along with the worn-out wheel-well cover beneath it. His sexy sedan was totaled. He looked down and realized that he was covered in broken glass and began to wipe himself off.

The sound of quick footsteps toward him materialized through the haze of his vision into his frantic coworker. Kevin knelt down next to the car, reached in, and pulled out the broken metal chair leg. Before Kevin could stand again, a man dressed in a trucker uniform was on top of him. A hard elbow to the attacker's chest gave Kevin enough room to swing the chair leg and connect with his head. Blood peppered Kevin's shirt as the jagged end tore through the driver's flesh.

"HOLY SHIT!" Matt screamed. *What the hell did Kevin say to the other driver?* Still a tad wobbly, Matt reached out to try and grab his coworker before he could do any more damage. There had to be a way to stop this fight. Assault charges would be the least of Kevin's worries if he went any farther.

Before Matt could grab Kevin, he moved toward his opponent and out of Matt's reach. Startled by the sudden approach of another individual, Matt closed his eyes and readied himself to de-escalate the situation. This person was most likely a passenger of the truck and not particularly happy with him and Kevin. Feeling hands tightly grip his shoulders, Matt knew his chance of talking this new person down had dissolved. Opening his eyes, Matt put his best foot forward. "Whatever was said, I'm sure it was a—OH MY GOD!"

He had come face-to-face with a beard soaked in blood and a large pink flap of skin hanging from the man's cheek that revealed his teeth underneath. The man gave off a shrill growl before pushing himself on Matt. Like a rabid animal, the man attempted to bite into Matt.

Using all his strength, Matt put his arms between himself and the psychopath. D*amn, this guy is strong!* Unable to break free or push him away, Matt had an idea. Thankful for his recent late-night, online-video search sprees, he knew just how to get out of this situation. Bringing his legs up, he forced the attacker to take on the burden of all of his weight.

Just as planned, Matt fell straight to the ground. Unfortunately, so did the attacker. Now pinned on the ground with his back against his car and the man on top of him, Matt had successfully screwed himself. Bits of flesh entangled in the attacker's beard fell onto his face.

Screaming for help, Matt was able to see Kevin through a gap under the bastard's arm. The fearful and angry eyes of his coworker looked back toward Matt before Kevin received a fist to the face that brought him back to reality. Matt watched Kevin block a second punch and send the driver stumbling back with a strike to the jaw. With a mighty swing, Kevin swung the chair leg at the driver, connecting with the man's head and collapsing the skull. The body went limp and fell like a rag-doll.

Sprinting to Matt, Kevin lifted the attacker off and slammed them into the side of the car. Taking a step back, Kevin grunted and swung the chair leg down. The back of the man's skull cracked as the metal leg broke upon impact. Tossing the broken leg aside, Kevin took up a defensive stance. The man screamed and charged. A right hook from Kevin knocked him to the ground. A finishing stomp caved the man's head in with a sickening crack.

Eyeing the motionless corpse, Matt was finally able to take a good look at his attacker. Blood covered his gray, ripped-open uniform. A torn sleeve revealed an arm covered in bite marks. Protruding from his ribs was the handle of what might have been a screwdriver.

"What the hell just happened?" he shouted, pointing at his attacker with eyes widened. "How the fuck was this guy even moving?" Matt then looked at the second corpse lying in the street. "Why did you bash in both their heads!?"

Staring at the corpse at his feet with a serious frown, Kevin said, "I'll explain later, but right now we need to move. It isn't safe here. We don't have time to wait around for the police, either."

Terrified and confused, Matt felt Kevin place a hand on his shoulder.

"Do you trust me?"

Matt stared into Kevin's eyes. His face was stern, a look that Matt had never seen on his usually happy face. Whatever was going on ... Matt had no idea why, but he trusted Kevin. With a nod, Matt felt the hand lift off his shoulder.

"We need to get back to the office. Do you remember which direction it was in?" Kevin asked.

Matt nodded and pointed to his right.

"Alright, let's start moving," Kevin ordered.

Matt looked back at his car. "I still think we should call the police, at least for insurance to have something to go off of."

Kevin stopped and looked back at Matt. "This is bigger than anything the police can handle." Chuckling softly, he added, "And do you really think insurance is going to believe a dead guy attacked you as your reason for the crash?"

Did he just say dead? How could he have been dead? Matt looked down at his phone. New cracks covered the screen. Questions raced through his mind. With a sigh, he slipped the phone back into his pocket and joined his coworker.

✳

Forty minutes had passed since they started walking. Having lost the rush of adrenaline, the pain Matt felt increased threefold, causing him to walk slower than usual. Every so often, a look of confusion or worry would come their way from a passerby. Most people that they saw on the street were still going about their daily business, blissfully unaware of the growing danger they were in. At one point, a blue-and-white police car blew past them in the direction of their car crash with sirens blaring.

"Can we please just call a cab or something? We could have been back to the office by now, and I really don't want to get fired for being back late from lunch."

"And risk getting into another crash? You're extremely lucky you're walking right now. In fact, you're lucky to even be alive."

Kevin was right. The impact of the truck had sent his car rolling. He remembered seeing the truck right before it had hit his car and Kevin pulling him out of the wreckage. Everything between those events was a blur. If there was another accident, he might not be so lucky. Maybe walking *was* the best option right now.

A crowd burst through the door of a department store across the street, interrupting his thoughts and grabbing the attention of both men. The people fought their way through the small doors, causing some to trip and become trampled beneath the stampede. Out of the stampeding shoppers dove a large woman in a red dress, who grabbed hold of a young screaming girl and, with animalistic fervor, bit down. Climbing over her was a security guard whose face was covered in blood and three other blood-covered shoppers.

The screams of the girl could be heard above the fleeing crowd. With the security guard holding onto her suit jacket, a woman in high heels slipped out of it and rushed into the street only to be hit by a passing car that had swerved to avoid hitting another fleeing shopper. A nightmare unfolded beneath the smiling face on the department store's sign. The woman in red moved on from her prey. Moments later, the girl that had been beneath her lifted herself out of a pool of her own blood, an inhuman scream erupting from her toward the sky.

A passing police car screeched to a halt in the middle of the street. Doors on each side quickly opened, and two officers emerged with guns drawn. Their shouts attracted the attention of three blood-covered shoppers. Walking toward the officers, they ignored all orders and warnings. A flash burst from the muzzle of the closest officer, causing one of the shoppers to slightly stumble and then break into a full run. The officer fired shot after shot until the shopper was on top of him.

Then the second officer opened fire, launching round after round into the approaching shoppers with equal effect. Hearing a click, the officer pulled out a fresh magazine while ejecting the spent one. A large force from behind caused him to drop the new magazine. He swung at the nearest shopper but was pulled down by another that had grabbed hold of his vest.

The sight was unbelievable. Matt's eyes darted from each act of gore and cry for help. Picking up speed, his heart raced forward. *No, no, no, no, no. I don't have my car. I can't outrun them all. I can't fight back. We're screwed.* "This is how we die," Matt blurted out, instantly drawing the attention of half a dozen zombies. Lifting her head from the bosom of her mother, a pigtailed girl looked directly at Matt. A chunk of bloody flesh and torn purple lace hung from her stuffed mouth.

Kevin grabbed Matt's arm. "Run!"

Having barely run half a block, Matt's body ached, but his fear kept him going. Keeping up with Kevin at this speed would have been impossible if it were for any other reason, although he wasn't sure how much longer he could go on. His side screamed at him for not going to the gym like his doctor had mentioned during his last visit—and every other previous visit as far back as he could remember.

"This way!" Kevin shouted, turning down an alley. "C'mon. C'mon!" he said to himself as he frantically went door to door, pulling on their handles. Behind them, a garbage can made a loud clang as it was knocked to the ground, spewing its contents over the alleyway. Zombies tumbled over the can and were trampled by those behind them.

Matt looked back and suddenly wished he hadn't. A man in a torn business suit was being ripped apart by three hunched-over figures. *This can't be happening*, he thought. *The dead rise in movies, not real life*. After watching a zombie movie, he would talk with his friends over drinks about how they would take on the dead with a gun in one hand and a machete in the other as fearless, invincible heroes. Now that he was being chased by the dead, he realized what he would actually do. The sound of shoes hitting cement began to gain on him. He couldn't tell how many were running after him, and he really didn't want to know.

With a screech, a rusted metal door pulled open.

"Get in, get in, get in, get in!" Kevin yelled as he hurried inside and motioned Matt to follow. The second both of them were inside, Kevin slammed the door shut and looked for a way to lock the door. Noticing a row of bolts running down the door's length, he slammed one closed. Ferocious pounding on the door rattled the hinges. Kevin closed the remainder of the bolts for good measure and stepped back. "That should hold."

Matt's heart pounded in his chest. Was it from the adrenaline? The fear? Both? He couldn't decide. His life had been awful before, but now it was a horror movie. He looked over at Kevin, who seemed strangely guilty—or maybe he was just tired. Matt allowed himself to catch his breath, then cleared his throat. But before he had the chance to speak, he was interrupted.

Chk Chk.

The two men spun around toward the source of the noise. Standing no more than twelve feet down a small, dimly lit hallway in a defensive stance was a shriveled man in a green apron. A single dying light bulb hung from the ceiling, giving just enough light to make out the nametag. His skin, wrinkled by age, was the color and texture of worn leather. Staring at them from behind the barrel of a shotgun were eyes as large and alert as an owl's. The man braced the butt of the gun against his shoulder. His arms trembled under its weight. Like a third eye watching them, the barrel moved back and forth between the two, causing Matt to hold his breath each time it was on him.

"You had better turn right back around and take your friends with you."

They both eyed the door behind them. It still shook with the ferocious pounding. Matt looked at Kevin as if he were back at the office where his coworker could find an easy solution. Kevin gave Matt the same look. Realizing that neither of them had any idea of what to do, they looked back at the old man and slowly raised their hands.

"You got that?!" shouted the old man.

"Not going to happen. We barely made it in here." Kevin stepped forward carefully and then flinched as a dozen tiny holes appeared in the wall next to him. His ears rang from the deafening boom in the tight hallway.

The old man pumped the shotgun and retrained it back on Kevin. "Like hell it's not! I've seen what you rioters do. Be animals somewhere else!" Muffled crying could be heard farther down the hall.

"There are other people here?" Kevin asked.

"Never mind them." The owner barked.

"Where are we exactly?"

"My shop, which you will not be allowed to steal from or destroy."

"We didn't come here to rob you. We were running from..." Kevin looked at the holes in the wall then back at the shopkeeper "...the mob. Your door was the first one we were able to open. They were right behind us."

The shopkeeper narrowed his eyes at Kevin and tightened his grip on the shotgun. Matt looked over and watched as Kevin's eyes slowly widened. His soft breaths became faster.

Matt closed his eyes as memories and worries collided in his mind. He would never get the chance to talk to Maddison again. The time they shared together must have meant something to her. He just wanted to go back to his desk and his boring life. Every day, he looked at her picture in his wallet and thought of reaching for the phone to call her. It always stuck to that: just a thought. He could never build up the courage to dial those beautiful numbers. Waiting for the shotgun pellets to tear through his body was as intense as the day he watched Maddison walk out the front door and out of his life. The passing seconds felt like hours.

The shopkeeper took in a deep breath and let it out slowly, lowering the shotgun and relaxing his body. "You can stay here until it calms down a bit out there."

Built-up tension began to take its toll on Matt's slender frame. Feeling safe enough to relieve himself of the self-inflicted burden, he tried to relax his body. He thanked their host graciously, and the two coworkers followed him down the hall.

Down the hall, they emerged into a small room with an old wooden desk tucked into the corner. Painted ages ago, the once-bright white paint had absorbed years of smoking and turned into a sad, spotty yellow. A small coffee table sat in the middle, covered in newspapers, magazines, and a box of cigars. Resting on top of the mess were five partially full water bottles. Against the opposite wall were four folding chairs. Two of them were filled by a family with a child in a purple sweater, who sat in the lap of her mother. Tears streamed from the mother's eyes as she held the small girl to her chest. In a space between them sat an old woman. Her head was laid back against the wall.

"If you can find a chair or a blanket in the shop, you're free to use it." The shopkeeper laid the shotgun on the desk and walked out of the room, coming back moments later with two ice-cold bottles of water that were accepted eagerly.

Matt sunk to the floor and twisted off the cap. He didn't realize how thirsty he was until the water touched his lips. The bottle was completely empty by the time the shopkeeper was able to pull out a chair and sit at the desk. In stark contrast, Kevin's bottle only had a single sip taken from it and now rested on the floor next to his feet. The old man cleared his throat. For the next ten minutes, they spoke about the start of the riot and how they had escaped with only the injuries they had acquired from the crash.

With a nod, Kevin motioned toward a door. Matt concluded the conversation with the shopkeeper, grabbed his coworker's bottle, and followed him out of the room. He closed the door behind him, walked down a short hall, and stopped at the first row of chest-high shelves. Happy to be out of the foul-smelling office, he looked around the room. The lights had been turned off, and the windows covered. Slivers of light poked through the cracks of the yellowing shades. He took a few steps forward and looked around. It was a quaint shop, yet surprisingly filled to the brim.

Quietly, Kevin walked up to a window and cautiously peeked outside. Through a small slit, he was able to see just across the street with only a small amount of difficulty. Crashed cars littered the street. Slipping around them like water around rocks were numerous bloodied and butchered figures. The sound of shattering glass caused him to readjust his footing to search for the source. A terrified scream came from a car as a zombie slipped in through its broken window. With great effort, Kevin tore himself from the hellish sight. Moving beside Matt, he leaned in close. "Things aren't good outside."

"What did you see?" said Matt.

"A bunch of those things are still out there. We'll need to stay here for a bit."

Kevin's eyes searched the floor as he crossed his arms. "Did you notice anything about the family back there?"

Recalling the image in his mind, Matt tried to find anything out of the ordinary. Seemed like an ordinary family. Given the circumstances, people huddling together in the back of a small shop wasn't the strangest thing going on.

Assisting his pondering coworker, Kevin answered his own question. "The child that the woman was cradling ... There was a towel pressed to her arm."

Since Kevin's comment about the dead after the attack in the street, Matt had been trying to come to terms with the idea of zombies. "Do you think one of them bit her?" Matt said.

"One of them could have attacked her. It's also possible she just tripped or ran into something in the chaos."

"If something did hurt her... If it's not a bite, she'll be ok, right?" Matt looked at Kevin with a furrowed brow. He barely noticed the tightening fist tucked beneath Kevin's folded arms.

Kevin looked back with pained eyes. "I wish it were that simple." Before any questions could be asked, Kevin placed his hand on Matt's shoulder, then walked back to the others in the room.

Now standing alone in the shop, a million thoughts ran through his head. Matt had never been more unsure and scared of the future than he was at this moment. One thought repeated in his head. It seemed to only increase each time it crossed his mind.

When would he wake up from this nightmare?

Every day he was awakened by the first rays of sunlight hitting his resting eyes. He would throw on his clothes and run to the oak tree with a glint of excitement in his eyes and a smile on his face. Zip would crawl out of its small earthen home and into the boy's hand. No matter where the boy went, the lizard would accompany him. When his family took a trip into the city, he would sit in the backseat with the lizard safely hidden away within his trouser pocket, giggling randomly as its tongue flicked at his finger.

V

LUST

With the last drop of his blood, the jar was filled. Screwing the lid on tightly, Hades stood and handed it to a nihanim in a blood-soaked gray sweater. He waved his hand, and Gray Sweater and two others went off, their assignments programmed into their skulls.

Kneeling and held in place by dead hands was a trembling young woman in a pink athletic jacket. Trails of tears streamed down her face, ruining her makeup. Her husband's husk lay face down beside her. Hades placed a hand softly against her cheek.

"Please," she cried to Hades, placing her hand on his, "Let me go."

Blood still flowed from the cut on his wrist, running down his fingers and dripping onto the cement.

"No!" she screamed as Hades clenched her head. The screams were soon silenced as blood filled her throat.

Unbeknownst to Hades and hidden from view were prying eyes. They had noticed him two hours before and had been trailing him ever since. Dilated by lust, they devoured each act of gore with sick pleasure. A brief, devilish smile crept across their face as blood erupted from the woman's mouth. The chance to act was now. Straightening out their clothing and adjusting their hair with slender fingers, they readied themselves. The observer's heart pounded as they made their way to the door.

The woman's shriveled hand fell from Hades'. With the wound healed and blood replenished, he released his grip. She joined her husband with a solid thud. Her hand bounced against the ground and landed against her betrothed.

A noise behind Hades grabbed his attention, and he turned to meet it. Walking defiantly through the horde of nihanem was a figure dressed in black. Her short skirt swayed with each heavy step in her ankle-high boots. Imprinted on her body-hugging tank top was the image of a skull with four bat-like wings. The nihanem moved toward the teenage girl but stopped as Hades eyed her curiously.

Stopping within arm's length of Hades, she tilted her head upward and looked him dead in the eye. "You're going to let me join you."

Hades looked down at the strange girl standing confidently before him. The top of her head barely met his chest. His fingers toyed with the dagger hilt protruding from his belt. *Such a bold rat*, he thought. The nihanem stood around her like sharpened teeth on a bear trap wired to strike. "And why would I do that when I could simply slice open your throat and add your corpse to my army instead?"

"Because you need me."

The nihanem took a sudden step toward her, but her gaze was unwavering. Not even the slightest flinch occurred as a corpse to her right let out a hollow scream. This girl is either brave or incredibly stupid. Hades quickly gripped her throat and withdrew the dagger. She could be a trap sent by the others or even one of their descendants. A trace of disgust flashed across his face at the very thought of the possible union. He shook the idea from his head.

No, they would have attacked him on sight.

He considered her offer in silence. The only sounds that could be heard were of the scattered spurts of chaos in the distance. His grip tightened but was met with no resistance. Through squinted eyes, he examined the human. Her eyes were locked onto his while her hands rested calmly at her side.

This could be interesting, he thought before forcefully releasing her. "And why would I need you?" he snarled.

"I know how you can spread your virus faster and create more zombies."

Hades crossed his arms. "Look around you. My army has grown without a problem."

"You haven't been directing them anywhere. It's all random. Something focused would work much better," the mystery girl advised.

"Say I don't kill you now. What ideas could you possibly have?"

The girl bit the edge of her lip as she searched the ground. Her eyes flared open, and she reached toward her breast. Pulling a phone from beneath her shirt, she swiped and poked at the screen. Just as Hades had reached the end of his patience, she looked up at him.

"I know just where to go. How does a thousand people trapped in one place sound?"

A single dark eyebrow rose on Hades. "If you know of such a place, you may just prove useful."

Walking past him, she bid him to follow. The blade slipped back into his belt. If this was a plot geared toward toying with him, the slow death she would receive would make her corpse useless for his army. He eyed the nihanem standing around him, breathed deeply, and then trudged off to accompany the human.

Thoughts of his past raced through his head. He had promised himself that he would be a servant no more, yet here he was, bowing to the whim of a being that was even weaker than the tyrants that still haunted his dreams. The wooden soles of his buskin clacked on the pavement while more than one hundred shambling nihanem scraped the ground behind him. Curse the others. If they hadn't diminished his *Essence*, he'd at least be able to make these corpses walk properly.

Hades was lost in thought until he nearly bumped into the girl, who had stopped suddenly.

With balled fists, she stared at a large building in front of them. "Attack here."

Ignoring her order, he closely eyed the building. It was immense. Its white walls were plain aside from the single orange stripe that ran around the base. Its color had faded with age. "What is this place?"

People walking alongside the building turned and ran for the entrance at the sight of the approaching horde. Those closer to the edge ran off into a sea of unmoving cars and disappeared.

"It's a place that profits off the misery and pain of others. The people within deserve this," she stated.

Hades watched as the curious eyes of children appeared in a window on the third floor. "What's your plan?"

"There are three doors into the building. Send zombies into each entrance, and no one will be able to escape," she said with confidence, pointing toward each location.

"What part do you play in your plan? Do you sit idly by as my army does all the work?"

She flashed Hades an annoyed glare. "Of course not. I'm going in as well."

Hades smiled slyly. "Personal objective?" He moved toward the building. "I'll be watching you." The horde behind him began to split into three channels. He looked back at the girl and took a wild guess. "Something happened here that made you turn on your own kind."

The girl, now only a few paces behind him, fingered a band of purple beads around her wrist. "They took something from me ..." She fixated on a single bead. "And I'll never forgive them for it."

Hades faced the building. "What is your name, human?"

Surprised by his curiosity, her fingers released the bead. "Lindsey ... but my friends call me Liz."

"Pray your plan succeeds, Lindsey. Fail me, and I will hunt you down. Not even the *Void* will be able to provide you refuge."

Without another word, his three detachments moved toward the entrances. Hades slipped between the bodies and stayed within the center of the fleshy mass. Still confused by Hades' threat, Lindsey took front and center of the horde. An idea crossed her mind, and she suddenly sprinted toward the entrance, a façade of fear masking her grim intent.

A guard, pale as the walls protecting him, watched her approach from behind the thick glass doors. Slamming into the door, she screamed to be let in. Wide-eyed, he frantically fumbled with a ring full of various keys until he had a small brass key between his fingers.

The horde of nihanem were no more than ten yards from Lindsey and getting closer. Her screaming became increasingly shrill with each step they took. As if sending a telegraph, the key tapped against metal as the guard struggled to get the key into the lock. Five yards away. Grinding the tip of the key along the surface, the man managed to slide it into its home. With a click, the door unlocked, and he pushed it open just enough for her to slip through.

The guard struggled to shut the door, facing stiff resistance due to the automatic door closer. Dead hands pounded on the glass and gripped the edge of the door. Despite this, the guard still managed to nearly close it. Now, Lindsey saw her chance and slammed her shoulder into his side with all her weight. Instead of crashing to the ground, her light frame only offset the man and caused him to slightly stumble. This break in focus gave the dead outside the ability to pull the door open wide enough to grab the guard's sleeve.

"No!"

The repeated screams and cries for help were lost on Lindsey. She watched as more hands found their hold on him. The screeching of fingernails being pulled along metal barely rose above the moans and screams of the horde outside. Within seconds, he was pulled from the building and disappeared amongst the dead.

With the door now open, the nihanem poured into the building. Like a stone in a stream, the rotting river flowed around her. Her wish was finally coming true. The zombies would slaughter the filth within. But there was one person she needed to find. Preparing for the ordeal, she took in a deep breath.

Out of the corner of her eye, she saw movement down the main hall. Emerging from a room was a small child. Her blue gown was the color of the sky on a warm summer day. Messy golden hair fell about her shoulders. Locking eyes, the girl gazed at Lindsey from behind a fluffy brown teddy bear. Tears streamed from the girl's eyes.

For a moment, time seemed to stand still. Evil filled this place. After everything they had put her through, how could it not? Her hatred raged inside her like an unrelenting storm. Yet there was a calm. Creating this peace, wiping the hate from her mind, was this child.

The guard at the door had thrown her and her mother into the cold. The monster had to die. This girl, though ... she radiated innocence. She played no part in the atrocity. No part in the pain. With only her eyes, the girl called out to her for safety and comfort.

The storm faltered within Lindsey. Losing their hardness,

her eyes gained a glimmer of compassion. Just one person could be left alive. One less body to be given to the horde. She could hold the child's hand and walk them to the door. She didn't have to die with the rest. Innocence did not deserve this fate.

Lindsey released her breath and walked toward the child. She could protect her. Give her a life that was better than her own. As if the girl understood, she began walking toward Lindsey.

Hope filled the small girl's eyes. Without warning, a mutilated hand emerged from the chaos in front of the girl. Gripping the child's face, the zombie slammed the back of the girl's head against the edge of a door frame.

Sudden shock wiped the glimmer from Lindsey's eyes. Going into a full run, she desperately made her way toward the girl. With each step, a new lifeless barricade stood between her and the child. Shoving and evading the obstacles, she reached the child. Hunched over the girl, a zombie in a torn green jersey clutched the child's head and tore flesh from her arm using its teeth.

Sensing company, it looked up toward Lindsey. Like a wolf guarding its meal, the zombie snarled at her through blood-covered teeth. At that moment, Lindsey felt more helpless than she had in years. She could do nothing to stop the mutilation of this child. The feast continued before her.

Stop. She wanted the harm to this girl to stop. "Stop ... Please stop." It came out like a quiet whimper. At first, she couldn't tell if it was a thought or if she had actually spoken it.

The noises of tearing skin chilled her spine. Straightening her back and standing tall, she looked down at the unholy creation and spoke with strength. "I command you to stop. Let this one be."

The zombie became still, and Lindsey froze, unsure if she had just made herself the next meal. But she had to remain strong.

The zombie released the child and slowly stood up. Adrenaline flooded her veins. The corpse towered above her. Blood dripped from its chin, and she could feel it patter on her boot. When it leaned in, she could smell the overpowering stench of death. An inhuman scream from behind took her to the edge.

Fingers slowly made their way onto Lindsey's shoulders and grasped tightly. The zombie's teeth chattered. She stared intently back into the dead eyes which now studied her. A soft chuckle pulled her from the fear. Quickly turning her head, she found Hades smiling. Lindsey's fear ignited into rage.

"The girl didn't have to die!" Lindsey shouted.

Hades' smile faded. "A fire does not distinguish between who it burns. You ignited the spark in this place. All the lives within it you condemned to the flames." He stretched his hand out toward the child's mutilated corpse, now crumpled on the floor. "She is no different from any other piece of kindling."

Lindsey's gaze followed the outstretched arm and rested on the girl. Jerking into motion, the girl slammed her palms against the ground and forced herself up like a fleshy marionette. Blood-soaked hair clung awkwardly to her face. Hiding behind a few strands of soaked hair, a bloody, pulp-filled eye socket showed just how ferocious the attack had been. Lindsey prayed that the wound had occurred after death.

Removing his hand from her shoulder and tightly gripping the back of her neck, Hades looked down at Lindsey. "Try to hinder me again, and I won't hesitate to turn my nihanem on you." With surprising strength, he shoved her forward.

Lindsey stumbled but lost balance, landing hard on her hands and knees. By the time she was back on her feet, Hades was nowhere to be seen. She fixed her shirt. With a very audible "Hmph!" she strutted off down the hall. Her boots clacked against the hospital tile.

Once a place filled with beeping machines and a cyclone of white and blue uniforms, the facility was now filled with death and ruin. Most rooms contained little evidence of resistance. Doors, already open, led to easy prey. Patients made immobile by disease and injury lay helpless as the rotting fire engulfed the building. Their cured corpses added to the growing horde. To her left, five zombies threw themselves against a door. Between the animalistic screams of the dead, she heard the cries of those inside.

"They all deserve it," Lindsey mumbled to herself as she glanced over a hospital map. How could they not? They all contributed one way or another. Praising those that claimed to heal but only hurt. Propelling them further and causing more damage. But there was one person she had in mind who truly deserved the fate that the rest of the building was condemned to. She just had to find them before the horde did. Her nail tapped on the map's marble surface. "There you are. Room 329B."

Across the hospital, Hades found himself in a place of mystery. Confusion and wonder fought for supremacy of his mind. His eyes snaked their way from item to item. He knelt before a glass case. Resting upon each shelf were tiny buildings trapped within globes. It felt strange in his hand. Turning it upside-down, the item came to life as small white particles fell from their previous resting place. Startled, Hades cast it away. Two nihanem sprung into the room and stomped on the object before stepping back and growling at the broken, shattered target between them.

Hades leaned in, cautiously inspecting the object. The carpet became soaked by whatever the globe had stored. *How far have humans come?* he pondered. Glass and miniature white balls littered the area surrounding the destroyed item.

Eyes wide, he finally realized what he had stumbled upon: eggs. These globes were incubators filled with human eggs.

His head darted to the right. Small versions of aquatic birds stared blankly toward him. Behind them on another shelf ... fuzzy blankets. To his left, miniature metal tags with various names hung from a strange thorn-covered post.

A grim smile spread across his face. He could deal a blow to the humans by eliminating them before they even had a chance to poison the air with their breath. He spread his arms out wide and thrust them forward. A flood of nihanem stormed past him into the room. Only his laughter could be heard above the crashing of shelves and shattering of glass.

Far from the chaos, Lindsey stood in front of a dark oak door on the third floor, unaware of the destruction occurring below. Nestled in a wing far away from the patients was room 329B. A gold placard hung beside the door. Engraved into it was a name that had haunted her ever since that nightmarish day that took place twelve years ago. Her fingers traced the lines etched into the metal.

Mouthing the name to herself, the fateful day played out in her mind. A scalpel rolled in her fingers. The anticipation continued to grow with each moment—and with it, the speed of the scalpel.

A noise from within the room broke the spell. Gripping the handle, she thrust the door open. Screeching from the brass hinges tore into the silent space.

The room was dark. Feeling around, she was able to make out a light switch and flicked it on. Standing triumphantly in the center of the room—surrounded by two towering file cabinets and two shabby chairs—was a mahogany desk. If it was in a different office, she might have admired the beauty of its Victorian features. Unfortunately, this desk came with memories of her mother: the very place where her mother had been condemned

Staring at the chair behind the altar, her memories came rushing back to her. Standing behind the desk, she saw the doctor as he had been back then. Those cold brown eyes gazed across the desk at a woman dressed in a hoodie and worn-out jeans. Beside her sat a young girl in an oversized purple sweater. Tears streamed from both of their eyes. "Please! There must be something you can do!" they pleaded.

Casually, the doctor picked up a phone. Lindsey couldn't make out his words over the screaming of the woman. The doctor's gaze remained unchanged as security entered and dragged the woman and her child out of the room.

A closet door caught her eye, and the ghosts of the past dissipated. The heels of her boots proclaimed each step she took. The closet door burst open, and emerging from it was a wide-eyed woman in blue scrubs. Lindsey stumbled backward as the woman pushed her aside and ran out into the hallway.

Rage took over. Lindsey bolted down the hallway. The ache of her legs should have slowed her down, but the fire inside thrust her forward. Catching up to the woman in blue, Lindsey tackled her and jammed the scalpel into her back. "TELL ME WHERE HE IS!" Lindsey aggressively screamed at the top of her lungs. "WHERE IS DOCTOR NOSPARCHEZ!"

Grabbing a handful of hair, Lindsey yanked the woman's head off the ground and plunged it back into the tile.

"Talk, you bitch!" Lindsey shrieked.

The woman lay motionless. Frustrated, Lindsey looked down at the woman's back; her blue shirt had practically turned red. Countless holes tattered the blood-soaked garment. In shock, she looked at her hands. Blood dripped from her fingertips. Then she saw the hilt of the scalpel. The tip, along with half of the handle, was lodged in the woman's skull. She gazed upon it for mere moments before a sobering realization played through her mind.

She only remembered stabbing the woman once.

A warm aroma tickled the boy's nose. Smiling wide, he leapt from the bed and scampered to the kitchen. Upon the stove, a raging fire licked at the tarnished bottom of a copper pot. Breathing in deeply, the boy attempted to guess the ingredients in what he could only imagine was mom's famous stew.

His attempts were to no avail, but he had to know what was in it. Maybe it included dulculum? His favorite shirt was the same light purple hue as that sweet vegetable. Unfortunately, they uniquely were without a smell.

Normally, his father would lift him up to allow him to peer into the pot, but the man was nowhere to be found. His foot tapped impatiently on the wooden floor. Papa might not be around, but he wasn't alone. The lizard crawled out from under his shirt. Grabbing onto it, the boy lifted his small friend up to the edge of the pot. The boy's face suddenly beamed. Dulculum.

VI

PRODIGAL SON

Against the cold and dusty cement floor, sleep slipped through Matt's fingers like a distant memory. Each attempt brought him back to a room engulfed in flames. Flowing with maggots, a corpse snarled and snapped inches from his face. Just before it seemed that all hope was lost, tongues of fire burst from his palms and licked at the decayed flesh of his ferocious attacker. As if covered in oil, flames overtook the assailant, effectively turning it into a torch with teeth.

Like riding a never-ending rollercoaster, his heart beat against his ribcage, frantically begging to break free, waking him in a cold sweat. This recurring dream should have been the only thing tormenting him, but somehow images of the sarcophagus kept creeping up on him.

Reaching into his pocket, Matt pulled out the mysterious notes. What could the message possibly mean? No matter how many times he read it, the words never took on any new meaning.

"It could be a metaphor," Matt mumbled to himself. Although with the dead rising outside, maybe a god had really been trapped inside of the stone box in that room.

The Greek god Hades didn't command death, though; he

just ruled over the Underworld. But religious stories had a tendency to shift over time, and Hades could have been seen differently two thousand years ago. Matt had never been a particularly devout person, much to the discomfort of his mother, but maybe the Greeks had it right.

Still clutched in his fingers, Matt rested the notes on his stomach. *Kevin might have ideas of his own*, he thought. Pocketing the notes, Matt got up. Careful to not bump into anything, he moved his way around the room, looking down each aisle of the dark store. Kevin was nowhere to be seen. Maybe Kevin had changed his mind over the course of the last few hours and joined the others despite being steadfast in his decision to sleep as far away as possible. *Might as well check there.*

Feeling eyes on him, Matt looked about the shop. Perched on a counter near the back was an old register which stared down the curious guest. Matt slipped behind the counter and entered a short hall, escaping the compact guard's gaze.

Like a child woken in the night, Matt stood outside the closed office door. Would it be worse to knock or simply walk in? What if someone opened the door, and he was just standing there? He never went into a guest room once the door was closed. That was at his house, though; this was a random group of people.

Filibustered by his own brain, Matt awkwardly faced the closed door. Sounds of movement inside lifted his paralysis, and he grabbed the doorknob, readying himself to slowly open it and poke his head through.

As he turned the doorknob slightly, the scream of a tortured mouse erupted from the handle. Halting his progress, Matt pressed his lips together and weighed his options. He could continue to open the door and pain the mouse further, release the doorknob and wake the entire room, or stand here like a moron until morning. The cold brass of the doorknob suddenly felt like a grenade in his hand, and the pin had already been pulled.

Standing here until morning started to look pretty good. Unfortunately, the decision was no longer his to make. The doorknob squealed as it spun in his hand, and the door flung open. Aggressively bursting from the room, a great figure rushed through the doorway, nearly slamming into Matt. The figure jumped slightly and remained a blockade.

Matt instinctively stumbled backward. "I am so, so sorry to disturb you. I was looking—"

"Perfect timing. I'm glad you're up. We'll be leaving soon," Kevin stated firmly.

Relieved to find Kevin but hesitant to go out into the night, Matt pushed back. "Wasn't the plan to leave in the morning?" Matt leaned over to get a look past Kevin, but his coworker moved to the side and quickly closed the door, clearly blocking his view.

"There will be fewer people moving about the city right now, so we'll be able to cover more ground."

Matt scratched his head. He wasn't thrilled by the idea of going out into the dark, but it made sense. "Alright. I'll just grab my water bottle from the office, and we can get going."

Kevin pressed his hand against the doorframe and leaned against it. "No need. I already spoke with the shop owner, and he said we can take anything from the shop for our travels. Incredibly kind of him. Just try to keep the noise down for the kid when you're shopping."

Matt suspiciously looked at his eerily calm coworker through squinted eyes. *Kevin asked me before if I trusted him. I honestly do, but this ... this is pushing it.* Not wanting to cause a ruckus, he turned and walked back to the sales floor. With hands on his hips, he looked around without an idea of where to start. He'd need a bag to carry whatever he grabbed, but plastic bags, he knew, would not only be cumbersome but also create a ton of noise. "Maybe this shop has backpacks," he mumbled to himself.

Twenty minutes later, he stared in disbelief and embarrassment at the best option he could find. Hanging triumphantly on a shelf were roughly a dozen purple fanny packs. Leaping out of an embroidered puddle was a yellow fish with a cartoonish smile, surrounded by a ring of text that read "Lake Michigan is a SPLASH." Without taking his eyes off of the probably dated pouch, he motioned Kevin over to him.

Curiously, Kevin made his way over. "Find something good?"

"I, um ... definitely found something."

"Well, don't leave me hangin'. What is it?!" Kevin said excitedly, making his way down the aisle with a childlike smile.

After nearly thirty minutes of cramming foil-wrapped treats, water bottles, and various travel medical supplies into the packs, they were ready. Weighed down with defeat and plump fanny packs, the two men stood at the door. Kevin adjusted a strap on his shoulder. "Did we really need to use *all* of the packs?"

Matt ignored the question. He didn't want to think about the three *he* was wearing.

Carefully, he angled himself to peer through the drawn shades, trying not to disturb any of the blades. The coast looked clear, but that could change at any moment. "If you really want to leave, now's the time. Not sure why we couldn't just wait until morning."

"The quicker we get back to the office, the better."

"Once we're there, promise me you'll tell me why we needed to go back there. I'm sure there are hundreds of safer places to go."

Kevin looked down at the tools in his hand. Choosing to keep a large pipe wrench, he handed a crowbar to Matt. "Fortified by brick, mortar, and false securities. Sure. You might be out of the storm, but there will always be leaks. Make yourself waterproof, and no storm can touch you."

The weight of the crowbar and the coldness of its touch reminded Matt of the pen Maddison had once handed him. The heavy metal pen that signed the death of his marriage. Taking a deep breath, Matt pushed the thought from his head. Now was not the time to get lost in memories. "Ready when you are."

Kevin nodded and opened the door. A chorus of chimes sang above their heads. Wide-eyed, they both shot their attention to the small notification device and then at each other. A throaty howl from the street erupted from the backseat of a red sedan parked down the block.

"Damn it!" shouted Kevin as he left the shop. Further screaming in the distance spurred a barrage of mumbled curses as the duo ran down the street. "Details. It's always the little details."

Stopping at the red sedan, the two men were welcomed by the soft thud of a zombified woman's face as it pressed itself against the glass. Its arm waved maniacally as it grasped at the air through a partially open window. Smashing the window with the wrench, Kevin grabbed the fiend, tore it from the car, and removed most of its head with a single swing of the hefty tool.

"I don't see a key!" Matt frantically shouted.

"Just get in. We don't have time for this." Kevin ordered. He grabbed the remains of what might have been the woman's family and threw them onto the sidewalk behind him.

Running around the vehicle, Matt tried the front passenger door. It opened without issue. "The doors are un—"

The shattering of glass cut him off. Kevin reached in through the driver-side window and pressed the unlock button, causing all the doors to click. "Hop in!" Kevin blurted out as he slid into the vehicle and immediately started to feel around beneath the steering wheel.

Matt closed the door. While he would have loved to pay attention to his coworker displaying another questionable talent, something else took priority. Three unstable individuals had emerged from a nearby building and began making their way toward them. "Whatever you're doing, do it fast. We're running out of time."

Looking up from his work, Kevin swore and started fiddling vigorously with the wires. Using bone-exposed arms to pull itself along the ground, one more zombie emerged from the alley to their right; a tangled trail of entrails dragging behind it had replaced its legs. Farther down the street, an increasing number of others stumbled in their direction.

A sudden pounding on the back windshield caused Matt to nearly jump out of his seat. Jolting his head toward the sound, he was greeted by the shattering of glass. Screaming, Matt shielded his eyes. Meanwhile, the crackling sparks of electricity beneath the steering wheel transformed into the muffled roar of the engine kicking in. Kevin quickly put the car in drive and floored the gas pedal. Rubber tires spun against the cement until the vehicle lurched forward.

The wheels protested their handling, squealing with each swerve around the dead in their path.

"Which way, Matt?!" Kevin shouted as an intersection approached.

Matt desperately looked toward each street. "Left! Go Left!"

The force of the turn flung him against the door. Through the chaos of motion, Matt noticed a hooded figure on a rooftop that seemed to be looking directly at them—or possibly even through them. He couldn't tell. Reality came rushing back as the car jolted violently over something; in the side mirror, he saw a one-legged corpse roll across the pavement.

Strangely feeling like a kid in the back of a school bus, Matt fixed himself in the seat. They wove through walking corpses with torn open stomachs and banners of skin hanging off their bodies. Lunging for the vehicle, one lucky zombie thunked against the outside of Matt's door. This was not how he thought today would go.

"You've got to be shitting me!" Kevin yelled. Tires squealed as Kevin sharply turned the car to avoid a thick crowd of the restless dead. With the road blocked on either side, Kevin took the only path remaining: he pointed the car toward a thin alleyway and floored the gas pedal.

"What are you doing!? No, Kevin, no!" squealed Matt.

Having nicked the tail end of a curb, the sedan awkwardly leapt in the air. Pounding the ground and jerking the passengers inside, the vehicle narrowly avoided a weathered wooden telephone pole loitering in the alleyway entrance. Pulling hard on the steering wheel, Kevin veered the car away from a rusted blue dumpster.

Trash cans whizzed by Matt's open window while illegible graffiti marked their progress. Having swerved around a group of ghouls, Kevin held tightly onto the wheel.

"Look out!" Matt screamed as the sedan barreled into a pile of garbage bags strewn about an overflowing dumpster. Garbage bags exploded like confetti, sending trash and moldy leftovers into the air. Upon impact with the windshield, a lidded plastic cup burst open, releasing a wave of orange soda.

Temporarily blinded by the soda and other debris, Kevin hit down the wiper stick. Flying across the windshield like bats out of hell, the wiper blades made quick work of the sugary shade. Swearing loudly, Kevin slammed his foot on the brakes and turned the wheel sharply. With tires screeching, the car skidded across the pavement.

CRASH!

The driver's side of the sedan smashed against the metal guard rail protecting a brick wall. Kevin pressed his hand over the left side of his head and groaned.

Thankful for his seatbelt, Matt's chest hurt from where the strap tightened to keep him in place. Looking to his left, Matt eyed the building responsible for creating a right turn in the alley. *At least he managed to turn the car the right way.*

Feeling the front-right side of the car go down, Matt turned his head toward the source of the weight. Using the car for support, a hefty man in a filthy chef uniform hobbled toward Matt on one and a half legs. Startled, Matt pushed his back into the seat. "Go!" The vehicle jolted forward, causing the zombie to roll along the side of the car until it finally fell to the ground behind them.

After what felt like an eternity filled with screaming, screeching, and second-guessing, they arrived back at the office. The vehicle was a disaster; one side mirror was missing, two tires were quickly losing air, and both sides had sustained enough damage to practically remove the paint. Blood, dried by the passing air, clung to the dented metal.

The two men breathed heavily as they looked up at the glass building they called work. Shielding their eyes from the smiting rays of the morning sun, they surveyed the scene before them.

Matt furrowed his brows. The office seemed oddly at peace. Aside from a few cars in the parking lot, it looked like the chaos outside had barely touched his glass prison. After a moment of studying the windows for signs of foul play, a disappointed groan escaped his lips, and he slumped back into his seat. "After everything going on, I somehow thought this place would look like something out of a horror movie. Windows destroyed. Smoking from a fire. Something."

Kevin slowly looked over toward his pouty companion and then burst out laughing. "The scariest thing in the world is happening right now, and that's what you're focusing on? Bro, you have one of the weirdest methods of handling stress. After all this is over, you should go and see someone about that."

Matt rolled his eyes and chuckled. "And you're the one who wanted to return to the office while the dead are rising." He stepped out of the beaten-up vehicle, unclipped the fanny pack still around his waist, and tossed it onto the backseat. "Which of us really needs therapy?"

"Can't argue with you there," Kevin mumbled to himself, eyeing the building. It seemed taller than usual to him. Each floor was going to be a crapshoot. They only had to get to floor six, but any one of those floors could be filled with zombies. "Matt, how would you feel about staying out here while I run in?"

Matt quickly shot back, "Hell no. I was barely able to handle the zombie that came out of the truck on my own. If even one or two come by, I'm screwed. Even more so if there's a mob of them. I'm sticking with you until we find a safe place to rest. Whatever you came here for, let's just get it and go. If we're lucky, we might find a way to get out of the city."

"It could be filled with zombies, and you wouldn't know it until they were right on top of you. Out here, you can see them coming for a good distance," Kevin counterposed.

That was the worst idea Matt had heard all day. "Oh boy. I can now see my painful demise approaching sooner, with even fewer places to hide."

"There are cars and nearby buildings."

"You mean the buildings that could be filled to the brim with walking corpses or with someone who is a bit too trigger-happy?"

"You can talk them down," Kevin reassured.

"The corpses or the person with a gun?"

"If I had a gun, you'd be a corpse right now."

Smiling like an ass, Matt tossed his crowbar into the back seat and made finger guns at Kevin. "Even a better reason to come with you. To keep you from getting that gun."

There was little point in continuing the squabble. Kevin wasn't going to be able to shake off his coworker. Defeated, he grabbed his wrench, and together they walked toward the office front door. They peered through the glass doors into the lobby. It looked completely empty. Not even the old security guard could be seen in his usual place behind his sleek marble desk. The leather seats lining the front of the room—normally filled with nervous applicants and bored employees on break—were eerily barren aside from a single tipped-over water bottle beneath a seat. Cautiously, they entered the building.

To their left, a line of elevators waited patiently for passengers that were never going to arrive. Their shiny metal doors would never reflect the face of an empty-eyed employee again. To their right, two large doors leading to the ground floor offices were closed, accessible only by typing a code into a little black control panel on either side. Adjacent to those doors on the left was a normal-sized door labeled "STAIRWELL" in big white lettering across the dark wood finish. Kevin approached the elevators. Above the door before him, a small orange light remained lit.

Matt looked over at Kevin. "Are you sure you want to take the elevator? If the noise of it moving doesn't attract attention, the little *ding* noise certainly will when the door is about to open. We'd be screwed."

Barely acknowledging Matt's concerns, Kevin nonchalantly pressed the elevator call button. Almost immediately, an electronic bell chimed, and the door before them opened up. Matt jumped back and readied his fists.

Just like the lobby, the elevator was empty. Kevin poked his head inside and tapped the button for the topmost floor. "Come on," he said and walked toward the stairwell door.

Baffled and wishing he hadn't left the crowbar behind, Matt looked from Kevin to the closing elevator door and back. "You just alerted everything that might be inside the building that we're here."

"I know." Kevin smirked and turned the handle.

The door swung open, knocking into a surprised Kevin. Barreling out of it was the elderly security guard with a ghastly wound across his neck. Spidery hands grasped at Kevin's throat, missing his neck but firmly gripping his collar.

Kevin awkwardly swung the wrench and clipped the old man, causing him to stumble and release his grip. Quickly taking a step back, Kevin swung the heavy wrench downward into the crook of the guard's neck, dropping the man harder than a bag of stone. Kevin looked back at Matt, winded only due to his racing heart.

Matt watched the scene unfold from the center of the lobby. Out of all the people in the building, he had hoped Charles was able to escape and find refuge. "Behind you!" he shouted as the old man picked himself off the ground.

Charles' head sickeningly hung against his back. Kevin kicked the risen corpse in the chest and sent it flying backward into the stairwell door, cracking the wood. Before Charles could fall to the ground, Kevin delivered another powerful kick into his chest, cracking multiple ribs and sending the zombie completely through the door.

Kevin pushed through the splintery portal, breaking off jagged edges of the wood as he climbed through. Standing above the recovering corpse, he smashed his foot down onto the head until nothing remained. All motion ceased.

Studying the body of the newly headless guard, he was satisfied. "All clear," he muttered breathlessly.

After a brief discussion, they both agreed that resting on the steps for a moment was a good idea. Once they were both ready and Kevin's shoe was somewhat cleaned off, they began the ascent. On each floor, Kevin pressed his ear to the door and listened for movement. Muffled groaning with the occasional scream could be heard coming from floor two. Floor three was silent. He didn't even have to press his ear to the door to know what was on floor four; a large ensemble of screams, growls, and pounding could be clearly heard through the thick steel door. Kevin smiled to himself over his elevator diversion. Floor five had a similar situation as floor four, but was noticeably less intense.

Finally arriving at the sixth-floor landing, Kevin approached the door and placed a cupped ear against it. Both men held their breath. After a few seconds, Kevin gave Matt a thumbs up. Absolute silence.

Bracing the door with one arm, Kevin slowly turned the knob and opened it just a crack. Nothing in sight. He opened it the rest of the way, and the two coworkers entered the room.

Row upon row of shoulder-high cubicles filled the large space. Lining the right side of the room were offices, each with a tall glass window and their own personal doors to keep management safe from the employees. Taking up the entire back wall was the crown jewel of them all: it was the only office that had a full wall replaced by a large, thick glass window—with blinds for those extra secure meetings that everyone listened in on. It was also the office of his wife-stealing boss, Thomas.

Noticing that a few of the smaller offices had lights on within them, they decided the external aisle farthest from those offices would be the safest choice. Without another word, the coworkers followed their chosen path, making sure to keep low. Their cubicles were on the opposite side of the office floor. While just a short distance to cover, the path looked to be miles long, no doubt amplified by the new circumstances.

Each row of cubicles was a mystery box of danger. One wrong move and it could be their last. One zombie they could probably handle, but if there were too many—or if they attracted the attention of the hordes below them—their chances of victory or escape would fall drastically. Each step had to be taken with the utmost sense of caution. Even if there wasn't a single zombie on the floor, they had to treat this operation as if they were special forces attempting to infiltrate the conference room for a brownie without anyone noticing.

Mundane office noises that were slightly annoying at most now became serious possible threats. The groaning of the heating system, the whirring of an old computer tower, the ghostly typing sounds that no one could ever explain, Candace, the creaking of the building ...

Matt popped his head up from behind a printer and quickly dropped back down. "Kevin," he whispered, "I don't think we're alone in here."

Without breaking his focus on the path in front of them, Kevin leaned back. "What do you mean?"

"I could have sworn I just saw Candace walk into Thomas' office."

Kevin's face was a mix of concern and disgust. "You sure?"

"Just caught the back of her head before she went in."

Kevin popped his head up over the cubicle wall. "Shit. The blinds are drawn." Looking at the ground, he began biting the corner of his bottom lip. "If she really is here, we might get lucky and she'll be unaffected. If she's turned, we might be able to simply grab what we need and get out without her noticing us."

"And if she spots us?"

"Pray we can take her out before she makes noise."

After nodding at each other in agreement, Matt rechecked the coast and motioned to Kevin that it was clear. The slow mission continued. A few minutes later, they were at the end of their row: two rows away from the big guy's office.

Kevin checked the aisle. "All clear," he whispered. "I'll be right back. Stay here."

His desk was six cubicles in. Staying low, he entered his small space, moved over to his chair, and opened the drawer.

"No no no no no," he whispered to himself. Reaching into the drawer, he pulled out a sticky note.

'Told you I wanted to inspect your package. Come see me when you're ready, big guy.'

Below the message, in a deep scarlet, was the imprint of the thief's lips.

Crumpling the note and tossing it to the floor, it took all his strength to contain the flaring of his rage. "Candace," he growled. He made his way back to Matt. "Follow me," he ordered. Brandishing the wrench and driven by anger, he moved to the next cube row. Quickly, he dashed to the left of the boss's door. Once Matt was beside him, he pivoted on his foot so he was standing directly in the doorway.

Aside from the occasional beam of light piercing through factory-produced holes in the blinds, the room was completely dark. Standing in the middle of the room, facing away from them, was a thin figure dressed in a dangerously low-cut skirt and a tight red top. In its hand was Kevin's box.

Passing the wrench to Matt, Kevin took a step forward. "Candace," he softly hissed. Her head turned slightly toward him. "Candace, I don't have the patience for your B.S. right now." Forcefully, he extended an open hand toward her. "Give me the box."

Gingerly, she placed her hand in his, further lowering his patience.

"Candace, not the time," he growled.

She took a step toward him, and her face entered a beam of light. Dried blood covered her face and neck. Her grip tightened on his hand.

"Matt! The wrench!" he cried.

Startled, Matt fumbled the wrench. It tumbled to the floor and landed with a loud and solid thud. Matt quickly dropped down and grabbed the wrench. A hand burst from the shadows and grabbed his wrist. Matt turned his head only to be greeted by the ghastly white face of his boss. Screaming, he pulled away hard enough to break free. Using only his arms, Thomas hungrily dragged himself toward Matt.

Kevin heard the screams of his coworker, but he had his own troubles to deal with. Locked in a struggle with Candace's corpse, he had to somehow get the box out of her hand and keep her from injuring him. He jolted his arm downward as she scratched at him with her long fingernails.

Kevin looked down at the box in her hand only to come face to face with her bare chest, hardly covered by her almost entirely unbuttoned shirt. "Really, Candace, that's what you were doing?" he strained through gritted teeth. Pushing her backward, Kevin grabbed her wrist and slammed it repeatedly on the corner of a large mahogany desk until her hand broke and released the box.

With both of her arms free to attack, Candace became more ferocious. Looking for any way to get an edge, Kevin looked around the room. On the opposite side of Thomas' office was the full-length, ceiling-to-floor window. Even though the blinds were drawn, it was worth a shot. Grabbing her by the arm—with all of his rage behind it—he threw Candace at the large window. Despite her light frame, the force of the impact from her body shattered the glass, and she fell to the parking lot below.

Breathing heavily, he turned to Matt. Swearing up a storm, Matt stood over the motionless body of his now-late boss, pulverizing it with the wrench. Blood spattered his face and shirt with every blow.

Kevin strolled over to the show. "Matt, I think you got him."

Still swearing, Matt stopped the metallic barrage and let Kevin take the wrench. "Wish he'd still been alive for that," Matt said. He looked down at the body and scrunched his face. Thomas' bare ass was out, and his pants were completely around his ankles.

Kevin flipped Matt's kill over with his foot, causing both men to wince. "Figures," he muttered to himself. "Let's get out of here." He scooped the box off the floor, and together they walked back toward the stairwell.

Sounds of slurping and laughter filled the dimly lit room. The boy sat at a wooden table beside his father while his mother smiled at him from the other side. Before him was the largest bowl in the house, filled to the brim with his mom's famous stew. He could barely keep the steaming broth in his mouth between the bouts of giggling.

With a smirk, his father wrapped an arm around the boy. Playfully, he winked over at his wife. Together, they looked at their son and excitedly shouted, "Happy birthday!"

With a mouth full of dulculum, the best the boy could muster up was, "Ay ew!" He thought himself the happiest and luckiest boy ever in existence.

Spooning out a small chunk of his favorite purple veggie, the boy plopped it on the table, earning him confused looks from both his parents. Out from under his sleeve, Zip emerged. His mom's eyes widened. Confused, his dad looked at his wife and then leaned over to get a better view.

The lizard leaped from the boy's hand, lightly plopped on the table, and began to nibble on the tasty chunk. The mother's piercing scream startled the boy. Quickly shoving him to the floor, the father stepped closer and then smacked the boy's green friend off the table, knocking the bowl of stew to the floor along with it.

VII

SLOTH

19 HOURS AFTER REGENIFACT

Screeching metal against rails drowned out the insufferable chatter around them.

"I don't know how much more I can bear," Hades groaned to himself. As the subway train came to a halt, its doors opened, and the bipedal ants within wearily scampered out. A small hand weaved its way around his arm.

"Patience," Lindsey chuckled. "Just a few moments more and the fun can begin. Just try not to dirty up your new clothes." Due to the success of the assault on the hospital, Hades had granted the girl another chance to show him her usefulness. On the way to Lindsey's next idea, she had spotted a clothing shop; her plan, she had explained, would never work if this stop wasn't made. She had claimed that this stop was crucial and would be quick—only an hour or two. Hades gave her 10 minutes.

Lindsey clung to his arm as if they were newly engaged. Her stained clothing had been replaced with a black, backless tank top and a pair of dark blue skinny jeans with tears going up the front. Her boots had been cleaned and shined by the wonderful cashier, who had also been so generous as to give them the entire purchase for free in exchange for their life.

Hades stood unwillingly beside his lovely experiment in sturdy, yet comfortable, black steel-toe boots and dark gray jeans. A black leather jacket covered his shoulders. The soldier's knife, along with a scrap of stained cloth from his tunic, had been discretely stashed away within an inside pocket. Lindsey had tried relentlessly to have Hades wear a tight-fitted dress shirt and eyeliner. After he had torn off the collar on a dozen shirts and threatened to use his fists to give her a new color of eyeliner, Lindsey compromised with a black undershirt and a spritz of cologne.

"Cute couple," mentioned a passing woman, causing Lindsey to giggle and beam with delight. A groan from Hades only spurred her snake-like arms to constrict around his.

After the last of the exiting passengers cleared the doorway, they made their way aboard. Once on the train, Lindsey walked them to the back, passing row after row of connected metal benches padded with cheap blue fabric.

"Once we start moving, do exactly as we discussed," she whispered into his ear. He eyed the surrounding passengers. Most of them were on their cell phones, listening to music, or trying to sleep. Causing a ruckus nearby, a group of teens woke a previously sleeping old woman, who glared at them through a single squinted eye before turning to her other side and slipping back to sleep.

Nestled in the very last seat, sound asleep, was their first target. Lindsey motioned toward the doomed individual. Hades walked toward them, his arm now released from Lindsey's fleshy shackles. Each step closer made the target's foul stench more apparent.

Curled with their head resting against the window, the doomed soul slept, unaware of the looming threat. Hades slid into the seat next to them, quickly slipped out the knife, and ran it through their throat. No sooner had it been plunged into their neck than it was once again concealed in his jacket. What noises the person did try to make were covered up by the constant noise of the train. To keep the corpse from rolling out of the seat, Hades held it in place with his arm.

Lindsey surveyed the train. Not a single concerned eye in sight. Perfect.

Hades opened his free hand and extended it toward the recent kill. The body stiffened as *Essence* took hold of its new vessel and the nihanim sat up. Seven minutes later, the train came to a halt. Hades moved his legs aside and allowed his raggedy puppet to awkwardly move past him and off the train. Through the window, he watched as it found a corner and sat down, lying in wait for its master's signal.

The humans mindlessly traded places between the platform and the train. The doors, as if possessed by the spirit of a servant, closed as soon as the last person had decided their fate. With a great and sudden push, the train begrudgingly crawled forward.

Before losing sight of his nihanim, he saw a man in shorts and an orange jersey drop money into its lap.

"What a strange world this has become," Hades muttered to himself.

Woosh Woosh Woosh.

Each support beam that passed his window brought memories closer to the forefront of his mind. A rough face of a man, possibly in his fifties, smiled lovingly toward him. Delicate fingers ran through the man's silvery hair. The taste of peppermint fell light as a specter upon Hades' tongue.

The poles whipped by quickly, one after the other, creating a rhythmic combination of speed and airflow. Between each pole, a reflection flashed before Hades that was not his own. The silver-haired man sat facing the window with his arms wrapped around a woman with light brown hair. Hades squeezed his eyes and released a long breath. It had been too long.

That girl's memories had served him well and had enlightened him to this new society and its intricacies. Yet despite their assistance, her memories had continued to plague him like an aching tooth. An unfortunate side effect of a memory sync.

He took one last look at his reflection in the window. Looking back at him were his own eyes. Beside him, he could still see the ghost of Melissa. His gaze moved over her soft features. The world drifted toward silence. Strands of hair fell across her face, partially hiding one of her mesmerizing hazel eyes. Without voice, the haunt mouthed the words he craved. Like candy, her sweet smile brought him to bliss. She brushed the strands behind her ear. Quick as lightning, her light brown hair flashed the radiant color of gold. Hades punched the glass, cracking it slightly and causing many of the passengers to turn his way. But the glares subsided just as quickly as the people returned to their phones and conversations.

Clenching his eyes as tightly as he could, he removed his fist from the glass and rested it in his lap. How long had it been? It was impossible to tell. It could have been centuries, but to him, it felt as if it were mere moments. Even if attempting the ritual destroyed him, he had to try. For her sake.

Lindsey firmly tapped him on the shoulder. "What the hell was that?"

"Mind your tongue, girl," Hades snarled while opening his eyes and staring at the glass web he had created. "Assault me with your finger again and I'll remove it."

The young woman brushed off the god's threat. "This plan only works if we can keep a low profile. If we're noticed or make too much commotion, the train might stop." She looked around the metal compartment until she spotted what she needed. Held in place by a metal frame was a poster displaying a crude map of the city.

Like sickly veins, colorful lines weaved through a gray city, each with its own name. Blood clots dotted each line representing the train stops at which the life of the city could board. "There are nine more stops that we can make on this train."

Hades shoved the squeaky mouse to the side as he exited the cramped bench. "I grow impatient with your dull device."

"Each station that we drop someone off at creates a new point of infection. The city will fall quicker." Lindsey crossed her arms and leaned back against a pole. "But please, do things your way."

Gripping her shirt, Hades forcefully pulled her to him. His breath filled her lungs; the metallic tint of blood danced on her tongue. Like a landmine, her heart was about to explode. Lindsey's ravenous eyes darted between his venomous eyes and pale lips. She was sure that the words coming out of his mouth were vicious and could tear her to tatters, but all she could hear were the sounds of disgust in her head from the other passengers as he took her right then and there. Her fingers were lost in his slick hair. The frigid steel floor bit into her back.

THUD!

The cheap lights danced above her, and a ringing sound replaced the repetitive wails of the train grinding on the rails. The side of her head felt like the early memories of her father. She reached up and gripped the grimy edge of a bench and lifted herself into a sitting position. She looked toward Hades, but a blurry face blocked her sight.

"Are you ok, Mrs.?" Lindsey heard in a deep hoarse voice that reminded her of a cup of spiked hot chocolate on a cold night. As the world fell back into place, the concerned face of a man that could have been her grandpa repeated the question.

"I'm *fine*," she said while shoving him out of the way. The previously rowdy group of teens had descended upon Hades along with a few of the other passengers. An old woman stuck on the outside of the mob weakly jumped and used her purse to bridge the gap between herself and the leather-clad hooligan, managing to smack the god square in the head with each attempt.

Hades' face, contorted by rage, was easily seen even next to the tallest valiant passenger; he stood more than a head above them all. This soon changed after the human version of an overly inflated bean bag chair jumped off a bench and into the fray. Before she lost sight of Hades, Lindsey was sure a sliver of fear entered the god's eyes as he looked at the airborn behemoth.

Now stuck in a seated position and held down by the teenagers and the wrecking ball, Hades struggled without avail. "Let GO OF ME!" he screamed, but was drowned out by insults and other colorful phrases thrown at him by the crowd.

"Shame on you!" the old woman bellowed before whacking him yet again with her leather purse.

If only he could reach his knife, then these humans would cease to be.

Lindsey nervously looked down the car's length. Most of the idle passengers were now watching intently. Phones, like curious birds perched in their owner's hands, searched for different angles to record the best footage. One stylish high-school-aged girl turned away from the commotion only to pull out her phone and strike a pose. Huddled in the far corner, covering one ear with her hand and the other with her phone, was a middle-aged woman in a light red coat. The way she quickly peeked behind herself before hiding again in a corner reminded Lindsey of a frightened mouse.

Lindsey saw the entire plan unraveling before her very eyes. She had to act quickly. She clambered to her feet and locked onto the woman in red. The first step was easy; the second sent her head-first into a pole. Luckily, she caught herself—but barely.

With her head bent down and eyes closed, Lindsey steadied herself. She had endured multiple hells brought about by numerous faces. But no matter what was thrown at her, she had her survival kit. Makeup was her friend and had always got her through. It was just a bonus that the caked-on eyeshadow went so well with her black wardrobe.

Awkwardly, she pushed her way through the gathered crowd. "Excuse me," she hissed to a rail-thin man in a business suit two sizes too large. Jumping from either surprise or conditioning, he moved out of the way one step at a time, continuously checking to see if she had enough room. Looking over his shoulder, he locked eyes with the dead-eyed young woman before looking back down at the phone in his hand.

Lindsey closed her eyes and sighed. Brushing some of her loose hair behind her ear, she carried on.

By the time she got to the woman in the red jacket, the woman was already stashing the phone away in her purse. Lindsey reached out to tap her on the shoulder. The call had already been made. It could have been to anyone: the police, a family member, a restaurant. What was she going to do? Ask the woman who she had called and then demand that she call them back? Retracting her hand, Lindsey sorely slumped onto a bench.

Using her crossed arms as a cushion, she rested her chin on the back of the chair in front of her. With all the noise produced by the train and the crowd, Hades still claimed the spot as the loudest maker of noise.

"I'm killing you first, you withered whore!" he bellowed.

Lindsey smiled slightly at what followed.

Hades was a different breed. Millions of steps above the usual guys she chased. Some wore chains, while one had black eyeliner. One had tattoos from head to toe, and another had scars left from mind-cleansing blades. They all claimed to want her yet showed it with the loving caress of their fists. No matter how hard she tried, she was never able to earn their affection. Never able to keep their arms around her. The only thing she earned were the marks they left on her.

Despite being a god, the bruises he inflicted upon her didn't show any different from the mortal-inflicted ones. His words were like fangs toward her, and she left herself open to them each time. If she showed him her use, this time could be different. It might not be love now, but maybe it could be one day.

"Now approaching ..." squeaked a robotic voice above her head. The catching of the brakes pressed her chest into the back of the seat. Nonchalantly, she watched the people standing on the platform outside whizz by. The train screeched its song of arrival before coming to a pronounced halt.

Like salmon waiting for the dam to break, passengers around the car rushed from their stations toward the exit; some still craned their necks to get one last glimpse of the spectacle. The doors slid open, granting the fish their freedom. Instead of swimming free, the disembarking passengers at one door awkwardly stumbled backward upon each other. Two men and one woman dressed in black uniforms and bullet-proof vests forced their way onto the train.

"Fuck ..." Lindsey whispered to herself, "the bitch in red did call the cops."

Roughly a head taller than Lindsey, the female officer looked like a child compared to her partners. She kept her head low, skulking behind them. She nervously pulled the brim of her black cap down, causing strands of previously tucked-away hazelnut hair to fall from beneath it. She mouthed orders and motioned toward Hades.

The two men approached their target. Each of the moistened faces in the struggling mass before them had turned a bright shade of red, a confession of just how difficult it was to keep the tall, dark, and violent attacker subdued. Sweat plastered Hades' long hair to his forehead; he could barely make out the approaching opponents. Flicking his head, the hair moved just enough to uncover his eyes, and he looked from one man to the other with his head still cocked to the side.

Broad-shouldered and with eyes shadowed in darkened glass, the new men looked like muscular monoliths over the heads of his restraints. The odds didn't look good. Still tucked away in his jacket was the knife. If he could get a single arm free, the tide of this battle would be in his favor.

"Wooooo!" Cheers erupted one by one from the group of valiant citizens once they realized who was behind them.

"Gunna get what's comin' to ya, asshole!" spat one over-zealous twerp directly into Hades' ear.

Every scenario played through his mind. Each outcome was ill-fated. All but one.

Reminiscent of the ancient waters of the Red Sea, the bodies parted to make way for the city defenders. Unlike the fleeing slaves, Hades eagerly awaited his capture by his pursuers. The god of death looked worn and pathetic while stuck in his seat.

A large hand gripped Hades' shoulder. With all the care of a bull in a china shop, he was ripped from his sedentary confinement. Spun around and thrust into the window, he awkwardly held himself up with one knee on the metal bench and his other foot barely supporting weight on the floor.

Deep breaths were all Hades had at his disposal to ease him through this excruciating degradation. The officer pressing him into the wall shifted to the side as his counterpart tightly gripped Hades' left wrist and twisted it until it was behind the captured god's back.

Click click click.

Cold metal dug into Hades' skin as the first rigid handcuff tightened around his wrist. A flash of light from farther down the train beckoned his attention. Pictures. Not only was he subjecting himself to capture, but the event was also being documented by the humans. Practically the entire train was watching him. Smiles, along with the occasional angry glare, were scattered amongst the onlookers.

One face stuck out. A clash of fear and longing was painted across their face. Lindsey.

Diverting his eyes from her, Hades looked out the window. The window was practically a mirror due to the darkness outside of the train. The brute pressing him to the window had definitely seen battle. A long scar marred the right side of his face from his chin to his temple. That one would need to be dealt with first. He felt the weight of an officer on his back as his right wrist was torn from its place and forced to join his left.

In the reflection, a woman dressed in similar attire to his captors could partially be seen behind them, anxiously toying with a holstered gun on her hip. Her face was mostly covered by her cap. Another flash from her side caused her to look up in its direction, revealing her face. Hades' eyes shot open. Putting all his weight on his knee, he pulled his other foot in and thrust a powerful kick into Scar's gut. Falling backward, Scar clipped his female companion and came down hard onto the edge of a bench.

"*Raaaaa!*" Hades roared and smashed his free elbow into the face of the other officer behind him. Taken off guard by the sudden aggression, the remaining male officer lost control of Hades' left wrist, which allowed the god to spin around. Running forward with his left arm held out as a barrier, he rammed the man into a pole. He reached into his jacket, brandished the dagger, and thrust it into the officer's chest, who threw back his head and screamed in agony. Quickly turning the blade and ripping it out, the man's screams were silenced. Hades spun the dagger in his hand and plunged the blade down through the man's eye.

What felt like a war hammer crashed into Hades' side. A

recovered Scar had charged at Hades and used his shoulder as a battering ram. The force caused Hades to stumble before losing his balance and tumble to the ground. Drawing his pistol, Scar aimed directly at the toppled god. Hades grabbed a bystander's ankle and yanked their leg over himself, resulting in Scar's first fired round lodging in their leg. Wailing, the person fell on top of Hades.

Bang Bang Bang.

Round after round tore into the meat shield. Hades winced as one round went cleanly through the bystander and into his left side, piercing just below the ribs. He had to act fast. *Essence* seeped from his fingers into the bystander. *Damn*, Hades thought. *This bastard still has breath in him.*

Pushing the bystander up, Hades gave himself just enough room to tuck his legs underneath. With a great thrust, the barely breathing man flew through the air toward Scar. Unable to move out of the way, the full weight of the bystander knocked the officer off his feet.

Rolling backward and using his arms to project himself, Hades sprung to his feet. The scene before him looked like a modern-day Renaissance painting. For a second, it was as if the world had frozen. Dead-center in the tight confines of the train, Scar was struggling to roll the dying man off him. Five benches farther down the train, Lindsey, with gritted teeth and hands above her head, struggled with the female officer over the gun in her hands. Sticking out between them from underneath a bench were the boots of the first-felled officer. Framing the portrait and filling in the background were the screaming passengers. Piled like pigs for the slaughter, some ran for an exit that had already been sealed.

Breaking through the ice, Hades took a step forward and began sprinting forwards while directing *Essence* toward the dead officer. With all the grace of a seasoned performer, he dove over Scar, grabbing the knife from the eye socket of the now-sitting corpse, and rolled upon impact. Turning quickly around, he plunged the blade into Scar's throat, dragged the hilt across the center, and slid it out from the other side. Blood squirted from the gash to the fading beat of the man's heart.

Red life dripped from a blade which was nearly as hungry as the eyes of its wielder. Hades had waited lifetimes for this moment. A kindness was shown to Scar and his friend. That same kindness was something that bitch would never receive. Hades stood up, still facing his opponent. Wide-eyed, the final officer glanced at Hades and back at Lindsey. Was it fear that filled her or hatred?

Step.

The woman turned sharply, flinging the still-struggling Lindsey to her side, placing herself between Lindsey and the god of death.

Step.

In an attempt to break free, the woman wrenched the gun down past her stomach. Lindsey jerked forward only to be met by a strong knee to the chest. She cried out in pain and released the gun, falling to the floor.

Step.

Retribution was nearly within reach. Hades tightened his grip around the hilt of the dagger.

The woman spun around.

Step.

Hades reached out to grab the officer's throat.

She raised the gun toward him. Starting from the center of his chest and echoing throughout the rest of his body, Hades felt the sensation of something that he had once prayed he would never feel again.

"What did I do?" The boy brokenly cried to himself between heavy sobs. Curled up with his arms wrapped around his knees, he sat alone on the floor of his unlit bedroom and rested his back against the side of his old, worn-out bed. Steady tears and a trail of mucus flowed down his face. Using a corner of the brown blanket behind him, he wiped at his eyes and mouth. He looked at the mess left behind and feared what his mother would say.

The meal was perfect. Everyone was laughing. Muffled voices of his parents could be heard elsewhere in the house. Sorely, the boy looked toward his bedroom door, which had been locked from the outside, and wondered when his father would unlock it. Weakly, in a voice barely audible enough for even him to hear, he whispered, "What did I do?"

VI

OFFICE PARTY

49 HOURS AFTER REGENIFACT

"PUSH HARDER!" Kevin screamed as dead arms blindly clawed at him from behind a wooden door. The door should have splintered with how hard his shoulder pressed into it. Tucked into his right back pocket was his somewhat-cleaned bloody wrench.

"I'm pushing, you moron!" wailed Matt, pressing on the door with all his might. His face closely resembled the color and sheen of a teacher's apple.

Unholy screams and incessant pounding rattled equally the door and their eardrums. The motionless head of what used to be Ted from accounting lay at their feet; his single remaining eye seemed to be looking up at them.

"How am I a moron?!" Kevin screamed.

Matt lashed back. "Who uses an elevator in a zombie scenario?!"

"These aren't even zombies!"

"What the hell is that supposed to mean?!"

One of the hungry hands scored and latched onto Kevin's sleeve. "Son of a ..." Kevin spewed vulgarities as he used a free hand to grab the cold arm and pull it off. After a few good tugs, the hand ripped away along with part of his sleeve.

Matt, with all the kindness of a wounded bull, reiterated his question. "WHAT THE HELL DO YOU MEAN THEY AREN'T ZOMBIES?!"

"Not the time, Matt!"

"If we get out of here alive, you're telling me exactly what you do mean!"

Kevin rolled his eyes and banged his head against the door—twice. "Fine! Any bright ideas on how to do that?"

Matt craned his neck and looked around the room as best he could. Despite being L-shaped, the room was fairly small. A few waist-high, unpainted metal shelves sat against the walls. Cardboard boxes ready to be picked up by building maintenance were piled awkwardly on top. A few feet away from them, resting on the floor, was Kevin's parcel.

Not a single window existed to let in light; a single yellowing bulb missing its partner in an old hanging light fixture lit up the space from the center of the L.

Peeking out from around the corner, Matt saw what he was looking for. A cold fell over him as he realized it was their best chance at escape. "There's um ... There's a ..."

"There's a what, Matt?!" Kevin, now swatting away the hands of their pursuers, spat toward his colleague.

"There's a ... service elevator ..." Matt proposed sheepishly. Closing his eyes, he readied himself for Kevin's response.

Kevin turned his head and glared at Matt. If those eyes were laser beams, they would have incinerated the shame-filled man in an instant. "So, what do you suppose we do? Even if we manage to get this thing closed, these bastards will break through in seconds."

Matt spun around as quickly as he could and pushed his back into the door. Once he felt secure enough, he looked toward the service elevator and thought hard. His eyes darted to the cardboard boxes. He pursed his lips and shook his head. Maybe he could use the shelves to brace the door somehow?

He looked around for something solid nearby. The only solid surface was the wall on the opposite side. Not possible.

Desperately, Matt pondered every possible combination of items and furniture available to them. He looked back at the service elevator. There was one plausible idea, but Kevin wasn't going to like it.

"How's that side of yours?" asked Kevin.

Matt snapped out of his thoughts. "My side?" Puzzled, he looked down. He had collided with a few things while running through the office. Aside from his sore arm and probably bruised knee, his side felt generally fine. Suddenly, he was pushed forward and stumbled a few steps into the room. Fearful that the door had broken, he twisted his body and prepared for the worst.

The door was still intact. All he found was a smiling Kevin still bracing the door, his hand outstretched from shoving his partner.

"We could think of different ways all day." A massive shove from behind the door caused Kevin's foot to slip. He quickly caught himself and shoved back. "In the end, it'll be the same result. Grab my box and take the elevator down. Before you get off, send it back up to me."

Matt bent down, snatched up the small box, and walked toward the elevator. Both men stayed silent as the hum of the elevator grew louder. Matt stepped away from the metal doors and readied his fist. Then the doors opened without the expected ding. Some relief came over him at seeing the car empty.

He stood inside and placed his finger on the ground floor button. "You sure this is going to work?" Matt yelled toward Kevin.

"One hundred percent!" Kevin yelled back in a strained voice.

With that, Matt pressed the button, and the doors began to close.

"Whatever you do, don't open the ..."

Ch'ck.

The thick metal doors shut, muffling the words of his coworker. *I'm sure it was nothing,* Matt thought to himself as he leaned back and laid his head against the wall. The hum of the elevator was oddly relaxing. He breathed in deep and let it out slowly. Taking out his wallet, he flipped it open and gazed at the picture inside. "Maddison, please be safe," he whispered.

Despite the elevator only descending four floors to reach the dark, stale abyss of the office basement, it felt like the hands of time had nearly slowed to a halt. Matt savored each one of those elongated seconds. Green eyes smiled back at him lovingly. These were hardly the ones he remembered. The flat, ink-stained paper simply couldn't capture the radiance of her jade eyes.

Closing his eyes, Matt felt her smooth hand slip into his. The sounds of birds carried with them the joy of a hot summer day. Blankets, warmed by the sun, dotted the landscape of flowing green grass. Resting on his own rustic red picnic blanket, Matt watched chattery passersby to his left stroll down a winding gravel path. To his right, a thick head of hair, the color of fire-kissed oranges, danced against his chest, moved by a passing wind.

Using the tips of his fingers, he lightly traced circles on her back. Snuggling closer to him, she lifted her head and gently took his bottom lip between hers. She pulled slightly back, revealing a look brighter than the sun above them. Her eyes reminded him of swirling oceans. He'd been lost in their depths since the first time they met.

Ding.

The shake of the elevator coming to a halt jerked Matt from his daydream. He took one last longing look at the picture before closing his wallet and returning it to his back pocket. The doors opened, and Matt peered out into a dimly lit hall. Shrouded shapes lined the walls. Quickly building up his courage, he took a step out of the small box and into the darkness. Motion-sensor lights flicked on, lighting up the space and nearly sending him flying back into the elevator.

Office chairs, like soldiers ready for a procession by royalty, lined both sides of the hall. Old, cracked tile the color of spoiled cream nearly matched the wallpaper framing it. Gripping Kevin's box tighter, he surveyed the hall. No signs of foul play were visible. He seemed to be in the clear for now. As quietly as possible, he lowered himself into a seat. Upon giving himself a second to make sure he hadn't been discovered by any of the living dead inhabiting the building, he lay back.

Curiously, Matt turned the box over in his hands. *What could be so important in this that Kevin would risk our lives over it?* he thought. The edge of his nail played with the tape. Glancing over at the elevator, he began to scratch at the cardboard. Kevin was supposed to be right behind him. Where was he? Standing up, he took a step toward the door. Should he go up? If he was overrun, he would only be opening the elevator to God knows how many zombies. They'd push themselves around it and somehow end up in the basement with him. He couldn't do that. His free hand formed a fist while his thumb ran back and forth over it.

Kevin should have told him that they were going back to the office. Why didn't he think of going somewhere safe, like a police station or something? Both of them could have been protected by people with guns. But no, they had to go to the office. Kevin was most likely dead because he couldn't, for once in his life, be firm with what he wanted when it mattered. He should have ...

"Oh no," Matt blurted out, leaping from the chair and running to the elevator. He rapidly jabbed the elevator call button. He had a feeling that he had forgotten something. After a lifetime, the doors sluggishly opened. Without even looking to make sure it was clear, Matt slipped between the doors and turned toward the panel of yellow buttons. "Please be alive, and please forgive me," he chattered, pressing the button for the fourth floor.

Stepping off the elevator, he turned around just in time to watch the doors close and hear the mechanical workings of the elevator jumping into motion. Its hum slowly disappeared into the heart of the building until the song could no longer be heard.

Frozen in place by preemptive guilt, Matt prayed he was not the reason his coworker was dead. His eyes focused on the image before him. Against the cold steel of the elevator doors, resembling nothing more than a shadowy blur, was his lonely reflection. He couldn't help but feel that it was watching him.

Gradually, he raised his hand and watched as his reflection moved with him. "Matt," he coached to himself, "you're being stupid and only freaking yourself out more. There are zombies upstairs. You don't need to go searching for ghosts."

Forcing a quiet chuckle, Matt rested his arm by his side and closed his eyes. *Kevin will be coming out of those doors any moment now, and we'll get out of here.* His fingers dug into the box. *He has to.*

Calmly, he rolled his neck to the right until a multitude of satisfying cracks sang out from within, dispelling the stress of the apocalypse. He repeated his ritual to the other side, evening out the moment of relaxation. Rubbing his bent neck with his free hand, he gently opened his eyes, feeling like a slightly less tense man.

Noticing a strange reflection in the elevator doors, his eyes shot open, and he immediately spun around with a shaky fist raised.

At the opposite end of the hall, cloaked in shadows, was what appeared to be a person in an oversized hoodie. With the hood draped low over their head, he couldn't make out their face.

Matt's heart raced out of his chest. "Don't co—come any closer or I'll ... I'll ..." While there had been rage toward his late boss, his courage now vainly grasped at air. He skittishly shook his fist at the figure.

The nightmare slowly cocked its head. Like water, shadows flowed around the cloaked individual. Matt's spine frosted over with ice.

"Are you a zombie?" Internally, he cringed. *What kind of question was that?* Matt thought. None of the zombies he and Kevin had encountered so far remained stagnant. This had to be a crazy person. That was the only explanation. A zombie would have charged at and killed him by now. A crazy person would just stand there, wait for an opening, then kill him. "Do you want money?!"

Although barely audible, he could have sworn that he heard a quiet chuckle come from the cloaked figure. It sounded sort of feminine. Why did he almost recognize it?

DING.

Emitting a child-like screech, Matt clumsily leapt forward, away from the noise. With all the strength his tired arms could muster, he threw the box like a football toward the noise. The box slammed against the edge of the opening elevator door and ricocheted into the small car.

"Be careful with this thing," spoke a weary voice from within. As the doors fully opened, Kevin came into view; he bent down and picked up the box. His arms and face were covered in cuts and bruises. Using a hand still tightly grasping his blood-soaked wrench, he supported himself with the doorway. Gingerly, he moved out of the small elevator and into the hall. Eyeing the rows of chairs, he pulled out the closest one to him and dropped into it. He hung his head backward and placed the box and wrench in his lap.

Matt looked over his shoulder to the end of the hall. The figure had disappeared. He leaned to the side, hoping that he might see part of the psycho's sleeve poking out from behind the corner. Satisfied enough that the person had left but not enough to believe it entirely, he approached Kevin. He wanted to tell Kevin about the nut job, but that would have to wait. "What happened up there?"

"Put enough force on hinges, and apparently, they break."

Wincing, Matt surveyed Kevin's arms. "Did any of them bite you?"

"Bite?" Kevin muttered while examining his arms, swearing to himself over the further damage to his favorite shirt. "Doesn't look like it."

"At least I don't have to worry about you turning into one of those things." Matt chuckled nervously through a forced smile. He rested his back against a wall and, as nonchalantly as possible, looked briefly down the hall.

Running fingers through his ruffled hair and completely ignoring Matt, Kevin locked eyes with his coworker. "Enough about me. What did I miss down here?"

"Nothing. Nothing at all. It was completely quiet down here."

"Mhm," Kevin mocked. "Well, if that's the case, I know a place down here we can rest." Kevin wearily stood up and started walking toward the end of the hall.

Matt quickly moved in front of Kevin. "There are probably better places down the street to hide once we get out of here."

Kevin slyly raised an eyebrow. "Better than the company workout space?"

Matt's arms dropped almost faster than his jaw. "The what now?"

Kevin chuckled and playfully pushed Matt aside. "Knock it off. It hurts to laugh. Can't believe you've never heard of it. This place is one of the biggest reasons I stayed at this craphole." Slowly, he led Matt down the hall; the lights shot on one by one as they stepped into the darkened areas. After a few turns, they arrived at a windowless door.

"Never even seen this place before," mumbled Matt.

Kevin smirked while tapping away on a worn keypad above the door handle. "Prepare to have your mind blown." With a turn of the handle and a little push, the door swung open. "Boom."

The lights turned on, revealing a short hallway with two thin-windowed doors on each side. Past the doors, the hallway opened into a larger room filled with couches, cold drink vending machines, and a table with a rack overflowing with snacks. Like a child, Matt ran to the rack and drooled over the assortment of energy bars, protein brownies, rice cakes, and other workout treats.

Kevin walked up behind his coworker-turned-goblin. "Welcome to the best-kept secret of Circle Solutions. Once you're done clutching the grub, mind helping me with the door?"

With a sour face, Matt put down his hoard of foil-wrapped treats. "Sure thing."

Together, they walked over to one of the black couches. The piece of furniture looked well used. Most likely covered in faux leather, pieces of it had fallen off over the years, revealing a layer of white fabric beneath.

"You want this thing against the door?"

"Think you can manage? I'm a bit sore"—Kevin pressed fingers into the crook of his neck and massaged—"from everything that went down upstairs after you forgot about me."

Matt's eyes nearly bulged out from his head. "Of course, it's the least I can do." He looked down at the lengthy couch, at the door, and back at the challenge before him and scratched his head.

Kevin walked toward a small table and pulled out one of the chairs. "That would be a *huge* help. Thank you!"

Matt barely heard Kevin's gratitude over the sound of his

dress shoes slipping on the tile floor. Twisting the couch, he aimed it as best he could toward the hallway. With one hand on the couch's arm and the other on the couch's back, he lowered his head and pushed as hard as he could. Little by little, the textured boulder crawled forward. His footing occasionally slipped, which earned him a few jabbing remarks from his relaxing partner.

After much struggle, he began to feel confident that he'd made a good distance, but when he raised his head, he realized he'd barely gone ten feet, and the tip of the black beast had only just begun to enter the hallway. The blow to his ego nearly made him cry. He looked back at Kevin with pained eyes.

"Oh, my shoulder," Kevin whined with a grin.

Matt gave Kevin a look and went back to pushing on the couch. After what felt like an eternity, he needed only a few more good pushes before the couch would be firmly against the door.

Swoosh.

Like a flash, Kevin hurdled over Matt with a large silver object in hand. Running and jumping off the couch, he landed on the other side, pushed the back of a steel chair under the door handle, and braced it with his foot. Nonchalantly, he walked past the couch and his flabbergasted coworker. "Just push the couch against the chair. Big help. Thanks."

Nearly out of breath, Matt grumbled and moved his trial the remainder of the distance. With a soft thud, the suspended chair legs bumped the wood inside the couch. He promptly slumped to the floor and rested his back against the barricade. "Really?"

Kevin laughed, walking toward the vending machine. "We're even." Kneeling down, he used his fingers to feel around beneath the machine until he held up a small key and made a happy noise to himself. "Same guy fills this thing up every week or so, and he never takes this thing with him." Fidgeting with the key, he eventually heard a click, and the vending machine door popped open.

Intrigued and parched, Matt wearily pushed himself off the floor and walked to Kevin, who had practically buried his head in the machine. Glass and plastic bottles clinked about wildly under Kevin's invading arms. "Never bothers to fill the shelves with the same items no matter how many notes I give him," Kevin grumbled as he dropped a crumpled yellow sticky note on the floor behind him.

By the time Matt reached his coworker's side, Kevin was carefully pulling his arm out of the machine along with two bottles. "These things are amazing," he said, handing one to Matt, who graciously accepted the cold drink.

Together, they tore off the caps and drank. Kevin was right; these really were the best. The cold drink poured into Matt's mouth, and he couldn't get enough. Thin lines of the glorious liquid ran down his chin and dripped onto his shirt.

Then a sound from the closet in the corner caused him to lose his concentration. The drink spilled into his lungs, forcing him into an uncontrollable cough.

Kevin tossed his almost empty bottle to the side and grabbed the wrench off the floor. Approaching the closet, Kevin hovered his hand above the doorknob and looked back at Matt, who was still in a fit of coughing. Bracing for the worst, he turned the knob and ripped the door open.

His stomach grumbled in protest. Hours had passed since the ruined dinner. The want for sustenance nearly matched his craving for a hug. Not a soul had come to comfort him, to offer leftovers, not even to scold. The only thing that came to him was the pattering of rain against his window. The door remained as it had: locked. He sat on the floor against his bed, unable to move for fear of making the day worse.

Heavy footsteps could be heard entering the house. The strange voices that the steps carried sounded scary. Should he hide under his bed or call out to his mother so that she might wrap her loving arms safely around him? Minutes felt like days. Each alien step resonated off the walls. They seemed to grow louder and louder as they roamed the house. That was until they stopped at his door.

With widening eyes, the boy watched his bedroom door. The sound of a key fumbling with the old lock should have brought a glimmer of hope to the boy's eyes; instead, it sent him crawling until his back met a wall. The door quickly swung open to reveal a large, scruffy-faced, muscular man in a dark gray military uniform and heavy black boots that went up halfway to his knees. Angrily, the man stomped toward the boy.

All the boy could do was cry out for help as a large, gloved hand reached for him.

IX

HADES

With the strength of a lion, a firm hand gripped the back of his collar and lifted him from the grimy train car floor. Frightened feet, a few food wrappers, and the remains of a single used piece of gum whose missing remnants stuck annoyingly to his cheek were all he could see. But otherwise, Hades could barely see anything, much less move. Whatever the huntress did to him, it had stilled his body to the point that he thought he might be dead. What he wanted to do more than anything was scream. Every muscle in his body felt as if it had been torn apart and sewn back together again. Despite the urge, all he could do was emit a pathetic groan that sounded closer to boredom than pain.

Before exiting the train, he was able to make out the crumpled form of Lindsey from the corner of his eye. Useless. *Should have known better than to put his faith in a mortal. Fickle creatures.* Scar and his other slain accomplice should be defending him. Where were they? He could no longer feel the *Essence* that had filled their frames. He could feel nihanem in the distance, but none were close enough to come to his aid.

"Must you really allow my head to strike each ... and every ... stair?" he growled.

"If I knew you were going to make random noises the entire time, I'd have given you more. What happened to you being the silent one?"

The cool morning air and the sounds of passing cars greeted Hades as he emerged from the bowels of the city. While he would have been interested in surveying his surroundings, the disgusting sidewalk and his captor's boots would have to do. With his arms and legs dragging on the ground, he felt like a doll. Absolutely powerless. She was able to take him from the steel worm and up to the streets of this human colony without struggle. If this truly was his end, how dare she humiliate him in this way.

The ends of his fingers began to flare up with a new sensation of pain. As the new pain gradually made its way up and past the bends of his fingers, he found that he was able to move them ever so slightly. He hid the motion from her notice. Once he'd regained enough of his mobility, she would suffer for this dishonor.

"... acquired. Need an extraction at rendezvous Tau."

The sharp corner of a brick building bit into Hades' shoulder as he slammed into it. The sounds of the street were muffled the deeper they traveled into what seemed to be the filth of this colony. Overfilled and rusting green dumpsters lined the alleyway. Their stench soured inside his nostrils. Broken, grimy cardboard boxes and loose rubbish littered the ground. Glass clinked against the cement to their right from behind a dumpster.

"Find a new home," the woman heavily advised.

A thin yet scruffy voice began to protest.

Without warning, Hades was released and dropped to the cement below like a rag-doll. Despite the more advanced plumbing systems of this age, the ground still reeked of piss. His long hair partially obstructed his eyes. The only view he had of the woman's interaction with the homeless man was of her backside and the legs of the unfortunate soul in front of her.

A swift knee to the groin brought the man's overgrown, dirt-covered face into view as he nearly collapsed to the side.

If Hades could move, he would have winced. The man's groan echoed within him. The woman gripped the mortal by the throat and shoved him against the brick. With each strike, Hades could hear the man's head ricocheting off the coarse brick wall. Bending down, the woman picked up the man's bottle. Glass shattered against the metal rim of the dumpster, followed by a blood-curdling scream. Finished with her lesson, the woman tossed the beaten and bloody man to the side. His shirt, made brown by the filth of the streets, hardly hid the grizzly circular gash in his side.

"Still want your pitiful home?" the woman cooed coldly.

As best as he could, the man clambered to his feet. Blood from his wound dripped from between his fingers as he held his hand against the gash. He ran past Hades toward the nearest alley exit. They briefly locked eyes, and the fear and pain that filled the man was unmistakable.

The woman turned toward Hades. "What? No bodies for you to use here? Nothing to hide behind?" Reaching for her holster, she pulled out her handgun, gripped the handle with both hands, and fired a round into the lower back of the fleeing man. He hit the ground like a sack of bricks.

With gun in hand, she walked over to the screaming man, grabbed him by the ankle, and dragged him to just a few paces from Hades. She placed her boot on the back of the homeless man and retrieved the veteran's dagger from a pouch on her vest. "Nice knife you got here. American military issue. This knife has seen some use." Raising the blade, she whipped her hand downward and released the knife, plunging it just under the poor soul's left shoulder blade. The man's screams quickly turned into tears as he pleaded for his life.

Hades, just starting to feel the new pain in his neck, was able to turn his head just enough to look the huntress in the eyes. What was once fury had slowly been replaced by a sensation that he hadn't felt in years. Fear. She was ruthless. This wasn't the woman he remembered.

Lifting her foot from the man's back, she moved it over the hilt of the knife and slowly pushed down on it. Once she was satisfied, she put the rest of her weight on the hilt and then shot the man between the ribs. She walked over to Hades, just out of reach, and knelt.

"Can you feel that?" she whispered. "His life is fading right before your eyes. I bet you could move your arm right now if you tried. Go ahead. Turn him. Reach out and have his corpse come to your aid."

She was right. He could feel it. The energy that filled his body was nearly fizzled out.

"DO IT!"

The pain was excruciating. Costively, and to his surprise, he was able to move his right arm and vainly extend it toward the dying man. "You know I can't resurrect the living."

Impatiently, the woman shot two more rounds into the man. Hades watched as the man's beaten frame went limp, and the god heard a final breath escape the man's lips. With Hades' fingers now extended, tendrils of *Essence* were sent forth from his fingertips and into the corpse. His power had been weakened greatly; had this been during the war, her taunting request would have been a grave mistake. But he had to try.

Like strings on a marionette, he pulled on his *Essence* and raised the nihanim as fast as possible. Pushing itself awkwardly off the ground, the nihanim looked at Hades' captor, opened its mouth until the cheeks ripped open, and screamed an unholy scream. Its shoes scraped the pavement as it shoved off the ground like a bat out of hell toward her. Suddenly, the top of its forehead exploded in a mist of red, and the nihanim face planted on the ground in front of Hades.

"As if I would make it that easy for you, rot-walker," she growled.

Hades placed his hand against the cement and tried to lift himself up. With a still-recovering stiff neck, he painfully turned his head to look at the woman; instead, he saw the incoming toe of her boot.

He braced himself as best he could. Strong fingers wrapped around his throat and lifted him from the floor. The boy, barely able to breathe, looked into the cold eyes of the soldier. No longer touching the floor, his feet searched desperately for something to ease the pain of the weight placed on his neck. He curled up his fingers and dug his nails into the soldier's wrist.

"Knock it off, rot-walker," the soldier harshly ordered before plunging his fist into the boy's gut.

The child's eyes watered as the walls of his quaint bedroom were replaced by stars. He clawed desperately at the tightening fingers around his throat. From their nests, the shadows began to spread and engulf the room. With arms and eyes growing heavier by the second, he wearily looked up into the eyes of the soldier, but only saw darkness.

X

STRIPPED

"We need it alive," spoke a male voice authoritatively from the hall. Immediately, the fingers loosened, and the shadows receded to their dens.

"Understood, Captain," the soldier said sarcastically as two more soldiers entered the room.

The soldier released the boy's throat, and he fell to the floor, gasping for air. Before he could even regain his breath, the second soldier had already pushed him to the ground and forced his arms behind his back. Aiming an odd-looking rifle at the boy's head was the third soldier.

The first soldier reached into a pouch on his belt and revealed a pair of handcuffs. Dropping a knee onto the boy's back, he reached down and slapped a cuff onto the boy's right wrist.

Clink.

Despite reaching its limit, the cuff moved freely enough on the boy's arm that it could easily slip off. Grabbing the boy's other arm and forcing his wrists to cross, the soldier clasped the remaining cuff around both wrists until flesh was the only hindrance to escape.

"Weapon secure," the first soldier stated, removing his knee from the boy and standing up.

Feeling a strong grip around his arm, the boy was hoisted

from the floor and into a standing position. Without another word, the soldiers led him from his room and through the house. As the boy passed the kitchen, he saw the bowl of soup he had yearned for all year still lying upside down with its contents spilled across the table and floor. His small lizard friend was nowhere to be seen.

The weathered wooden door squeaked loudly on rusted hinges as it was thrust open and slammed against its frame by the soldier in front. Stepping first into the cold night air and rain, the leading soldier directed the other two toward a bulky vehicle in the center of what looked like a small fleet that had landed in front of the cottage. The bright headlights of the vehicles illuminated the rain and lit up the yard as if it were the middle of the day. The boy squinted his eyes.

Soldiers were everywhere, and as the child tried to look around, he noticed that nearly all of their eyes were on him. To his right, he noticed a soldier with his back to him talking to his mother and father. Nestled in the arms of his mother was his little sister.

"I'm sorry!" he shouted. "Mother! Father! Please!" The wells of his eyes filled with tears. His parents averted their gaze from their crying firstborn. His little sister reached out toward him only to have her hand quickly seized and pulled back by his mother. If this is what his birthday would bring, he didn't want it. He would never become older ever again.

"FATHE—" The butt of a rifle cracked against his left temple. He fell to the wet grass as the world around him spun. Through the ringing in his ears, he heard a multitude of voices shouting. Above them all was the angry voice of his father. He raised his head to look toward the commotion, but his eyes failed to focus. His father's voice sounded like it was getting closer while his mother's voice shrieked in the background.

A soldier let out a grunt, and a blur stumbled toward the boy. A deafening crack rang out above his head. A second blur emerged from behind the first. Two more cracks above him deafened the boy, and the second blur hit the ground in front of him. As his vision cleared, he opened his jaw to let out a wail, but his ears heard nothing.

Bringing his knee up, he raised himself from the ground and shoved himself forward, but a quick kick to his back sent him headlong into the wet grass. He lifted his mud-splotched face and turned to his right, looking upon a still corpse beside him. A stream of tears carved a path through the dirt on his cheek. He wanted to be back at the table. He didn't care about the stew. He wanted to be surrounded by his smiling family. Now that could never happen ever again. Face down, with a single arm stretched outward, was his father. A bullet had removed his right cheek and eye. His coarse green shirt turned a dark shade of red.

"NOOOOOOO!"

Hands gripped his arms and lifted him. He twisted his neck to the point of pain to look at the one responsible. Standing firm with a rifle tilted down, a soldier looked back at him through indifferent eyes. A thin wisp of smoke still leaked from the tip of the barrel.

The darkness of night turned to ink and swallowed the world. The only image not absorbed was the object of his rage. Tears flowed freely as he screamed and thrashed about. The soldier behind him struggled to keep the boy contained.

With great force, the soldier containing him was ripped away, pulling the boy with him. A shower of blood washed over the child as he managed to catch himself.

"Take it down!"

"I've got a clean shot!"

"We need the weapon alive!"

The chorus of screaming men should have drowned out the boy's thoughts, but his mind was steadfast in its focus.

The murderer retreated backward with his rifle raised.

The boy looked down the barrel into the eyes of a monster. Just as the first flash left the muzzle, a large individual in a crimson shirt moved between them. Flash after flash created a silhouette of the boy's protector. Seemingly unphased by the barrage of bullets, the protector swiftly moved forward and lunged at the soldier.

The struggle was shorter than the time it took for the soldier to forever tear his family apart. A fountain of blood spewed from the now-headless neck of the murderer. Still gripping the silently screaming head in one hand and the lifeless corpse in the other, the protector turned its head to the crying heavens and spewed a nightmare of sound from its lips.

Like sparks from a fire flower, cloth and flesh leapt from the protector's body in the storm of gunfire. Unfazed by the shredding of its body, it hunched over and began to snarl. With inhuman speed, it sprinted toward the closest soldier and, once in range, lunged toward the target.

Frantically, the soldier fiddled with the dagger on his belt. Countless hours of drills vanished from his desperation-drunk mind as he yanked incessantly on the hilt still strapped to its sheath. "Take it ou—"

The protector landed and rolled on empty earth. Mud and grass clung to its blood- and rain-drenched body. Hawk-like eyes turned in the direction of their new target. A moment later, the soldier lay on the ground some twenty paces from where he once stood, guarded by a new masked foe.

The erratic shimmering of a strange sword glimmered off his smoked-charcoal metallic suit. Delicate ribbons of gold decorated him from his eyeless helmet to his boots. Poised in a defensive position, the swordsman carefully adjusted his feet as if he were about to sprint in a race.

The child, conflicted by awe and horror, stared at his guardian. Having slipped from the cuff, he reached out with a small hand. No longer did the hope of being reunited in the comforting embrace of a blanket on a bed with his family seem distant.

The guardian turned his head toward the boy. For that brief moment, the world seemed peaceful. Everyone would shout, "Surprise!" and laugh. His family could sit back down at the table and enjoy dinner together.

A flash of light sparked beneath the swordsman's feet, scorching the soaked earth beneath them. As if a bird of glass carried him, the swordsman flew toward the guardian. Sparks of energy propelled him forward, each step faster than the last.

SWOOSH!

The swordsman's boots kicked up mud as they tore lines in the grass; he came to a stop on the opposite side of his foe.

The tattered guardian wobbled slightly and reached out toward the child. As he had so many times before, the boy ran toward him. A thin, black line divided the man's shirt from below the shoulder to his hip. Like uneven stacked stones, his top half began to slide until it tumbled off to the side and his legs crumpled to the ground.

The boy dropped to his knees beside the mutilated corpse. Red eyes begged for tears, but only the rain ran down his face. Gripping the remnants of the stained green shirt, the boy shook the body in vain. His father's head rocked in the mud, the last eye blankly staring toward the heavens.

Distracted, the boy barely heard the growing humming sound until the tip of the glowing sword was inches from his skull. Following the length of the blade, he glanced briefly at the hilt. Its thin silver frame was adorned with deep grooves that flowed like water. Poking out from under a thumb was a small shield decorated with a skeletal hand—the Royal Hand crest. Electricity danced between the fingers of the gloved hand above him. Before the boy could roll away, the swordsman tightly gripped his shoulder.

✳

Hades screamed as electricity coursed through his body. The tip of a cattle prod dug into his bare chest and seared his flesh. The smell of overcooked roadkill mixed with the rust of the dank warehouse created a nauseating cocktail of despair.

"I never meant to hurt him!" Hades ground out through mashed teeth. Strung up like a marionette, his hands hung from chains encased in thick gauntlets of iron. A steel spike inserted through a hole in each gauntlet pierced his wrists and guaranteed his imprisonment. The tips of his boots desperately scraped at the dusty floor. A thin yet muscular woman retracted the prod. Her ponytail lashed at her sweat-soaked dark uniform.

"LIAR! Aphrodite wasn't enough. You had to take my brother from me as well!"

"I was trying to save her," Hades coughed up weakly.

"And the people of the city were collateral?" The woman closed the distance between her and Hades like a wolf to its prey. Stopping mere inches from him, her hot breath tasted more like a distillery than spent air. "Like Hell you were. She was just the beginning. Was the nineteen-cycle reign over your filthy empire not enough to satiate your appetite? This planet would have fallen like a sandcastle against a tsunami."

Sorely lifting his chin from his chest, Hades looked deep into the woman's smoldering silver eyes. "I would have sacrificed a thousand vermin to bring back the only one I ever loved. Because of the delay brought about by you and the others, I'll need a million. Help me, and I can bring them both back Artem—" A dizzying uppercut silenced Hades, splitting his chin open and creating an arc of blood in the air.

"I don't remember giving you the right to use my name," she spat roughly.

Hades' hair hung heavy with more sweat than water. He laid his head back and cackled. "Would you prefer your filth-given name instead, Diana?"

Artemis turned her back to Hades and walked toward a wall. Beneath a suspended bulb, bathed in dim light, stood a table with an arsenal of tools that would make even the most wicked of interrogators blush. On the floor beside it was Hades' shirt and leather jacket.

Looming over the table, Artemis put down the prod, picked up a water bottle, and took a swig. Clearing her throat, she turned her head toward Hades. "Even gold becomes gravel on your tongue." Returning the bottle, her liberated hand hovered hungrily above its buffet. Her fingers slithered over the objects, lingering on a ghastly device longer than Hades would have liked.

Satisfied with her choice, Artemis faced her prisoner, dragging the metal tip of her toy along the table with her. Menacingly producing a dagger, Artemis' smile was tissue paper compared to the blade. Like a mist upon a sea of fire, relief teased the ropes constricting Hades' heart.

"It pains me to have to end our riveting conversation, but I think we should make up for lost time." Raising her hand toward a dark corner and motioning downward, a burly man in a black military uniform stepped forth from the shadows. A rifle hanging on a strap at his side clattered as he walked to the back of the warehouse.

Hades furrowed his brow. Had this brute been there the entire time? How many more were in their presence, waiting on her command?

"I could give you the same death you gave Apollo, but that's a mercy you shan't enjoy." Like a shark, she began to slowly circle her bloody prey. The whirr of machines echoed from the rafters, and the chains supporting Hades began to clink and lower. Now supporting the weight of a battered frame, his legs felt like rotten stilts. The added weight of the constraints brought his remaining strength to its limit.

"The moments before Zeus so graciously rescued you have

been etched into my mind. With how often I flirt with the alternatives, I should be pleasuring myself to them." Her fingers wrapped around the hilt and became white as bone. "I wonder which fantasy we'll enact, old friend ..." Her boots sounded heavier as they came to a halt on the cement behind Hades. Too weak to move, he awaited the kiss of her blade.

"I think I was right about here," she hissed into his ear, "before we were so rudely interrupted!" With the force of a cannon, her heel smashed into his back, cracking a vertebra and knocking out any wind left within. With so little strength remaining, down was the only place he could go.

His exposed chest was the first to make contact with the frozen surface of the steel table. Although demanded, no scream could be mustered. The murky soup that was now his mind blurred his senses, yet the pain left by the bestowing needle was as clear as a torch on a starless night. Men and women in garments of white bustled about the blindingly bright room like rabbits in a snowstorm. Seeing a woman dart by with the tail of her coat flowing behind her, the boy wanted more than anything to cover up his exposed body.

To either side of the child, soldiers pinned him to the table while a bar was painfully laid across his legs and locked into place. Lifeless jaws jutted out from the corners of the table. Repeatedly, his left hand was forced into a stationary cuff only to be ripped from it after an off-sounding clink. Then the act repeated.

"This kid's hands are too small for the restraints," fumed a soldier. "This isn't going to work. We need to wait until he's grown. Little shit's not even old enough to be one of 'em!"

He was never able to get a good look at them, but their voice ... their voice he would never—could never—forget. Long after the razing of the facility and the rightful death by his hand, their voice continues to echo in his mind.

"Sergeant Drom," spat a voice that might have once been angelic but now sounded closer to a cough, "This *thing* is the reason why a man is dead. Without the intervention by one of the Royal Hand, you wouldn't even have the opportunity to drag your grimy boots into my operating room. Your carelessness could have jeopardized the entire kingdom."

"You read the report. There's no way that nihanim was his. Some cryptic with *Essence* to spare is out there. The way that thing moved ..." Sergeant Drom sighed audibly. "Aside from a select few, that's something our current stock can't even conjure. He's already been prepped. Just allow me to place him in a containment room until we can—"

"Utter another word and I'll have you brought up on charges of insurrection," spat the doctor. "It is wise to respect what you hunt, but do not think even for a moment that this thing is a Deotrite. From the point of conception, it defiled our society by mimicking us. They are a poison that must be sucked out and burned, lest we prefer this planet to succumb to it. They should be gracious that we even found a use for their kind. Now, you and your men hold its arms in place, or you'll be processed."

From the corner of the boy's eye, he could just make out the pained expression upon Sergeant Drom's face. His eyes darted about the floor as if pursuing an evasive mouse. For a moment, Drom briefly looked into the child's eyes and then averted his gaze as if the boy before him was a feast fit for flies. Drom placed one hand on the boy's wrist and the other on his arm. The man's fingers felt like shivering worms against the child's skin. Pressing firmly, Drom nodded toward the doctor.

What felt like a red-hot nail suddenly burrowed itself deep within the base of the child's neck. Reaching within himself, he tried to scream, but his lungs refused. As if pulled by a slug, the penetrating live coal moved up toward his skull through muscle and sinew. With each passing of a vertebra, a soft, humming vibration blended with the sound of scraping clay. Sticky warmth dripped down his shoulders and pooled on the table below.

Like a canyon forming in a field, the incision was broadened, ripping the flesh further. Between the torrent of agony, he watched gloved fingers pick up what looked like an over-cooked bronze beetle from the table beside his head.

"The charge is in place," confirmed a nurse.

The child's vision danced between the light and a hungry shadow.

"Close it," ordered the doctor.

A strange sensation warmed his wound. What felt like ants crawled within his flesh and consumed his pain. As smoke flees from a doused fire, the shadow retreated from his sight.

"Incision sealed," said a nurse.

"Position the collar," the doctor ordered.

A bitter cold weight rested on the boy's upper back and curled over his shoulders. Droplets of sweat clung to his skin and brought a saltiness to the abrasive air.

"Collar in position," stated a nurse.

"Commencing installation," said another.

The high-pitched whir of a drill blanketed the room. The first screw broke through his flesh and bore into his left shoulder blade. Using what remnants of energy remained, he fought back, only to have the hands of the soldiers further tighten on him. A second screw went through his right shoulder blade. Inches above the first screws, two more shredded his skin and muscle before tunneling through his collar bones.

Delicate shocks near each impalement elicited new waves of pain as the tips of the screws blossomed and secured themselves within him.

"Collar installation complete," stated a male voice.

"Finish your healing and get it out of here," ordered the doctor.

No longer able to discern the direction of gravity, the shadow returned like a tidal wave and swept over the child. Forever part of him, harboring a gem of annihilation, was the badge of his forced identity. Engraved upon it for all to see, stripping the boy of his name and conscripting him into the legion of the condemned, were the characters:

XI-24.

Tangy dirt and a light breeze woke XI-24. Peering out through the cracks of his eyelids, he looked about groggily.

"Pa's going to make me clean the roof if he notices I've fallen asleep in the field again," he groaned to himself. Using the back of his wrist, he removed the sour grit clinging to his tongue. That had to be the worst dream ever. Right above the shadow monster nightmare, *he thought to himself as he got ready for his morning tradition. Aches and pains that were worse than even the most grueling of harvesting days rocked his back and shoulders.*

Mid-stretch, his hand bumped against a smooth metal surface. His heart began to beat as quickly as the wings of a racebird. Erratic hands patted against bone-cold metal as panicked fingers traced it down his back. Images of the night before flooded over him: the spilt dinner, the cracks of soldier's rifles, the screeching of a drill, and his father's broken, bloody face. Focusing his eyes, the tall grass surrounding him transformed into thick metal bars.

"It wasn't a dream ..."

XI

CRACKED MATRYOSHKA

"Two days?" Matt spat out through a mouthful of protein cookie bites toward a thin woman curled up on the stiff-carpeted floor beneath a cheap, blue Circle Solutions blanket. Her toasted walnut hair sat in a messy bun upon her head. "Are you related to that Skylar chick in logistics?"

A weak smile grew beneath beaten hazel eyes on the woman's face. "You mean my sister, Brianna? I'm Skylar."

The speed at which Matt stopped chewing was only exceeded by the spread of the rosiness in his cheeks.

"Did she ..."

"No ... I haven't seen her since all of this started. She was supposed to meet me down here for a workout when I heard the first scream. I panicked, shut the door, and hid." Skylar looked down and somberly swirled the last sip of a creamy strawberry protein shake in its bottle. "I tried calling the police about a dozen times. Each time, I got the same automated emergency message."

Like a child holding a cup of cough syrup, she grimaced and brought the bottle to her lips. Scraping at the remnants of her will, she lifted the bottom of the bottle up and let the last of the faux-strawberry-scented sludge ooze into her mouth.

With the empty bottle still in hand, she tightened the soft cocoon around herself. "After the screaming stopped, I snuck upstairs to go look for Brianna. There was this off-sounding tearing noise, like when someone tries to tear a thick, wet book in half. That's when I saw people just ..." Her eyes began to gloss over as if she was staring at something distant through the floor below her.

Matt was so accustomed to his stone-faced hero of a coworker that he almost forgot how a normal person would react. Kevin should have collapsed at the sight of the truck drivers. That man's ability to brush off what they had encountered wasn't natural. Tasting iron, he ran the tip of a finger across his lips. He hadn't noticed when he had bitten into the inside of his lower lip. "Excuse me," he mumbled toward Skylar, standing up and walking to the snack table for a napkin.

For the sake of survival, he had pushed the image from the shop to the back of his mind. Despite Kevin's best attempt to use his large frame to prohibit Matt's view, Matt glimpsed a puffy, crumpled form. He told himself over and over that the little girl in purple was asleep. But just like repeatedly watching his uncle use magic to remove and reattach his thumb, he could never believe it. It didn't matter which aspect of his coworker's recent behavior he analyzed; something was off about Kevin.

Matt leaned against the edge of the table, put his hands in his pockets, and eyed the short hallway entrance. Kevin said he had to give someone a call over forty minutes ago. His eyes scanned the carpet as if answers were sewn into its fibers. Looking back up at the hallway, he locked eyes on the door behind which Kevin had stowed himself. The small window into the room was coated in a layer of taped newspaper. *Why cover up the window if you're just on a call?* Matt thought.

Attempting to peer through the paper was fruitless. All he saw was the reflection of his stupid mug. Thinking himself smart, he lowered himself to the floor. Ready to shove off in case the door suddenly opened, Matt hovered his head just above the scuffed tile floor. The smell of dust and factory-produced lemon infiltrated his nostrils. Cringing, he did his best to see under the door.

While he couldn't see very far into the room, he did see an odd fluorescent aqua blue light. He could hear Kevin talking, but the door muffled his words past the point of comprehension. Another male voice cut Kevin off and reminded Matt of a cross between a Muscle Car engine and a lifetime supply of cigarettes.

Maybe he's on speaker phone with the lights off?

Muscle Car seemed to be arguing with Kevin. Had to be serious with how heated it was getting. Like a river rerouted over a campfire, a smooth and cool voice stiff-armed the conversation. Silence followed. Aside from the eager crinkling from Skylar's next snack, the room was quiet. Kevin might storm out at any second, and if he did so, he'd just trip over his nosy coworker. Were those footsteps he heard or the beat of his own heart within his chest?

Resilient to the calming current, smoke still bubbled to the surface. Kevin began yelling once again. Matt breathed a sigh of relief, comforted by the knowledge that he wasn't at risk of being discovered. Just like before, Matt couldn't understand a single thing his most likely irate coworker was saying. Except he did pick up one word: his name.

Matt prepared himself. Kneeling below the covered window, he waited for Kevin to get particularly loud once again. He didn't have to wait long. Matt gently tested the doorknob. Kevin had a habit of overlooking important details, usually leading to him worriedly double- and triple-checking his work. While Kevin had chosen a fairly decent sound-dampening room and covered the windows, what he had not done ... was lock the door. Turning the knob as quietly as possible,

Matt waited for the quiet click of the latch and pushed the door open just enough to hear clearly and see what was going on.

The scene inside took him by surprise. A blue, ghostly table floated above what looked like an open, steaming thermos on the floor. Its luminous form was made even eerier by wisps of blue smoke crawling across its surface. Two similarly composed figures manned the table.

Losing his balance, Matt gripped the doorknob for stability. Unfortunately, the door had other ideas. Propelled forward by his weight, the door quickly swung open. His shoulder hit the floor as a loud bang from the door hitting the wall heralded his presence.

"What the fuck are you doing in here!?" shouted a surprised Kevin.

Matt, still picking himself off the floor, shouted back. "What am I doing in here? What the fuck are you doing in here!?" Pointing with an entire arm toward the center of the room, Matt highlighted the source of the blue light.

"Thought you said you had him under control," Muscle Car sarcastically growled.

Following the voice, Matt locked eyes with a figure similarly composed as the table. Muscle Car's appearance matched the voice. Dagger-like eyes partially covered by pinky-length, messy hair weaponized his thin face. A short, razor-wire beard added to Muscle Car's intimidating presence. His loose V-neck shirt was littered with minuscule holes and tears, creating a crooked trail to his cut-off torso floating on a cloud of swirling smoke.

"Zeus," piped in the figure next to Muscle Car while looking directly at his spectral companion, "entertaining his delusion puts him and everyone around him at risk." His slick voice carried a strength with it that was stiff enough to hold in place his greased-back hair. Perfectly pointed collar ends were the cape to his button-down dress shirt, and his folded-back long sleeves revealed toned, light-haired arms. Two un-done buttons at the top allowed a small portion of his bare chest to peek outward. His clean-shaven face, combined with his square jaw and small nose, reminded Matt all too much of a douchey rich guy.

Zeus, not taking too kindly to the interjection, snapped back, "Last I recall, Poseidon, it was your idea to go along with it!"

Kevin sidestepped to block Matt's view. "I'll explain this all later. Right now, you need to get out of here."

Having a decent knowledge of tactics from playing video games while decaying between jobs, Matt executed the perfect strategy. Leaning to the side, he nullified Kevin's body block-ade. "Every single time I ask, I get the same B.S. response. No more—" Matt froze.

Hovering above the table, slowly rotating, was the bust of a woman. Unlike the rest of the apparitions, this one was full of color. Matt felt like the blood in his veins had been replaced with permafrost. Ducking beneath Kevin's outstretched arm and evading his awkward grasp, he whooshed to the table. He gazed in disbelief at what he saw before him.

Dark-roasted coffee-bean hair flowed like an elegant wa-terfall down the back of her head. Low cheekbones rose from her sandalwood skin and cradled her dainty nose. Matt's focus slipped down to her slender lips before rising back to her sil-very eyes. She looked different, but she had a face he could never forget. "What is *she* doing here?"

"You really should have left." Kevin grabbed Matt's arm and began tugging him away.

"No!" Matt broke Kevin's grip. "Why is there an image of Maddison here?"

Kevin furrowed his eyebrows and reached for his spiraling companion.

Evading once again, Matt screamed. "Why do you have an

image of my wife?!" The ice in his veins quickly began to boil. "What the hell is going on!?"

"Damn it! He needs to know. We can't keep him in the dark any longer!" shouted a male tenor voice.

Hidden behind Maddison's floating head was a third ghostly individual wearing a tight courier cap and fitted uniform. On his chest pocket was a small embroidered winged shoe. His stubble beard further accentuated his frustrated frown.

"Nearly forgot you were there, Hermes. Nice of you to finally join in," sneered Zeus.

Feeling outnumbered, Kevin let go of Matt. He rested one hand on his hip and rubbed his temples with the other. With a weary sigh, he said, "Alright. Fine. Wanted to wait until we found a fix, but sure. Let's tell him now."

"About damn time," huffed Matt.

Kevin glared at his coworker. "Long story short ..."

"Full story." Matt barked. "And start with Maddison."

Agitated, Kevin shook his head and readied himself. "The person you know as Maddison goes by another name." Kevin looked over at the other meeting attendees, hoping to find someone attempting to stop him. Finding no back door, he continued, "Artemis."

"Ok, so she has another name. She was secretive. That still doesn't explain any of this!" said Matt.

"She's been missing for forty-eight hours," Poseidon butted in.

Under the glow of the blue light, the warming of Matt's face visibly faded. "What do you mean 'missing'?"

Zeus shot a quick, dirty look at his well-put-together associate. "Hades, a previous ally of ours, is the source of the nihanem."

Matt glanced at Kevin. "Knee-ha-nem?"

"The zombies," Kevin muttered.

Zeus continued. "I ordered the team to locate him, but not to engage. If forced to confront him, aim to subdue, not kill. That brings us to Artemis." Zeus ceased his locking gaze with Matt and went back to studying the floating head of Matt's wife. "Roughly forty-eight hours ago, she sent word that she had found Hades and was actively trailing him. We haven't heard from her since."

"Is ... is this true?"

Kevin couldn't bring himself to face Matt.

"It's ok. You can tell him, Kratos," Poseidon softly nudged.

Reluctantly, Kevin turned and faced Matt. "If it were any of us you see here, there wouldn't be a reason for worry. Artemis, though ... Hades ... killed her brother."

Poseidon cleared his throat. Partially relieved to pass the torch, Kevin nodded to him. "Long ago, we were a team. One day, a switch flipped within Hades, and he killed one of our own. Nihanem had overrun the city we were visiting before we could get to him. We tried to get Hades to back down, but he attacked. Apollo died in the fight."

"Eventually, we captured Hades and shut him away in a stasis chamber," Zeus said. "Artemis tried skewering the damn thing, but I stopped her. Keeping that box safe from her was a suicide mission within itself. She can't think clearly when it comes to Hades." Zeus shook his head. "We're not what we used to be after what Nyx did. Not sure how Hades has the pull on *Essence* that he does. Bastard shouldn't be able to raise an army, much less even make a corpse twitch. If Artemis did go after him, she wouldn't have stood a chance."

Matt walked backward until his back hit the wall. "So, what does this mean? Is she dead?" His wife had left him without warning. Watching her walk away from him on that cold day felt like the teeth of a rusty saw ripping through his heart.

For weeks, he had fallen into a seemingly bottomless pit. Like a whore after a war, he had locked lips with enough bottles to make a bootlegger blush. Lying across the bed with a half-drunk, vomiting bottle of five-dollar wine, he would stare up at the shadow-veiled ceiling. Ideas of how to win her back blended his brain. She was his everything. His hopes, dreams, and joy were all tied to her. He just needed a few minutes with Maddison and she would have changed her mind. But now, he'd been told that she might be lost forever.

"Until we see her body, we can't confirm anything. Hermes, Poseidon, and I have been going to her known locations." Zeus gazed across the table. "Speaking of known locations ... Hermes, any updates?"

"Yes." Hermes lit up. "Artemis had a system of warehouses and other various buildings across the planet. Ran some kind of militant group. Within this city's limits, I was able to gather enough intel to count five designated locations. I've already searched three. The last two are north of Kratos' location. One deeper in the city and the other on the northwest edge of it."

Zeus nodded. "Hermes, send the downtown location to Kratos. You and I will rendezvous and go to the northwest location together. Poseidon, continue preparing the humans for now. We need that emergency shelter stocked and defensible." When Zeus turned toward Kevin, Matt could see the worry in his eyes. "Kratos, bring Matt to Poseidon. Once he's safe, you and Poseidon will make your way to your assignment."

"And what? Just leave me there? No!" Matt cried out. "I have to hide somewhere knowing that Maddison might be hurt or even killed!? No! I need to make sure she's ok. Give me a gun. Hell, give me a baseball bat. I'm not going to just get benched like this is some game." He folded his arms and focused on Zeus. "You can either tell *Kratos* to take me along, or I'm going on my own."

Zeus' annoyed expression shifted into anger. "You're in no condition to fight right now!"

"What the fuck is that supposed to mean?!" Matt shouted back.

Kevin placed a hand on Matt's chest as if to hold him back. "I'll bring him with me. Keep him close." An internal battle raged within Kevin. "He'll be safer with me than on his own. We have another survivor with us. We can get her to Poseidon and move out from there."

Matt felt like a coin balancing on a string. Either side could tip first; he just prayed it was heads.

Zeus crossed his arms and closed his eyes. "Don't let him out of your sight. Escort the survivor before going to the assignment. Rendezvous back at base with a report. May the Abyss' thirst for you go unquenched another day."

High above, birds swam in an endless ocean of light. Their un-organized songs professing love and gaiety choreographed to an aerial ballet were more beautiful than that of any sym-phony. Slapped from the sky by an invisible hand, the chas-tened fowl were hastily escorted from the premises by currents unseen.

"Our gracious hosts are worried we might get to one," spoke a leathery voice from nearby.

Removing his eyes from the birds and looking to his left, XI-24 saw a shirtless man in a cage ten paces away from his own. The man was about his father's age, sitting with his back against the bars. A collar of tarnished metal similar to his own sat upon the man's shoulders.

"Why would you say that?" XI-24 inquired.

Slyly smirking, the man lowered his gaze from the sky down to the boy. "Because we did one time," he chuckled. "Must be new here. Can't really say it's nice to meet you, kid. I'm H-39, but you can call me Chatter."

XII

OASIS ON THE LAKE

Ripe tangerine rays from the fledgling sunrise bathed the city in new hope. Kevin, followed by Matt and Skylar, emerged from an auxiliary door of the office building. Towers of glass sparkled as far as the eye could see. Birds chirped happily from the scantily clad branches of auburn trees at the opposite end of the parking lot. For a second, the world seemed perfect. Ready for the journey ahead, they set off.

By the time the trio had reached their destination, the moon hung in the sky like a tarnished copper hook. Beneath its hazy light swam tranquil, clumped schools of clouds. A large white banner reading "The Museum of History and Science" flapped haphazardly in the wind.

Finally getting a bite, the tail of the moon sunk behind the museum's arrowhead roof as they climbed marble steps upon weary legs. Waiting for them in the opening of a large metal door was Poseidon, a cocky smile on his face. His royal-purple button-up shirt had a shine to it that only top dollar could buy. Matt's original impression of him was spot on: rich douche-bag.

"So good to see you again, Krate. What's it been? Sixty ... seventy years?" Poseidon teased Kevin.

Too tired to deal with his obnoxious host, Kevin slapped Poseidon's open hand and pushed through him to get inside.

When Poseidon looked down at his hand, an earthy green, foil-wrapped, spinach-and-fudge vegan protein bar sat there. It was warm to the touch. Poseidon grimaced at the unsavory gift and slipped it into his dress pants pocket. Waving the other travelers in, he scanned the area and then closed the giant door.

Matt followed Kevin into the main hall. Images of angels and the glory of heaven adorned the grand domed ceiling. Gold-painted trim acted as a corral to contain the magnificent artwork. Beneath the cherubs, a bustling new way of life carried on. People were walking every which way. Not a single rotting horror in sight. A boy no older than nineteen in dusty gray sweatpants and an oversized blue hoodie scurried behind a group of men, each of them carrying a load of various pipes in their arms. His long brown hair bounced above his eyebrows with each step.

Nearby was a fairly beautiful girl in skin-tight, torn black jeans; she swung her legs while sitting on a large circular desk. Messy hair the color of a tropical beach fell about her bare shoulders and onto her tight purple tie-dye tank top. Taking a few strands of her roughly cut hair, she wound them around her fingers and slyly smiled at the boy.

Matt saw the blue-hooded boy lose control of the pipes, and they crashed to the floor. The boy kneeled on the ground and frantically tried to retrieve them. His sunburnt face drooped beneath his shoulders. Laughter from the girl echoed off the walls and became a focused chorus. Without thinking, Matt knelt beside him and began to assist.

A sharp pain burned across his fingers, and he yanked his hand away. Looking at his hand, he saw a thin line running across all four of his fingers. Dots of blood began to seep through. Clutching his shirt to stop the blood, Matt took a closer look at the pipes. To his surprise, the pipes had been altered. While the first few inches of each pipe remained normal, everything past that point had been flattened into a long steel leaf with sharpened edges. Signs of hammering covered every inch of the blade's rough exterior.

"Sorry," the boy mumbled shyly.

Before Matt could respond, one of the men the boy had been following stood above them. "That's the second time you've dropped those today," the man said in a firm voice. "We can't keep sending you to the doc every time we move shit. Either know your strength or go see what they need in the Boulder."

Coming to the boy's defense, words tumbled out of Matt's mouth before his brain could even stop them. "Lay off the kid. The world is falling to pieces, and he's doing the best he can." He instantly regretted the outburst. The burly man loomed over him. With a rough umber beard and a red bandana over his head, he didn't look like the forgiving type. Fully expecting a kick—or at least a verbal lashing—he nervously awaited his consolation prize. To his relief, the man grunted and walked away, shaking his head.

Forcing a smile to ease the boy, Matt gathered the pipe swords and jogged to catch up. Clambering in his hands, the bundle sounded more like a runner wearing bells and chain-mail. Focusing on Mr. Bandana, Matt tried his best not to acknowledge Kevin's glare as he walked by.

Passing through various exhibits, Matt couldn't remember ever going this quickly through a museum in his life. Each well-lit-but-seemingly-dark room was filled with the most fascinating and beautiful spectacles. Focused lights hung above a small clay lamp in a clear case. Behind it, a colorful mural of an ancient Greek village transported museum visitors to another time. After exiting the fifth room, an odd thought occurred to him. While many of its historical exhibits were familiar to him, he couldn't remember a single time when he had visited this particular museum.

Entering the Civil War room, Matt was more or less instructed to lay the weapons down at the feet of a blue-uniformed mannequin. Its hand was proudly thrust above its head in an open fist where a sword had previously perched. Turning to head back, Matt heard the voice of Mr. Bandana.

"Thanks for the help."

Not wanting to get on his bad side, Matt politely turned around and reassured him it wasn't a bother.

Mr. Bandana said, "About Lewis back there … he's a good kid. His heart is in the right place." Wiping his hands together, he gazed over Matt's shoulder. "Should be putting a costume together and looking forward to taking a pretty girl to a Halloween party, not preparing himself to die fighting zombies. If we knew this was even possible, swine flu would have been a joke." Swearing under his breath, his eyes locked back onto Matt. "Haven't seen you around here before. Name's Dale."

Taking Dale's outstretched hand seemed to also be a mistake; shaking it was like feeding it to a toothless crocodile. "Good to meet you. I'm Matt. Just arrived with two others. We'll be resting for a few hours, then heading back out."

"You can't go back out there," spat a soft, breezy voice.

Startled, Matt swiveled his head in the direction of the mystery person.

Carrying a water bottle in each hand, a skinny, gentle-looking man in dirty jeans and a warm olive sweater approached. His bobbing, bushy black hair had grayed at the roots. Matt graciously accepted a bottle from him. The old man opened the second bottle and took a swig for himself.

"What? Nothing for me, Brandon?" Dale jokingly snapped.

A mischievous smile widened beneath the rim of the bottle. "Not this time." Looking back at Matt, the old man's hickory face turned serious. "This is the safest place you're going to find. Maybe two days ago you would have had a chance. Dang things spread like wildfire. If you're going to try to get to the city limit to fall into the sweet bosom of the military, you're going to have one hell of a time doing it."

"Brandon's right," warned Dale. "You're in the center of the shit show now. We've been able to hold back the bastards while still managing to send out resource-gathering parties. This place is locked down. You're better off here. Winter'll be here in three or so months. If we can hold 'em off 'til then, the fuckers will freeze out there."

"Unless they start building fires," Brandon remarked.

"Don't even," Dale chuckled.

Matt picked up a sword and skirted around Brandon. Nodding to the two gentlemen, he began heading back. "I'm sorry. Right now, I just can't accept the offer." Resisting further temptation, he went in search of Kevin.

Hoping Kevin had followed him was asking for too much. Standing in the center of the main hall, Matt spun in place trying to catch a glimpse of his coworker or a possible clue to where he could have gone. He'd be content with even finding Skylar to find out if she had seen something. A moment later, he spotted the laughing girl leaning against an information desk, busily scribbling on museum maps.

Fully expecting disappointment, he approached her. "Hi."

"Hey," she emptily replied without looking up from her work.

"You wouldn't happen to have seen where the people I arrived with went?" Matt inquired. "Specifically, the football-player-looking one? We just got here maybe thirty minutes ago."

Automatically, she folded up the map and placed it on a growing pile beside her. Fetching another map from the table behind the counter, she flipped it open and restarted the process. "Can't say I did. But if they're new here, Pierson probably took them to get checked out."

What a bitch. Matt wished he had asked someone else.

"Who is Pierson, and where would he be?"

"You might have seen him already. He looks like a rich guy. Sleazy hair. Somehow organized this whole thing." Grabbing her most recently completed map, she pushed one into Matt's hand. "The clinic is down the East Wing. Second floor. Follow the map and keep it with you. Anything else?"

Unsure if the information was worth the sass, Matt thanked her and carried on.

The map crinkled loudly in his hand as he walked, but it proved surprisingly helpful. Multiple rooms within the museum were repurposed and relabeled. In case of an emergency, there was even a designated safe spot with multiple recommended paths to follow. Locations of swords were marked with an upside-down T. As much as she annoyed him, the girl had done a good job on these.

Finding the clinic was a breeze. Previously the telescope exhibit, the artifacts and the replicas had been moved to a far corner and replaced with various rugs and mats. Pillows made from newspaper-stuffed gift-shop shirts lay on each rug, ready to provide potential patients minimal comfort from the hard floor. Screwed into the painted steel skeleton that supported a wall of windows facing the lake was a large plywood door. A hefty bolt on the door's right-hand side locked it in place.

"Matt!" Kevin shouted. Sitting cross-legged on the only yoga mat, Kevin's shirtless chest was being examined by a middle-aged Hispanic man in street clothing. "Need to tell you something!" Kevin mumbled something to his clinician, resulting in the man smiling at Matt and giving the two some privacy.

"What? Am I next in line for a physical?" Matt sarcastically chuckled. "You heard Zeus. We're just supposed to be dropping off Skylar and head out afterward. Possibly grab a few things to help us out." Like a game show model, Matt presented the sword he had borrowed.

"Yeah ... about that."

Matt didn't like the sound of that.

"Zeus reached out to Poseidon a few hours after the meeting ended. With Artemis' life on the line, he decided to check out our assigned location himself. Told him to update us once we arrived."

It felt like the air had been sucked from his lungs. He finally had the perfect chance to win Maddison back. He could swoop in and rescue her. Seeing him and his heroics, Maddison would swoon. But now he was being told that his chance at getting her back had all gone to hell because of the apparent need to get the bitch from the office to safety. He had an idea of where she could be. He had to go. With or without Kevin.

"MATT!"

"What!?" Matt snapped. Huffing like a riled bull, he tightened his fingers until they felt like they were crushing embers around the sword's handle.

"You need to calm down," Kevin ordered. Now resting on a single knee, he looked like he was ready for a fight. "Zeus wants to protect her as much as you do. For all we know, she might have just lost her MBT. He ordered us to protect the refugees and build up defenses. Hades' army is growing larger each day. The military has set up a perimeter around the city, but that's not going to save anyone this far in. The more people we can keep out of his grasp, the better."

Further irritated by Kevin's advice, Matt lashed back. "How is that our problem? There are five of us. That's even if we're including myself." Turning his body, he pointed at Kevin. "You dragged me into this. Whatever you and your band of inflated-ego tech nerds think they need to do, keep me out of it."

Kevin stood and held his hands up between himself and his irate partner. "Matt, you don't know what you're saying. Give me the sword. I can't let you go off on your own. Leaving this safe haven is suicide. You want Artemis—"

"Maddison!"

Reconsidering the breadth of Matt's frustration, Kevin continued. "Maddison. You want Maddison to be safe. As I mentioned back at the office, you aren't the only one. Running off and getting yourself killed isn't going to help her. I know how much you miss her. Honest. If she is still alive and you die, it's going to break her."

Break her? Why would that break her? Matt thought. Even if what Kevin had said was true, it didn't make sense. Maddison had left him. You don't leave someone if you love them. *That's just something people say to take the high ground in a breakup.*

Fishing Matt out from his whirlpool of thoughts, Kevin yanked on the line. "She still loves you." His spine straightened up. "I can't keep seeing you like this. None of us knew what she did until it was done. We all came together to take care of you. It's hard to believe, but she arranged it. She never wanted to leave you, Matt. If you want to see her again, stay here and stay alive. Help these people survive. She's out there somewhere. Make sure she has a place to come back to."

Following the length of his outstretched arm, Matt realized the tip of his sword was aimed at Kevin's throat. "I—I'm ..."

Sidestepping the blade, Kevin carefully grabbed the exposed hilt above Matt's hand. Matt allowed the hilt to slide from his grasp.

"You don't need to apologize," Kevin reassured. Gripping the handle, Kevin quickly lifted his palm and held it beneath the blade with his fingertips. Furrowing his eyebrows, he looked at Matt as if he had just been offended. "Let's uh ... get this thing back downstairs, shall we? Poseidon mentioned that there's a team building something near the entrance to the Boulder, and they need supplies. We'll start there. This place needs a lot of attention if it's going to survive the storm. If you can't do this for the people, do this for Maddison."

Matt mutely nodded and walked toward the window. The lake looked peaceful. He had always shied away from daunting tasks. Something inside of him wanted to burn the city to the ground and the rotting pests within it. Nothing made sense anymore. Maybe it was stress that fueled his rage—or maybe it was the sudden diet change to protein bars. Whatever it was, it wasn't him.

"Preparing for a date?" jested Chatter.

Rubbing his sunburnt, naked skull, XI-24 frowned at his volunteer mentor. With the longest reigning tenure, Chatter was the most experienced Death-Touched around. Bored with the lesson of the day, XI-24 looked into the distance at the tall, manned walls encircling their expansive, open-aired prison.

"When can I play with something else?" he whined.

"Something else?" Chatter questioned as he bent down to pick up the child's discarded knife. "Practice enough with your dagger, and it can do anything you want it to do." He handed the weapon to the boy. The lightweight dagger looked like a short sword in the child's small hands. "Get back into that skeel rider stance. Let's work on that upward jab."

XIII

EIDOLIC EXPEDITATION

"Ten minutes!"

Zeus looked up while holding a board in place for a nearly completed wooden barricade. Wiping sweat from his forehead, Matt tossed his hammer down and watched Lewis run by.

Within thirty-six hours of Matt and Kevin's arrival at the museum, both Zeus and Hermes had returned from their missions. Each of the searched locations failed to yield Artemis or clues to her whereabouts. Not wanting to give up, Poseidon had presented a well-accepted idea: surreptitiously tucked away under the museum's need for food, supplies, and resources, the search for Artemis continued under the guise of supply gathering runs. Two weeks had since passed.

"Ten minutes!" Lewis joyously shouted again. His shoes clapped against the floor as he ran past the two men and an intimidating clown statue that nearly reached the ceiling. Cracks and chips in its decade-old paint added to the statue's creepiness.

"Heard you the first time. We'll be there," Zeus said in a crotchety manner.

Chuckling, Matt wiped his hands on his freshly washed pair of community jeans. "The kid's excited to finally get some air."

Zeus crossed his arms. "If he wanted air, he could have gone to the roof. A scavenging run is no place for him."

"Hermes wouldn't have backed Lewis up if he didn't think his pupil was ready. Would love to see that kid handle a real sword." Devious flames lit up Matt's eyes. "Don't we still have a few from the Civil War room?"

"I'd rather have the kid use something that he's in tune with. If we give a saber to him, we might as well just kill him now."

Matt knew that Zeus was right. Through Kevin's classes, Matt had received training of his own and had gotten quite good with a pipe sword. Although he had the right idea about what to do in a fight against the undead, picking up one of the other Frankensteined weapons created by the refugees would throw him off.

Going on the supply run was still dangerous. At best, a skilled team could take down a group equal to their size or fewer as long as none of the nihanem ganged up on an individual. Anything larger than that and your shoes became the conduit to your fate.

"I'll meet you and the others by the entrance," Matt said. "Need to make a quick stop."

No more than five minutes later, Matt emerged from the latrine, zipping up his jeans. He doubted that he could ever get used to the communal stench and would trade anything to get the water to the city turned back on. Luckily, the museum was right on the edge of a lake, so buckets of water could be collected whenever the stored supply got low. Grabbing the pipe sword leaning against the latrine entrance, he walked over to the meeting point.

Standing huddled together and deep in conversation were Dale—wearing his lucky red bandana—and Lewis. Zeus stood off to the side, impatiently tapping his finger against his folded arms. All three of them wore the same cheap museum gift shop backpack. Having been careful not to damage his first backpack, Zeus still had possession of a coveted black version.

Slumped over on the floor like an unwanted child was a lonely bubblegum-pink backpack. Matt begrudgingly picked it up and slung it over his shoulder. Hearing snickering, he shot a glare at both Dale and Lewis: each wore a forest green backpack.

"Lewis, loosen your straps," Zeus ordered, halting the young man's taunting. "If one of those bastards grabs your pack, you need to be able to slip out of it. Nothing we find out there is worth more than a life." He signaled Matt and the others to follow him. "Remember," Zeus reiterated, "until we're back in here, do not talk unless it is vital for survival."

They approached the massive gate sealing the museum to find Poseidon already preparing to open it. After getting word that the coast was clear, he cracked open the iron seal and let the scavenger party out. Pausing in the doorway, Zeus whispered something to the doorman. Maybe it had something to do with Maddison. Despite his best effort, Zeus' perfectly angled head meant Matt couldn't even lipread the message. When they left the safety of the museum, the no-talking rule would be in place—and with it the high possibility that his question didn't meet the need-to-survive requirement. His curiosity would have to wait.

In the movies, people moving about a zombie-infested city fought tooth and nail for every step they took. The moaning dead would spill out of every crevice and cupboard without end, dressed in their Sunday finest. In reality, once the initial shockwave calmed, the living dead were drawn to the loudest sources of sounds like moths to a light. Here, the military threw anything they could at their infamous movie-star enemy from the outskirts of the city. Sound travels, especially when there's nothing else to cover it up. One of those sounds was the boom from a tank. Still, not all lures work perfectly.

"Lewis!" Dale whispered as intensely as possible.

Matt and Zeus stopped in their tracks. Matt's partially filled backpack rattled as he turned to look back at Dale. Following the direction of Dale's bushy face, he caught a glimpse of Lewis' green backpack before it disappeared into a building across the street.

"Knew he wasn't ready," Zeus growled under his breath. Motioning to Matt and Dale to stay put, Zeus carefully made his way across the street. Readying his own pipe sword, he entered the building.

Dale and Matt looked at each other, silently complaining about the recklessness of the youngest scavenger team member.

Attempting to peer into the building, Matt was only met by his reflection. Nervously, he looked over his shoulder. Just because the street was clear when they arrived didn't mean it would be forever. Company could arrive at any moment. They had to move.

Matt checked his watch. *They're taking a while in there*, he thought.

Dale nudged Matt. "We'll give those two another minute. After that, we're going in after them," he whispered. Matt nodded in agreement.

With thirteen seconds left to go, Zeus emerged. Even from this distance, Matt could see how aggravated he was. Tailing behind on an invisible leash was Lewis. Instead of carrying embarrassment or shame, he was zipping up his now-much-bulkier green bag. Just as his bag passed through the doorway, their luck ran out.

RINGINGINGINGINGINGING!

Alarms, somehow still active, screamed from within the store. Somewhere down the street, a single screech replied to the electrical siren. One by one, the bone-chilling calls of nihanem entered the previously dead space.

Looking toward their fearless leader for hope and direction, Matt and Dale only found terror. The first nihanem to round a corner was wearing anything but her Sunday finest; the unfortunate woman had most likely been attacked in a changing room in a nearby clothing store. Half of her arm swung like nunchucks on a rope of twisted, mushy-looking flesh below the uncovered white knob of her elbow. Exposed breasts wobbled about as she awkwardly hobbled toward the men on a mostly eaten leg. The only thing covering her athletic body was a thin, purple lace thong and dried blood.

Suffering from withdrawal, Matt was unable to tear his eyes away. Feeling a strong tug from one of his teammates, he noticed the growing horde behind her.

"Run!" Zeus shouted.

Cutting himself off from the guilty treat, Matt turned tail and retreated. Abandoning stealth, the four men sprinted down the street. Like a clutter of spiders sharing a plucked web, the undead seemed to pour out of every crevice and cupboard. Hands that had been distant moments before quickly became narrowly dodged traps. Writhing walls closed in upon them. In the race of life or death, their feet were the tortoise to the wailing hare.

Dale shoved the nihanim of an old man to the ground, jumped over the frail monster, and continued on. Safety could easily be found in any of the passed-by buildings, but their protection would be bittersweet, and the team knew it. They needed to find a way to escape the clutches of the living dead without turning themselves into a canned meal. While the dead could run forever, the living, unfortunately, were limited by the handicaps of lactic acid and anxiety. Their fuel gauges were nearly on empty, and they had to get off the street as soon as possible.

Spotting an alleyway, Matt felt like magnets in his chest had been snagged by their opposites. "This way!" he shouted.

Before anyone could argue, he bolted in the alley's direction. Forced to choose between potential escape and dying in battle due to the recklessness of another squad member, the three irked men ran after him.

Decayed wooden telephone poles became distance markers in a deadly race. Ignoring the frenzied pleas behind him, Matt pounded his soles on the cold pavement. Bursting out of the alley, a buildup of stiff leaves beneath a cement curb crunched as he barreled through it.

Matt's body detached from his mind, drunk on cortisol. Two streets west, divert one street to the north, and continue west down Nory Blvd. More of a rider without reins on a chariot than a captain at the helm, Matt's feet seemed to be directing him.

A quarter of the way down another alley, Matt's auto-piloted legs disengaged. Abandoned by his own intuition at the edge of a manhole cover, he should have felt lost. Instead, he dropped to the ground and dug his fingers between the threads of a cast iron web. Built up over years of neglect, city grime happily transferred from its stodgy home to Matt's sweaty skin.

"Wait up!" screamed Lewis.

"What the hell is wrong with you!?" heaved Dale. The swiftly approaching horde loudly entered their cramped public corridor, surging forward like a crashing tsunami of decaying bodies.

CLUNK!

Exhausted, Lewis and Dale watched slack-jawed as Matt descended into the bowels of the city. Holding up the rear, Zeus ordered the other two to jump in. Not seeing much choice in the matter, Lewis and Dale did as they were told.

Zeus lowered himself into the manhole, grabbed the heavy lid, and set it in place behind him. Certain that the cover wouldn't be enough, he slipped off his prized black backpack and pushed a strap through the grate. He stuck two fingers into the cold open air, pulling the strap through another hole and looping the other around a rung in the sewer's embedded ladder; then, he tied the two ends together and prayed that the nihanem's motor functions would impede their ability to pursue.

Farther along in the sewer, Matt waded through what he told himself was knee-high, fermenting gym-sweat slush. Reflecting off the uneven city-soup surface, warm brown light entered the sewer through storm drains and dimly filled the concrete tunnel. Like a hound on the trail of an apparition, Matt was determined to see this through.

Black sludge and over-steeped cinnamon tea sloshed about, creating endless, tightly packed echoes. With no obvious manhole cover to lift, Matt allowed himself a break from the gagging humidity and the next pre-programmed process. Then he noticed a storm drain opening leading to the street above. It was just a foot away. Cool, toasted vanilla autumn air refreshed him more than any glass of chilled water ever had before.

Closing his eyes, he calmed his racing thoughts. *Smells really do work wonders*, Matt thought, recalling his visit to the Sensory Simulation exhibit back at the museum. If he came out of today alive, he vowed to find a candle shop and keep some wax in a container for an instant holiday.

The moment of relief that Matt had so quickly become infatuated with spun into agony. Instinctively, he covered the placement of the pain with an open hand. Expecting his own hair, he instead found a hairy version of his wife's alligator skin skirt tightly pulled over a rigged, boney frame. Latched on tightly, Matt struggled to break free. Following an arm the color of mold-covered blueberries, the blender-kissed face of a man emptily stared at its catch. Yelling for help, Matt was answered by an ear-splitting scream from the predator.

Using his pipe sword, Matt hacked at the dead man's arm. While successful in mincing an area of flesh on one side of the nihanim's arm, he couldn't break through the bone at his current angle. Attempting to brace himself, Matt's sludge-caked shoe failed to stay on the slimy sewer wall.

Matt sensed additional hairless spider legs reaching for him as they brushed the back of his shirt. Tilting the sword toward the opening, Matt thrust it through the slim window. Despite piercing his attacker, its claw refused to release.

Thwack!

Liberated by a well-aimed chop from Dale, Matt stumbled forward, stepping on a patch of submerged muck. He lost his balance and belly-flopped into the brown river. Ripping free the lifeless hand entangled in his hair, Matt whipped it deeper into the subterranean maze.

Swinging his sword, Dale managed to slice through a second hungry undead hand, leaving just a fraction of an index finger writhing aimlessly. He repeatedly plunged his sword into the visible monsters and continued until all movement of the puppeted corpses ceased.

Breathless from the ordeal, Matt turned to Dale. "Damn good aim." He vainly attempted to wipe off the sewage covering his face.

"Who said I was aiming?" Dale tiredly scowled.

Shocked, Matt gawked at the amputated arm and then in the direction of the discarded hand. *That could have been my head,* he thought. An odd shadow fluttered on the wall near the hand's watery grave. Sticking oddly out of the wastewater, a ledge no longer than Matt's shoulders and no wider than the average cell phone caught his attention.

Zeus and Lewis eventually caught up to their companions and tried to make sense of what had just happened. Unsympathetic to the close call, Lewis loudly remarked how they wouldn't be trapped in shit city and have to dodge hands from outside if it weren't for someone's inability to stay with the group.

Ignoring Lewis' ironic jab, Matt approached the ledge. Four perfectly drilled holes lined up like vertical bean-bag goals. Aligning his left hand with the holes, Matt slid his fingers inside.

Each crevice, despite feeling like concrete, was as smooth as ice. In each hole—roughly one and a half inches in—Matt could feel the scratchiness of a razor's edge against the bump of his knuckles. Pushing his fingers in as far as they could go, the texture of the crevice changed under his fingertips. Instead of cement, these small spots felt like metal. Testing the surface lightly, Matt confirmed they were buttons by their springiness.

Curious, Dale waded over. "Matt, you find something?"

"Maybe?" Matt replied with uncertainty. Taking a deep breath and tightly wrapping his free hand around his pipe sword's hilt, he prepared for the worst. Matt pressed the hidden keys to the tune of suspense, giving in to the whims of his appendages.

Crack!

Unsure whether he had done something right or was in shock from the sudden severing of his fingers, Matt gingerly retrieved them from the holes. Aside from the slight skinning of a knuckle from his sudden startle, all digits were accounted for. A moment later, a section of the wall retreated six inches backward and silently glided to the left until it was entirely tucked away. The movement revealed a secret doorway.

Poking his head in, Matt was startled yet again by the immediate flooding of light from LEDs in every corner of the room. For the first time in his life, he felt like a secret agent. Row upon row of military-grade firearms stood at the ready upon hook-lined shelves. Resting on the floor beneath each weapon were boxes of ammunition.

"Holy shit. Is that a G36C?!" Lewis excitedly squealed,

pushing past Matt.

Giddy, Dale also approached, politely requesting Matt step aside before entering. Matt remained by the door, completely and utterly stupefied. Never before had he taken a trip into the smelly intestines of the city. Either his bad luck streak had finally ended, or subliminal messaging from tv shows implanted this gem into his brain. Whichever it was, he couldn't complain. An arsenal like this could ensure the survival of the museum. *Hell,* he thought, *it could turn the tide of a war.*

Walking in front of Matt and blocking his view of the room, Zeus firmly clamped his hand onto his squadmate's shoulder. "How did you know about this place?" he discreetly demanded.

Matt garbled and stuttered a response.

Displeased, Zeus shoved Matt against the wall and reiterated. "Matt, I need you to answer me. How did you know about one of Artemis' caches?!"

Resting peacefully in the summer-heated grass beneath a crescent moon, the middle-aged woman almost looked peaceful. Red, clean-cut stumps remained where her hands previously resided, breaking the image of the fairytale. Forming a wide circle of the bereaved, heavily armed soldiers stood at the ready.

Mourning beside the deceased, XI-24 tried again to resurrect the corpse. He raised his bruised arm and aimed his hand at his target. Barked demands and insults from the presiding officer failed to spur the desired results from the child. Dragged by a chain wrapped around his hands like an abhorrent beast, Chatter was led into the circle by a group of soldiers.

The red-faced officer drew a gun from his hip and trained it on the child's friend. Trying harder to command the corpse, XI-24 raised both arms and focused as hard as he could.

BANG!

Smoke spilled from the barrel toward the sky. Chatter fell to the ground, biting his tongue to hold back the agony. Rage-filled, XI-24 screamed under the chorus of a thousand drums as the soldiers opened fire.

The officer sneered and turned to exit the ring. "Give this dog a drink," he proudly jeered.

Shredded, the woman's corpse lay in a heap less than an arm's reach from the officer's boots.

XIV

CRUCIFIXION

SPLOOSH!

Shocked by the penetrating cold, Hades gasped for breath only to have the sweet, rusted air replaced by another high-powered blast of water. Heavy, sodden pants clung to him like a frigid second skin. Blood-speckled water spastically rippled in a shallow pool beneath the chair he was strapped to. Beneath the puddle's surface, the spattering gurgle of a thirsty drain hardly bridled its growth.

"Almost lost you that time," Artemis cooed as she shut the valve on an IV.

Hades looked up at the half-spent bag of blood dangling from a flimsy pole. A growing pile of empty bags lay at her feet. The last of the generous drought of red life flowed down a thin tube and seeped into his veins through a barbed needle in his arm. His grizzly wounds slowly sealed and faded into scars that were indistinguishable from the hundreds of others marring his body.

Artemis looked at her toy with disgust. "Never thought I'd appreciate that abhorrent trait of yours."

"Where are you securing your supply from? These bags aren't filled with animal blood or some other concoction. I can feel it." A sly smile grew upon Hades' face. "This blood is human and fairly fresh."

"If I was in your position, I wouldn't concern myself with the source of anything."

"And you call me the monster. How far you've fallen," Hades sneered.

A powerful right hook rocked Hades. Its force would have knocked him from the chair had he not been tied to it. Instead, the chair violently fell to the side. The metal chain attached to his left arm loudly clunked as it drew taut, halting his descent and stopping the chair from falling to the floor. He winced. The chain was connected to a gauntlet whose locking rod had been inserted through his arm; now, that rod pressed against the bones beneath his wrist. Cherry-red blood flowed from the inside of his cheek and over the jagged edges of broken teeth.

Artemis reached up, grasped a section of groaning chain, and leaned back on it. Link after link passed through a hefty metal clasp bolted to the floor. Using her weight, the huntress was able to hoist her prisoner back into a proper position. Then she released the chain and furiously stomped toward Hades. His chin rested on his chest as a soft chuckle bounced his shoulders.

Gripping his hair, she yanked his head up until her scorching eyes burned into his. "My actions could never measure up to you and the rest of your vile species. Entire cities perished by your hands. Nihanem left countless children without families. Defenseless people in shock were mutilated by their defiled loved ones!"

Fire begot fire as Hades returned her glare. "None of us ever chose which gift the *Void* would bestow upon us, only how we would use it. Those touched by Death had a choice to make as well, but we never had the chance to choose our own paths. Deotram collectively decided to TAKE THAT AWAY FROM US!" Spittle flew from Hades' snarling lips and onto Artemis' face. "We became the creations of society's fears! Our hands were forced into calluses and stains so yours could remain soft. Did my *kind* ever have a choice? My actions were guided by chains. Your crimes were committed freely."

The huntress cast Hades' head aside like a futile hand of cards, retrieved the pistol holstered at her hip, and pressed the tip of the muzzle into her prisoner's forehead. Her free hand trembled as her body coursed with adrenaline. "When we adopted the names of these primitives' gods, we agreed to put the ideas of the old world aside. All of us wanted you dead, but Aphrodite saw something in you." A thin trickle of blood slithered along the rim of the muzzle before flowing down the bridge of his nose and off the side of his flaring nostrils. "You repaid our kindness by slaughtering her, Apollo, and the rest of that city. Consider my actions their retribution."

"The city was a meager price to pay to rescind their doing. Apollo was simply a consequence of your interference. You all cast your lot that day. Once the remainder of you have been disposed of, I'll finish what I started."

Amid the silence, the sheen of tears in her eyes betrayed Artemis' true emotions. "You may have taken Apollo from me, and I don't know how you managed to get to Hephaestus, but I swear to the *Void* itself that you'll give him back to me before you cease to foul the air on this side of the *Veil*." She removed the muzzle, revealing a dark red circle on Hades' forehead that quickly began to bleed. Artemis stood tall while retaining eye contact with her prisoner.

A deafening bang and a bright flash of light suddenly reverberated off the steel columns in the warehouse. Hot lead shattered Hades' right kneecap and upper tibia, and he fought back the urge to scream as wicked warmth spilled down his leg.

"The very moment I'm free, I vow to break every tether you have left to this world, including that DAMN PYRO!" Hades growled.

No longer able to contain her rage, Artemis backhanded him with the hefty pistol. "You already broke him! I'd rather you killed him than use another of your rot-walker tricks. Zeus wants you back in your pod, but timeless sleep doesn't compare to the pain you caused me. I'm going to savor stripping the flesh from your bones for the rest of my life, even if it means wrenching out the last drop of human blood to do so."

Chains clinked as Hades fought his bindings. "Don't tire yourself out, bi—" A biting upwards knee from Artemis cut off Hades. Had he not predicted her reaction, his nose certainly would have been escorted to the back of his brain.

Now burning hotter than a leather seat in the desert sun, Artemis holstered her pistol and barked at a mercenary in the corner. "Get him out of the chair and raise him until his toes can't kiss the floor!"

Like a well-trained pit crew, the mercenaries swooped in around Hades. Thick rubber soles tapped and scraped on the concrete while at least a dozen individual footsteps shook the metal catwalk circling the high-ceilinged room. No sooner had they arrived than the god had been freed from the chair. He could hear the groan of machinery above him. With the chains no longer clipped to the floor, Hades was lifted toward the ceiling for his treeless crucifixion.

As soon as his entire weight was supported by spikes through his arms, the machinery stopped. His legs dangled like lead chimes. *These rats are too coordinated,* Hades thought. The muscles in his shoulders felt like stale bread being twisted. He looked at his leather jacket beneath the table. As long as there was still hope, he could endure her wrath for a thousand lifetimes.

The mercenaries scurried back to their posts, leaving the room in silence. In the chaos of the moment, he had lost sight of Artemis. If his well-equipped guards had rotated, the shadows cloaked their movements. For what seemed like hours, he stared at his jacket, waiting for the sting to come from behind. It was one thing to be cognizant of when and how the pain would be inflicted; it was another level of torment entirely to be left to meditate upon his fate.

SCREEEEEE!

The sound of rusted metal grinding on a concrete floor screeched behind Hades, breaking him from his rumination. Slow footsteps closed in. Expecting the sting of a knife or the penetrating tendrils of electricity, Hades prepared himself for the worst. Instead, a light touch graced his back, circling about on his scarred skin. Moving like whispering feathers along his back, the fingers traced braided lines over his protruding ribs and onto his chest.

A head draped in flowing golden hair ducked beneath his marionetted left arm and glided into view. The top of her bowed head nearly rested against the center of his chest. Soft breath and cloud-light hair warmed his filth-covered, scarred skin. The scent of a vivifying bouquet begged to unfurl the sails of his heart.

Hades observed the woman through owl-like eyes clouded in disbelief. Images of a dark stain spreading outward from a ghastly tear in purple cloth flooded his mind. Blood ran down the worn blade of an iron dagger, dripped off its wooden hilt, and onto his crimson-wet hand. Clamorous streets in an ancient city turned into chaos and gore. Delicate snakes of gold swam in a hot royal pool, drinking the slowly coagulating waters.

"I ... I..."

Something sharp dug into his flesh, just three inches to the left of his belly. Sharp pain resonated outward from the source. Despite mustering the rest of his strength, a groan of anguish escaped through his clenched teeth.

"Murdered her?" The golden-haired woman looked up at him, revealing Artemis' scowling face and tightening jaws. She roughly twisted the buried knife, causing Hades to lose his dwindling composure, throw back his head, and roar in agony.

"I think she would have sounded something like that if you hadn't ruptured her lung."

Standing on her toes to bring her face closer to his, Artemis used the leverage to push the blade deeper. "You could have at least attacked her from the front. Given her a damn chance. Instead, you took the coward's route."

Wells long thought dry burst open. Tears ran down Hades' face. Already broken, the memory continued to pour from the dam. Aphrodite's eyes of cerulean glass blazing beneath him transformed into lifeless orbs directed toward the heavens. The weight of her head nestled against his breast as he cradled her with a single arm.

CRACK!

A bullet whizzed past Hades, nearly striking Artemis in the left arm. Artemis snapped her head in the direction of the projectile's source. Screaming like a koala on cocaine, a boy no older than fifteen, wearing black clothing and heavily ornamented with piercings, stormed toward Artemis. Maintaining speed, he raised a silvery handgun toward Artemis. A chorus of bangs and booms around the room showered the teen with lead, removing his jaw and tearing flesh from his body.

His gun discharged with a flash, sending a stray bullet on a collision course with a catwalk support beam, which ricocheted in a hail of sparks and shallowly lodged itself in a nearby wall. The boy's body smacked the floor like a wet sponge and skidded to an abrupt stop. The remains of his jaw loosely clung to his skull by a twisted strand of flesh.

"How the hell did he get in here?" Artemis said while ripping her knife out of Hades. Without missing a beat, she pointed at a mercenary on the catwalk. "Raise the prisoner and get this bastard's body out of here!" Turning back to face Hades, she watched as he was lifted toward the ceiling. The attached IV bag briefly followed until the weight of the bag and its adjoined stand ripped the barbed needle from Hades' arm.

With a pistol drawn, she strode over to the boy's corpse. She used the tip of her boot to lift the corpse's head and get a better look at its face. "Find how he got in!" A dozen men armed with rifles dashed toward the intruder's entry point.

Their search was brief. A flood of nihanem burst through the heavy steel door. The mercs closest to the door were lost in an instant, while those that chose to fight in the immediate vicinity were quickly overwhelmed. Their previous display of firepower was akin to a bottle rocket compared to the continuous barrage released by the defending mercs. Their concentration of fire and precision practically halted the undead advance.

Then the sound of metal tearing turned into a loud crash as a new flood of ravenous corpses emerged from the catwalk. A burly, masked henchman on the catwalk used his rifle like a club against three nihanem with some success, until he was tackled over the railing and lost in the decaying sea below.

Still standing over the dead boy, Artemis fired round after round from her pistol into the horde. Her shots were precise, but as nihanem fell left and right, they were replaced by two more snarling corpses. Quickly ducking the swipe of an overweight pale nurse to her left, Artemis stooped down, grabbed the creature by its tight blue scrubs, and rolled. The nurse flew like a tethered swan over the mouse-like woman and smacked head-first into the cement, cracking her forehead open. Artemis landed her roll with a knee on the ghoul's back, putting her last two bullets into the back of the nurse's skull before looking up.

Like a jilted lover fueled by rage, Artemis sprinted toward a mercenary fleeing toward the back entrance. She caught up to the deserter with ease, her speed comparable to a trained athlete. The man lost his balance when she slammed into him with a strong shoulder and rolled like a ragdoll on the ground. Unwilling to confront his attacker, he quickly found his bearings and desperately crawled toward the exit.

Treating the man's head like a football, Artemis punted with all her strength. The mercenary's head snapped to the right, an audible crack sounding from his neck. Ripping the rifle from twitching hands, she readied the weapon, fired a single round into the man's head, and then turned toward Hades with a scowl.

With his head turned, Hades was just able to make out his captor from the corner of his eye. Artemis had a rifle trained on him. The nearest nihanem could reach her in three paces; unfortunately, he knew she could make the shot before the corpse even traveled one.

Sparks jumped off of her weapon while dust and concrete shards popped like popcorn from the wall behind her. Loudly swearing, she dove behind a steel pillar.

Like a prairie dog shyly peering out from its burrow, a head of thick black hair poked out of a small gap in the horde. A tail of smoke wagged from the barrel of a M4A1 that was tightly gripped in steady hands. As quickly as they had appeared, the gunman dropped below the shoulders of the ravenous mob. Artemis returned fire, tearing through the faces and chests of nihanem where the guerilla fighter had appeared.

A spray of bullets loosely aimed at the mercenary from the catwalk grated the air around Artemis until one tore through her arm and another grazed her neck. Hades looked at the volley's source, expecting to see Lindsey. Instead, he was greeted with the image of a boy with shoulder-length, dusk blue hair wielding a stockier rifle. Just like the dark-haired fighter, the blue-haired oddity was quickly sucked back into the belly of the rotting beast.

Now twenty five feet above the fray, Hades could make out individual scratch marks on the rafters. Without a commander at their helm, the two spools of chain continued to reel in their catch. Hades could feel the stakes piercing his wrists, begging for an exit as his arms were pulled in opposite directions.

Mentally lassoing in the last of his scattering focus, Hades directed his attention toward a large, decayed bus driver on the catwalk. Uncurling its fingers from around a merc's rib bone, the nihanim stood up and turned its head toward the lift control panel; the merc collapsed at its feet. Drunken footsteps trampled and tugged on the entrails hanging from a broad gash across the nihanim's slowly peeling stomach. Pushing through its rampageous siblings was an uphill battle, but it finally reached the keyboard and looked down.

The first bone to break was in Hades' right wrist. He could feel his hand slowly being torn off. Losing focus, he saw the heavy hand of the bus driver mindlessly pound on the panel. Blood trickled down Hades' arms and along his autumn-leaf red chest. He couldn't take much more. Out of all of Artemis' torture techniques, this unintentional method was by far the worst.

The driver began to slam on the panel with both hands. Suddenly, the large corpse lurched to the side, and from around its body, small hands gripped the panel and swiftly pressed a button.

CEEEERRRK.

The machinery went silent. Like a gift from the *Void* itself, the reels began to reverse and bring Hades back to the ground. Once barren, the floor beneath him was now a battlefield painted red. War cries from men and women were overlaid by the earthy growls and demonic shrieks of the undead.

Bullets zipped about the room. Most found their home in one of the countless living dead, while orphaned bullets found refuge in bricks or the ceiling. Three nearly back-to-back mercenaries held their own as a seemingly never-ending wave of horrors charged toward them. The one closest to Hades seemed to be calling the shots: a stocky, middle-aged woman with tied-back, shoulder-length blond hair wearing black, full-body military garb. Like a well-oiled machine, they danced in perfect harmony. As soon as someone needed to reload, the other two took turns firing in their teammate's stead.

Whether she was aware of the guerillas hiding among the dead, Hades didn't know; she stood in the open, barking orders until a barrage of rounds ripped through her neck and upper chest. With bulging eyes and her mouth open in shock, she stumbled backward and collapsed. Tumbling between the soldiers, her finger held the trigger, firing a short, arched burst. The bullets drew a line up the wall toward Hades, resulting in a shower of sparks as one of the rounds slammed into and ricocheted off his left gauntlet.

The end of the ride couldn't have arrived sooner. As the tips of his boots began to touch down on the dusty cement, he allowed his injured right leg to go limp. With all of his weight managed by his left leg, the last of his diminished strength quickly waned. With the iron gauntlets still covering his hands and the growing weight of the burgeoning piles of chain on his arms, he had no way of conducting a blood regeneration. In his present state, he couldn't even fight. Slowly pivoting in place, Hades positioned himself to face the closest vertical surface to rest against.

Hades moved like a sloth through tar. At his disposal was a left leg made of balanced marbles and a right leg stuffed with shards of glass. With a single thought, he could summon his puppets of flesh and bone to his aid. To be carried by a handful of his nihanem would be a luxury sweeter than wine, a luxury that he couldn't afford to enjoy with Artemis nearby. Every last nihanem had to be focused until she was either killed, captured, or expelled. Preferably the first.

Hades slid his back down a support beam, barely minding the cold surface of it against his skin. Having more collapsed than gracefully descended, he righted himself. His gauntlets clinked and clanked on the cement with his effort. Finally sitting, Hades dropped his hands to his sides and rested his head against the beam. He had been steadily losing blood from the wounds sustained after his last forced blood regeneration; now, he needed to find a source of fresh blood—and soon.

"How in the Abyss am I going to get these manacles off?" Hades said, his voice frail.

He raised his left hand to study the contraption. The gauntlet drooled thick red liquid like a hungry dog. It was insultingly simple yet sturdy. If one of his soldiers lent a hand, he could get out of this on his own. Thinking back to the hefty bus driver and its failed execution of the simple task of pressing a button, he decided that he'd rather bleed out than lose a hand.

Gunfire erupted just above his head, leaving his ears ringing. A familiar face knelt beside him to his right. Letting the rifle hang from her shoulder by its strap, Lindsey brushed strands of hair behind her ear. Her mouth moved, but the shock to his ears had yet to fade. Below twisted eyebrows, Hades gawked at the human.

Although his arms had begun to go numb, Hades could feel Lindsey tinkering with the gauntlet on his right hand. She looked somewhat different. Almost leaner. Looking closer, he could see a different shine to her eyes, too. Before, she had radiated hate and a disturbing lust. Now her eyes were like arrows. As he pondered these details, the ringing in his ears began to fade, and he heard one of the most dreaded phrases in his life.

"This is probably going to hurt," Lindsey said, yanking on the stake running through his right arm.

Torn muscle and skin gripped the iron stake like starving children. The scratching of metal against bone reverberated through his hand and up his arm to his elbow. Hades squeezed his eyelids together and groaned in agony. His left leg pushed on the dusty floor, pressing his back into the support beam.

Gently, Lindsey removed the gauntlet from his right hand.

A ghastly, circular hole in his wrist bled profusely. Bits of white poked out from the merlot-red mush inside. The unsealed wound's internal screaming practically drowned out the wails and gunfire in the room.

Attempting to grab Lindsey as she crossed over his legs to his left side, Hades realized he couldn't move his hand. It swung limply at the end of his arm like a fish on a pole.

Helpless to stop his rescuer, Hades apprehensively braced himself. Knowledge of the oncoming pain did nothing to reduce its severity. He stomped on invisible grapes with his left foot until the pain subsided enough that the white sprites in his vision disappeared.

Removing the final gauntlet, Lindsey looked at Hades. "Can you walk?"

"What does it look like?" snapped Hades in a pained, gravelly voice.

Lindsey tucked her shoulder beneath Hades' armpit and threw his left arm around her. "We're going to stand in 3 ... 2 ... 1 ..."

Together, they pushed off the floor with their legs. Lindsey grunted under her cumbersome load made slippery by his caked-on blood and sweat.

Hades released a warrior's roar as his wounded ankle and shattered knee took on some of the weight. Drained by the ordeal, he now had an idea of how the human felt with her shaking legs.

"We need to head toward the table over there." Hades nudged toward it with his head. "I can't leave here without the jacket under it."

"We'll find you another one."

"I need what's inside it!" Hades angrily protested.

"Once we're in the hallway, I'll have someone get it. I promise. Right now, we need to get you out of here."

"This way!" shouted the blue-haired boy, waving to them

in an aggressive "come here" motion.

Still looking toward the table, Hades swore and allowed Lindsey to lead. They moved toward the colorful-haired anomaly. Hades' mind spun with questions, remembering the ambush in the train car and Lindsey lying on its grooved floor like a discarded ragdoll. The rest was still fuzzy. "I thought you were dead."

"I thought you'd be easier to find," Lindsey bounced back.

"The fight happened only a few hours ago. Your tracking skills are either remarkable for someone untouched, or Artemis has gotten rusty."

Moving past the blue-haired boy, he directed them toward the door where the nihanem still flooded in.

"Scott, stay behind and cover us," Lindsey ordered. Scott nodded and took up the rear. After a few steps, Hades' words finally caught up to her. Lindsey paused and looked at him. "The incident on the train wasn't a few hours ago." A sliver of woe softened her hard features. "That was two and a half months ago."

Before Hades could say anything, a blood-curdling scream let loose behind them. Looking back, he watched as Scott fell backward beneath a dark spray; using a short sword, Artemis had split the young fighter open from hip to shoulder in an upwards, diagonal strike. Before he could even hit the floor, she gracefully carved a course through the air, resulting in the removal of Scott's head.

"SCOTT!" Lindsey screamed as her friend's head smacked the floor and rolled away, stopping a few feet from his body. His mouth loosely hung open while his eyes darted about before coming to a final halt. Practically frothing at the mouth, Artemis hurtled over Scott's headless corpse and charged at the pair.

Hades had never expected to see this strange human again. He wasn't sure how Lindsey found him—or, more importantly, how she had managed to direct his nihanem. What he was sure about was that she could serve one final purpose. Removing his left arm from Lindsey's supporting shoulder, he placed his wrist against her back.

Having closed the gap between them, Artemis was now mere feet away. She pulled back her sword and lunged, thrusting the tip of the blade forward. The fire in her eyes was the same as it had been all those years ago. Hades shoved Lindsey as hard as he could, sending jolts of pain throughout his arm from his gaping wound.

Lindsey's eyes widened like an owl's as she tumbled forward. With Artemis' weight behind the attack, the blade of the sword entered her target's back and cut like butter through flesh. Obstructive bone shattered in the path of its might. Just as a diver breaks water for air, so did the tip of the blade burst through the skin on the opposite side of its victim before retreating back into the depths.

Lindsey's scream drowned out the surrounding chaos. Betrayed, she locked eyes with Hades. A thin, four-inch-wide line grew red before the first drip broke the dam.

There wasn't even a point to looking down, and he knew it. Artemis was as skilled with a sword as she was with a gun. Pressing a boot against her target's back, Artemis pushed Hades off her blade. Hades stumbled two steps before collapsing to the floor.

Using the tip of her boot, Artemis flipped Hades over and pointed the sword at his throat. Blood ran along its edges and dripped onto the dying god. "Now"—she pressed the tip of the blade against his skin—"this feels exactly like the day you destroyed our little family."

A fountain of lead erupted and zipped around Artemis. One bullet managed to strike her above the left hip while another grazed her left arm, creating a long gash on her forearm.

Artemis shot a glance toward Lindsey, whose steadiness was almost as lost as her composure. "Wait your turn, you bitch!"

Staring shameful death in the face, Hades saw his chance and took it. Mentally calling out to his nihanem, he commanded the nearby corpses to turn toward Artemis and charge at her. Startled by the sudden change, the huntress quickly surveyed the new battlefield dynamic. Then she gripped the hilt of the short sword with both hands and plunged it down toward Hades' neck.

OOF!

Artemis flew over Hades as a single nihanim tackled her, rhino-like, from behind. Holding tightly to her sword, she was able to slay the corpse on top of her just as the eye of the undead storm closed in around her.

Hades released his captive breath. A small dot of blood grew on his neck. *Too close*, he thought.

While the horde dealt with Artemis, Hades drained the blood from Scott's nearby headless corpse. He looked over at Scott's skull and his frozen expression. The same pain-nullifying sensation festered around his wounds, but this time it felt different. Blood regenerations typically brought a feeling of ascendency. Looking into Scott's eyes, he felt the unnerving sensation that he was draining an equal.

Hades stood up and tested out his hands. Satisfied—and partly amazed—with their functionality, he crunched his fingers together into fists.

Muted gunfire from reinforcements could be heard coming from outside. Unfortunately for Artemis, they weren't going to be able to save her. Still sore but filled with rage, Hades sprinted into the fray.

Like a goddess of war, Artemis danced a deadly waltz amongst the attacking corpses. Through slashing and weaving, Artemis managed to stay untouched. Sensing incoming fire, she grabbed a corpse to use as a shield and continued her performance. Hades' meteored fist connected with her jaw and broke her trance.

Like a spring, she recoiled with vicious swipes of her sword. Hades evaded her strikes and sent nihanem into her path to disrupt her attacks. Kicking a larger nihanem into her, he gave himself enough of a window to flank Artemis and hit her from behind. Each punch or kick thrown by Hades was stronger than the last. Stepping off the bent knee of a corpse, Hades launched himself into the air, barely evading the lethal kiss of Artemis' sword. He spun around and used his momentum to land a bone-shattering kick against his adversary's blocking arm.

Artemis swore, rolling on the ground and landing on her knee. She charged forward but suddenly lost the air in her lungs when a knee from a rotting woman in a raggedy yellow blouse plunged into her stomach. Without giving her a moment to react, a hand—flesh hanging from its bones like meaty curtains—cracked against Artemis' left temple. Artemis lashed back with her sword only to be stopped mid-swing by a swarm of hands on her arm and blade. She clung to the sword and pulled with her might to free it.

Like a ghost in the mist, Hades appeared before her and delivered a dizzying uppercut. Pooling all his rage into his next attack, his boot became a battering ram against his losing opponent. The strike sent her tumbling backward with enough force to break the sword free from her grasp. Thrusting his hand forward, thirty of the closest nihanem converged on Artemis.

The bodies covering Artemis resembled a discolored, writhing cocoon. Walking up to the mass, the bodies parted, leaving the mercenary kneeling. A legion of bluish, rotting hands covered her body, keeping her restrained. Her skin was now a bright shade of red. Veins coursing with adrenaline bulged from her temples and arms.

"Just kill me already, you corpse fucker," Artemis growled. "I know I'll see Apollo and Aphrodite where I'm going. The others will take you out."

Reaching out through the pile behind Artemis, Hades commanded the blood-soaked hand of a corpse to wrap its fingers around her throat. "You always did talk too much," Hades said as he towered above his previous captor. "Your death will come soon enough. Until that time, you're useful."

The hand around Artemis' throat tightened its grip and forced her jaw upward until she stared into the eyes of Hades. The motion caused her to gasp for breath.

"The moment I know where the others are"—Hades knelt down with both of his feet flat on the floor and gazed into Artemis' soul—"I'll kill you myself," he hissed.

The rotting vice around the huntress' neck continued to tighten. Rage shifted into desperate fear as her eyes began to bulge. Her chest shallowly surged and snapped back in quick repetitions. Her hands balled into fists, and the veins in her arms dilated like animals attempting to break free from beneath a heavy net. Moments after her gasping ceased, her eyes rolled into the back of her skull, and her body went limp.

Tears from the heavens hid XI-24's lamentation. Scratching at his hands like a trapped animal was a teenage soldier that could have been a distant childhood friend in a better world. Blood slithered out of the soldier's mouth and eyes as it was summoned by the tune of a forbidden song.

Feasting on the hot wine, XI-24's wounds healed. The teen struggled to contain the contents of his grumbling stomach, sickened by his own abhorrent ritual. Squadmates, supported by nihanem, passed by apathetically. Distant gunfire silenced foreign screams. Each briefing told XI-24 that the enemy were monsters, yet on each mission, the only monster he ever saw was himself.

XV

GRATITUDE

Hades cringed at the sight of the grizzly scars on his wrists. Basking in the morning light from a row of dusty windows, he looked around the newly discovered room in his exploration of Artemis' facility. Already standing about him, and still clumsily shuffling in the dank space, were a dozen of his most capable nihanem. His scarred chest showed through his opened, scuffed-up leather jacket; he had yet to find a decent shirt on his puppets or in the facility. Pulling down on the sleeves of his jacket to conceal the ghastly marks, Hades gazed over the dusty shelves and scattered cardboard boxes.

Following the capture of Artemis, one of the humans accompanying Lindsey discovered holding cells on a subterranean level. The only inhabitants discovered within were a mother in her early thirties and her clingy offspring. Their skin and hair had darkened from grime, and their clothing hung like sheets on their wiry frames. Their once-lavish clothes were torn and reeked of feces, with pieces of torn cloth from the mother's dress holding the child's hair in pigtails. After releasing them from their cage, the mother had placed her hand—sans ring finger—on Hades and thanked him with tears in her eyes. Without pause, he dispatched them and ordered their corpses to find the nearest fire and lie in it.

Throwing the unconscious huntress into their now-empty

cell seemed fitting.

As he turned to leave the insipid space, the sparkle of light reflecting off glass caught his attention. Sitting at eye level on a dusty bookcase shelf was a lonely picture frame. Picking up the frame exposed a line as wide as a finger in the dust. Toasted walnut wood peeked toward the ceiling through the thin hole in the gray blanket coating the room.

The brimming smile of a woman running in a flowing white dress lit up the frame. Flowers hung in the air around her, blurred by motion. Her fair skin nearly blended in with the dress while her long, curly hair shone through a ghostly veil; her hair was the color of a stolen sunset. Hades' fingers tightened on the antique wooden frame, and he ground his teeth. Despite her altered appearance, Artemis was unmistakable.

Just a step behind her stood a slightly taller man in a fine black tuxedo holding her hand. His slicked-back, black hair shined like smooth marble. Struggling to keep up with his electric bride, the groom resembled a faltering kite. Hades gazed at the groom. Walking toward the window, his breath quickened. The man's face had barely changed after all these years. Without the furrowed brows and permanent scowl, the bastard was almost unrecognizable. The sound of cracking wood squeezed out from beneath his pinot noir, blood-engorged fingers.

"So, the Dragon still breathes," Hades snarled to himself, chucking the picture frame at the wall across the room.

Just as Lindsey put her foot in the doorway, a spinning comet struck the wall next to her, exploding into a shower of glass and wood debris. Every muscle in her body recoiled. Prying her stone-stiff body apart with a mental crowbar, she felt the sudden tension melt away, and she proceeded to approach the fuming god with pursed lips. "You wanted to see me?"

"How did you control my nihanem?" Hades said while still

facing the window.

"What do you mean?"

"They listened to you. How did you do it?"

"I kind of dragged one, and a bunch of them followed," Lindsey said sheepishly.

Already on the tipping point of rage, Hades glared at the human over his shoulder. "There are other humans with you. My nihanem should have killed them on sight. How in the Abyss did you command them not to!?"

Taken aback by the lashing from the person she rescued not even five hours ago, Lindsey fired back. "I didn't do anything, you ungrateful prick! When the first zombie saw us, I told it that the people here were with me, and it just wandered off. I didn't read off some incantation or whatever." She spun back toward the door, her heels squeaking against the white- and blue-marbled linoleum tiles. "Next time you send one of your shambling shits for me, it had better be for a decent reason."

Moving to block her exit were two nihanem.

"Get the hell out of my way!" Lindsey fiercely demanded.

Hades looked down through glass shards at the face-up picture lying on the floor. Taking a deep breath, he faced Lindsey, who was locked in a struggle to budge his undead soldiers from the door. "You mentioned that the events in the underground transport transpired over two months ago. After three weeks, most would call off a search." Hades unconsciously chewed on the corner of his bottom lip. "Why did you keep searching?"

"I didn't," Lindsey said angrily into the chests of the blockade members. "When I woke up, you were gone. For the next few days, I searched every prison I could find. Most were either turned into holdouts or overrun by zombies with the prisoners still alive in their cells. One became a fortress run by the inmates who had been set free to give them a fighting chance.

That's where I met the others here with us."

She looked down at the side of her index finger. A small and painful white line, created by her nervously grinding thumbnail, quickly faded. The warmth of the sunlight hitting her neck reminded her of a warm towel from her last trip to the spa. Feeling the tension dull in her back, she decided to do her own searching of the room.

"After a week and a half of following leads, we gave up. Scott had the idea of us getting into military and survivor hold-outs and then helping your zombies breach them. If you hadn't started directing us, we never would have found you." Crouched down and huddled over a taped-up box, Lindsey played with the edge of the stubborn strip of tape sealing it shut. "You could have done that sooner and been less creepy about it," she said through a sassy smirk.

Hades—once again looking out a window—watched as two mercenaries retreated into a modified Humvee. The car shook as the walking dead flung themselves against it. An arm popped out of a hole in the roof. Grasping a handle on the bottom of a hatch, they pulled it shut. Like cockroaches, the dead crawled onto the vehicle. The vehicle shot forward, ripping it from the clutches of the murderous horde.

Two corpses still held on by the hole in the roof. Flashes of light burst from under the nearly closed hatch. Managing to put their torso between the mercenary and the hatch, the ni-hanim slid in face first. The Humvee veered to the right with a pair of legs sticking out of the hole like discount bunny ears. A moment later, the Humvee crashed through the brick wall of a building down the street.

Hades wryly smiled. "I never ordered any of my nihanem to guide you."

Puzzled, Lindsey stopped twirling a blown glass trinket in her hand. "Yes ... you did." Letting the glass slip from her fingers, she stood back up. "About two weeks ago, you had a zombie go to a rooftop across the street from where the others and

I were staying and just point in a direction.”

“I couldn’t have sent one of my nihanem for you. I didn’t know where I was, much less where you were. Even if I did know where you were, I wouldn’t have called for you.” Even though the reflection was faint, Hades could see the anger and hurt build up on the human’s face. “What did this ... zombie ... look like?”

Lindsey’s gaze bounced between the glass trinket in the box and the back of Hades’ head. “Every time we saw it, it was wearing a large, dark purple hoodie or something,” she growled.

Furrowing his brows, Hades leaned against a white, painted windowsill. “You saw them more than once? Did you get a good look at their face?”

“Why the hell would that matter?”

“It matters.”

“We mostly saw it at night. It appeared every few days or so. Taylor noticed it late in the afternoon one time. She said its face was as black as charcoal.”

Hades ran his fingers through his slick black hair and sighed. The two nihanem blocking the door shuffled about until they stood like statues along a short pathway. “I need time to think.”

Lindsey rolled her eyes, muttered, “Whatever,” and stormed out of the room.

Looking at the crowd of his creation below, Hades mentally flicked through the library of his thoughts. Could he have been reaching out to that human without realizing it? He shook his head. *No, that can’t be it*, he thought. The nihanem would have gone directly to her and had her follow. That didn’t leave much to go off of, but there was one person who came to mind and fit the description. His fingernails tapped against the cracked, painted wood. If it was them, why would they be helping him? Whatever their reasoning was, their mistake wouldn’t save them from their ruin.

"Is Lindsey still here?" peeped an oil-thin voice from the doorway.

Hades turned and saw a cinnamon-skinned face poking through the door. With short black hair that stopped just above her ears and a slender nose, the petite girl reminded him of a drenched coyote. "Just missed her," he grunted.

"If you see her, pass the message that we found where that doctor she's searching for is at."

Hades turned around and rested on the windowsill with his arms crossed. Having been gently enticed by one of the ni-hanem, the girl now stood in the middle of the room. Seemingly supported by the cold hand gripping her arm, the girl's face quickly drained of color.

"How did you come across this?" Hades strongly inquired.

Not more than ten minutes later, the thumping of a single pair of heavy boots against tile moved briskly through the dimly lit, lifeless facility. Seeing a sliver of light escape through a cracked door, Hades nudged the door open and walked inside. The robust smell of gun oil, heavy enough to slicken walls, immediately invaded his nostrils. Before him was a medium-sized room with rows of metal cages filled with firearms hung on metal prongs.

Hades wrinkled his nose. *Of all places to be, of course she had to be in here*, he thought.

Like a diabetic in a candy store, Lindsey intently yet cautiously perused the various items on display. Hearing footsteps stop behind her, she took in a deep breath of air and groaned. "Turn back around. I'm not going with you. If that ungrateful prick needs me, he can come to me himself."

Silence. Lindsey ran her finger over the grooves on top of a rifle. Feeling some spark between herself and the weapon, she lifted it from the wall and positioned it in her arms like an awkward barbell. She raised and lowered the rifle. Unlike her carbine, this one had a little more weight to it. She placed her hand over the magazine receiver. Her thumb tapped against the side of the rifle while she searched the bottom of the cage.

Having yet to hear her pest retreat, Lindsey loudly sighed. "If you're still here by the time I find the damn ammo for this thing, I'm going to ..." She turned and locked eyes with Hades.

Hades' knuckles cracked as he tightened his fists. "Going to what?" he growled.

Momentarily startled, Lindsey puffed up her chest, wishing to stand her ground. "Find ... you myself. This rifle is much more suited for you."

Hades' eyes narrowed. Normally, he wouldn't allow a human to get away with threatening him, no matter how careless it might have been. He almost admired her boldness. After a moment, he relaxed his stern gaze and gave a soft chuckle, which lightly shook his upper body. "Keep it for yourself. I prefer something a bit more personal."

"Noted," Lindsey said through a solaced smile. "So, um ... what are you here for?"

"Doctor Nosparchez's location has been discovered. His radio messages have betrayed him. Meet me in the main chamber in fifteen minutes. Bring your weapon and a decent knife with you."

Lindsey nodded and watched Hades casually stroll about the room as if it were a museum. "Fifteen minutes. Got it. I'll go tell the oth—"

"Your companions are staying here," Hades said sternly. Finding a rack of military knives, he grabbed one, removed the sheath, and looked it over from side to side. The jagged edges of its serrated blade reminded him of the ancient dagger he was issued while enslaved. Hades scowled at the memories before brushing them aside. Sheathing the dagger, he walked toward the door. The zipper pull on his open leather jacket jingled with each step. Before he slipped out the door, he swore he heard a small "What the fuck?" from Lindsey.

Roughly twenty minutes later, Lindsey walked into the large room where Hades had been contained. Beads of sweat clung to her warm face, and she found herself panting like a dog. Weighing her down was her rifle in one hand and a knife—as requested—in the other. More than ready to snap at him for not specifying this room instead of the incongruous ballroom, she licked her lips.

"Unsheathe your knife and come here," Hades ordered. A horde of nihanem positioned themselves side by side in neat rows like well-trained soldiers. Hades stood halfway down the first row, facing a particularly ugly corpse from an angle with his back to her; the movements of Hades' task swayed his upper half.

Confused and somewhat intrigued, Lindsey approached him, going around to get a better view. What she saw made her squeak. Carving away on the dead man's right arm, Hades had removed a hand and exposed two thick bones in the corpse's forearm. Hades' knife was covered in nearly the same amount of blood as his hands. Glancing down at the floor, she found the missing hand soaking in a thick maroon puddle. With her eyes, she walked down the row. Each corpse's right arm had been gruesomely modified in a similar fashion.

Steel grinded against bone like fingernails on a chalkboard, sending chills along Lindsey's spine. After five inches or so of bone had been completely exposed, Hades began sharpening the ends of the bones into spikes. "I'll show you what to do on the next one, then walk you through your own after that," Hades said.

"What ... are you doing?"

"A little trick from an old friend." Testing the sharpened point with his thumb, Hades went over it one more time before moving on to the next bone. "Where we're going, we'll need any advantage we can get."

Hidden behind a veil of shadow, the hunter studied its prey. Confident in understanding the prey's pattern, the patient man executed his plan. Sticking to cover, he made his way to the patrolling rebel.

Dagger ready, he slipped behind the inconspicuously garbed target. He plunged the blade up to its hilt into the base of the rebel's skull, instantly killing the rebel. XI-24 caught the back of the dead man's head with his free hand and sent Essence into the corpse. Carrying on as if nothing had happened, the nihanim casually continued along its previous path.

Slipping back into the darkness, the infiltrator moved on to his next target.

XVI

LINSEED BOUQUET

"Isn't this all a bit soon?" Poseidon whispered to Zeus.

Overhearing the conversation in the row before him, Kevin leaned forward and quietly contributed. "These kids wake up each day thinking that it'll be their last. They're just making the most out of the present." He rested his forearm on the back of Poseidon's chair, his weight causing it to creak. "Besides, this is kinda cute."

Turning to face Kevin, Poseidon commented back, "But a wedding?" He shifted his gaze up toward the clear plastic podium at the back of the Renaissance exhibit in the Art Wing. Parting a rolling sea of guest-filled, copper-colored folding chairs, the pathway leading directly to Lewis and his gorgeous bride, Aurora, was decorated in torn pieces of newspaper.

Lewis cupped Aurora's hands. He was dressed in the finest of black museum-labeled blazers and dark blue jeans. Smiling sweeter than wine, Aurora's sandy hair was curled into a loose bun atop her head. She wore Lewis' jean jacket, zipped up just below the bottom of her cleavage, and a pair of almost fitted, faded jeans. She looked stunning.

"They've only known each other for, what, slightly more than two months?" Poseidon jeered.

Kevin rolled his eyes. "This is the happiest I've seen anyone here since we came across the cache of guns. Normally,

I'd say getting married this early on is a bit too fast-paced, but joy is a rare commodity right now. Celebrating something familiar might bring them a hair of normalcy."

"Shhhhh!" policed Hermes from the right of Poseidon.

Sitting in an aisle seat directly behind Hermes, Matt tried his best to focus on the ceremony in the colorful, painting-filled room. The banter of the strange group he had become a part of made it hard to hear, but the constant clinking of the strange flashlight clipped to Zeus' belt against the side of his chair was a bugle to his frontal lobe. As weird as the group was and as brief of a time they had been around him, these people felt like family. Maybe it was bias, but Kevin was his favorite.

Matt still thought about what he had seen back at the shop. Did Kevin kill that little girl and the rest of the people in that room? He hadn't been successful in getting a straight answer from Kevin about their fate yet—and he probably wouldn't get one ever. All Matt could really do was trust him.

"Shhhhh!" Flustered, Hermes' face, somehow still tanned, had grown a touch rosy. "Haven't been to a wedding in ages, and Aurora just said her vow. Do you know what she said? No? Neither do I. Do you two ever stop talking?"

Zeus, having been stoic and quiet the entire time, cracked a smirk.

Standing behind the couple as their wedding officiant was Skylar. Having officiated her sister's wedding, she was the first to campaign for the position. She exploded with excitement when the engaged couple approached her. Running unopposed had its privileges.

Reaching into his jacket, Lewis retrieved a small piece of printer paper and unfolded it. He began to read: "Growing up, I saw a world of possibilities. Hundreds of paths to choose. Millions of choices that followed. Finally, at the college I had dreamed of going to, I felt like everything had fallen into place.

Then the dead began to rise."

Giving the softly laughing crowd a moment to simmer down, Lewis carried on: "Suddenly, my world shattered into a million micro-sized puzzle pieces. Without a reference to go off of, I sat in the scattered destruction. That's when I met you. Just as lost as I was, you combined your puzzle pieces with mine. Little by little, you showed me that our pieces could be brought together. Quickly, a picture began to form. While we may have only known each other for a short time, it feels like we've known each other our entire lives. The picture that was a mystery then is now one of the most beautiful scenes I have ever had the blessing of laying eyes on. Now, as I stand before you here today, I see that our puzzle is far from finished. The edges have keys, and their matching pieces are out there for us to find."

Bringing her hand to his lips, Lewis kissed it gently. "Aurora, I once saw hundreds of paths with as many possibilities as there are stars. None of them would have brought me the same joy as the path to you. You are my guiding star. Hand in hand, I want to share the rest of my life with you."

Skylar nodded to a small boy in a green superhero shirt and then spoke. "May I have the rings, please?"

Running upon light-up shoes, the boy approached the podium. With a smile, Skylar retrieved the wire rings from the child's cupped hands and whispered something to the boy. Giggling, the boy walked back to his seat.

Skylar turned to Lewis and handed him a ring. "Lewis Kendall, do you take Aurora Brandt to be your lawfully wedded wife?"

Beaming, Lewis gazed into Aurora's eyes. "I do." He slipped a ring onto Aurora's finger, and her eyes began to sparkle.

Skylar then turned toward Aurora, handing her a ring. "Aurora Brandt, do you take Lewis Kendall to be your lawfully—"

Aurora slipped the ring onto Lewis' finger. "I do!" she shouted, wrapping her arms around his neck and planting her lips on his. Cheers from around the room filled the packed exhibit, the loudest being from Dale. The crowd masked the rest of Skylar's lines, and she struggled to get through due to her own laughter. Still, Matt had a pretty good idea of what they were.

POP!

Poseidon's idea of keeping a lock on the museum's wine supply paid off. Aromas of dried citrus and white grapes wove their way between the mingling crowd. With the chairs folded and out of the way, people moved about like bees in a hive. Sipping room-temperature champagne out of a Styrofoam cup, Matt admired a large painting of flowers in an ornate vase. Even after two hundred years, the brush strokes looked as fresh as if they had been made yesterday. Soft light from a small fixture above the piece caught some of the larger paint strokes and cast miniature shadows.

"Bored with these people already?" Kevin said, joining Matt.

Nodding to Kevin and then returning his gaze to the painting, Matt rolled his eyes and smiled. "Just can't stop thinking about Maddison. I know what you're going to say. That I'm being selfish. While those two were going through their vows, I kept finding myself holding my hand open as if she were still beside me."

"We'll find her. I promise." Kevin bumped his shoulder into Matt's, causing the wine to slosh around in Matt's cup. "Try to relax a little. The last thing you want is to pass over something that could lead us to finding her because you were too stressed to notice it." Kevin took a sip from his cup and swished wine around in his mouth before swallowing.

Matt grimaced at his coworker. "How can you even do that? This stuff tastes like mineral spirits."

Peeking into Matt's cup, Kevin laughed. "Shouldn't have poured yourself that. Stuff tastes like ass. Semi-sweet red is where it's at."

Matt verified the contents of Kevin's cup, then surveyed the room with confusion plastered on his face. Noticing someone approaching, Kevin bid him adieu and strolled off. Passing right by Kevin on her way to Matt was Skylar. She locked eyes with him, a shy smile growing on her soft face. Stopping beside him, she nervously twisted herself to face the painting with him.

With the end of the world going on, you would think survivors would be working nonstop to collect supplies, fortify defenses, and fight off the living dead. Surprisingly, you'd be wrong. The survivors within the museum all struggled against the same beast: boredom. Thick walls and high windows meant only a few doors had to be made secure. Barricades and other defenses were constantly being improved in case there was a breach.

Jamie, previously a security guard, figured out how to remotely lower the metal security gates installed above nearly every door. After her discovery, everyone soon dove into an apocalypse economy, making weapons or preserving food for trade. With long hours between tasks, people had to find some way to occupy their time. Luckily, the building was still filled with plenty of non-cannibalized artifacts. Aside from attending training courses, museum dwellers perused the halls to enjoy the sights and tales pulled from history and science.

Sharing the same pastime, Matt, too, walked the halls. Favoring the History wing, the majority of his free time was spent reading the yellowing pages of books on display or imagining the lives of featured peoples. On the days he didn't haunt the halls of history, he was in the Art wing with Skylar. Despite their Hellish reality, she still found warmth in paintings and life in marble. Kevin often poked at Matt, saying that his widest grins only happened after being around her. Matt always brushed him off, but he had a feeling that Kevin was right. The longer Maddison went without being found, the more his doubts grew and told him to move on. It felt wrong, but those strolls with Skylar through the library of canvas and copper were the highlights of his days.

"So, did, um ... What did you think of the ceremony?" Skylar's focus darted back and forth between Matt's eyes and the painting. "It's been a while since my last time. Bit nervous. What did you think of me?" Her eyes widened like an owl's. "Up there. What did you think of me up there?"

Skylar's rosy cheeks hid behind a Styrofoam wall as she sipped on her most likely empty drink. Matt couldn't help but blush as well. "Hardly even noticed the other two people with you up there."

"Stooooop." Skylar giggled, playfully shoving Matt.

Sheepishly smiling, he leaned over on his tippy toes to look into her cup. "*You* are completely out. I heard that a bottle of red wine was floating around. Let's see if we can find it." Nudging his head toward the table on the opposite side of the room, he winked at her. "Heard that a red's rich flavor truly comes out in more quiet rooms. Something with the sound-waves suppressing the tannins or something."

"Oh, really now? I do think we should test that hypothesis," Skylar quipped.

Like children, they made their way through the crowd toward the refreshment table. Spotting the last red wine bottle, something tugged on Matt's attention. He looked through the crowd and spotted Kevin, whose eyes rolled to the table and then darted back to Matt. Understanding that they were both after the same treasure, the two ran as politely as possible. Matt was closest, and the last of the good wine was as good as his.

A piercing scream from the hall stopped the two childish

men in their tracks. Like a master thief, the ghastly alarm simultaneously stole the voices of the loquacious crowd. The two coworkers looked at each other again, no longer competing for the bottle. One of the partygoers jogged to the hallway and cautiously poked his head out just enough to get a peek down both directions. Another scream crashed through the hall from the direction of the main room. Its almost human quality entered Matt's ears and slid down his spine like ice.

Like a cart on a track, Zeus flew through the stunned forest, grabbing a pipe sword out of a box by the door as he passed. Gunshots melted over screams of agony and anger from deeper in the building. Unsure what would greet them, Zeus and three dozen other armed wedding guests ran down the hall.

Before Matt could say anything, Kevin had gripped his arm. "Get as many as you can to the Boulder. Once it's safe, we'll let you know. If you see a single nihanem, drop the gates."

"Wh—what?" Matt stuttered. He hadn't seen Kevin this serious since the blue meeting.

Before dashing out the door, Kevin quickly turned to face Matt. "Grab a pipe sword. Nothing else. Remember our training!" Then he sprinted out the door, grabbing from the box a blade made from a sharpened street sign.

Adrenaline coursed through Matt's veins. *Everyone says you have a natural response of fight or flight.* When confronting the dead outside, fighting was an easy choice. But with the possibility that those things were within the safety of the walls, he suddenly didn't seem strong enough, and his legs begged for flight. Warmth filled his palm, and when he looked down, he discovered Skylar's hand in his. Fear filled her eyes and forced her every breath.

Fight ... Matt thought to himself. *I choose to fight.*

Tightening his fingers around Skylar's hand, he briskly led

them to the hall. He grabbed a sword and faced the remaining guests, rallying their attention. "Just like we practiced. Go straight to the Boulder! Arm yourselves along the way when you can! Those that can fight, you know what to do!" Just a little under three months ago, he was pushing paper in an administrative job. Now, he was about to lead a group of people through a possibly zombie-filled building. With his first step, the trial began.

Reaching the main lobby, Matt gazed upon a war between the living and the dead. People armed with various weapons fought hand-to-hand with mutilated intruders. Flashes of light from gun muzzles briefly illuminated the hanging flesh and protruding bones of the nihanem.

With their chest cavity ripped open and internal organs clinging for dear life, an older man in a tattered workout shirt swung at Zeus. Zeus ducked under the attack, swept behind the beast, and sliced diagonally through it from below the waist to the crook of its neck. The nihanim toppled over, its spine severed and its face writhing with a demonic scream. Zeus brought his foot down on the foe's head, but his attack was thwarted when a nihanem of a teenage girl tackled him from the side.

The passage leading to the Boulder was on the opposite side. All Matt had to do was lead his group around the edges of the fray and into the hallway. The fighters were doing their best to push back the horde. The barriers were all in place, facing the main entrance and ready for a breach. There was just one problem: the dead weren't streaming in from the front entrance on the west side of the building; they were flooding in through the eastern hallway. Without the barricades to keep the dead off the fighters, it was a losing battle.

Telling everyone to run with him, Matt burst into the room toward the front entrance. He ran between barricades, taking a curved path around the information desk. Although the dead were close, the fighters held them back just enough for the doorway to be within reach.

With thirty-five feet left, he was startled by a shallow cry emanating from behind. Like mice scattering from a hawk, Matt's group shattered into a chaotic orgy of panic. Behind the legs of the fleeing people, a woman in a cropped leather jacket lay face-down on the museum floor. Her short amber hair covered her face. Huddled over her with its hand jammed into her back was a blue-faced nihanem. Not even an ounce of emotion could be found on the dead man's face. Ripping its hand out from the woman, two jagged, protruding bones resided where a hand should have been. It dislocated its jaw and roared to the heavens.

Nearly tripping over his own feet, Matt spun and sprinted toward the Southern Wing. The line had broken. All that mattered now was getting to safety. Tightly holding hands, Matt and Skylar ran as quickly as they could. Footsteps pounded on the floor behind them. Unsure if they were friend or foe, Matt released Skylar and swung his sword as hard as he could.

SLICE!

Tumbling to the floor, the nihanim of an overweight child slapped the tile. The top of its skull cracked open, allowing its yellowing brain to splatter like a jello mold on the ground. Quickly surveying the room, Matt saw the few remaining fighters slowly retreating toward him. Like ants with a mission, nihanem ran past the fighters toward the main door.

Matt shouted down the hallway, hoping the message would make it in time, "Jamie! Drop the gates now!"

Half a dozen living corpses passed the entrance hall's threshold. Something wasn't right. These undead were supposed to be mindless. What was attracting them to that hallway? Had people run down there, hoping to escape?

More and more undead made their way toward the main entrance. As soon as one nihanim was defeated, another ran from the line to take its place. Like a sign from God, the metal gates began to lower. There was no way Jamie had heard him from inside the Boulder, and that meant she had used the remote. Like a bullet, reality struck Matt. His escape was now timed. Everyone who didn't make it inside before the gates closed was as good as dead. Looking back toward Skylar, who was waiting for him farther down the hall, Matt yelled, "Go! I'll see you in there!"

Biting down on her lips, she shook her head.

"Go!" Matt screamed.

"Fuck!" Skylar yelled. She turned and ran.

A huge mass barreled toward Matt.

"You can birdwatch later," Kevin spat as he passed Matt. The other three, along with Zeus, Poseidon, Hermes, and the last remaining fighters, followed close behind. Seeing the charging wall of decay behind them, Matt joined the group.

Each window for getting to safety behind the gate and to the next exhibit grew smaller and smaller. Stumbling into the Egyptian exhibit, the fleeing team ran around and vaulted over any obstacle that was in their way. As they ran around the bend, their fear materialized before them. The security gate clinked heavily as it hit the floor. The undead were right behind them. They needed to act fast.

Zeus and Hermes prepared for battle while Poseidon frantically eyed the room for an alternative route.

"This is not how we die," Kevin said as his fingers found a hold in the gate's many holes. Bending his legs, he tried to lift the gate. Metal groaned in defiance. "Fucking help me!" he barked at Matt and the others.

Looking at each other, they all quickly bent down and started lifting.

With the motor working against them, lifting the security gate was no easy task. The sounds of breaking metal and screaming nihanem echoed through the exhibit, reminding them of their reason to hurry. Unsure who was complaining more—the metal or the people—the group managed to raise the gate to Kevin's hips.

"Get under!" Kevin ordered through gritted teeth.

Not wanting to argue, the team ducked under one by one, making sure to grab the gate from the other side. Once the last person had passed under it, Kevin released the gate. Matt's fingers and arms cried out from the sudden weight thrown upon them. After Kevin ducked under the slowly lowering gate, the others let go, allowing it to drop heavily to the floor. Only a few more rooms and they'd be safe.

After lifting three more gates, the team was exhausted. They were finally in the last room before the Boulder. Angry voices could be heard from up ahead. Recognizing Dale's voice, Matt ran on weary legs.

"This isn't the time to be a hero!" Dale yelled, red-faced. "Let someone else get in there. You two have something to live for. Don't do this!" Dale stood in front of a large cage composed of various welded metal objects.

As he approached, Matt recognized the people inside: the just-married couple, Lewis and Aurora.

Lewis, wielding a makeshift sword made from part of a stop sign, stood firm. "This community came together for us. We want to defend them," Lewis retaliated.

Seeing Poseidon, Dale walked to him and pulled him over. "Tell these kids to unlock the cage and let someone else get in there."

Poseidon eyed the couple before looking back at Dale. "The undead aren't far behind. This isn't the time to fight about who does what." He turned toward the newlywed couple. "Your intentions are admirable. This auxiliary cage is meant to draw attention away from the central defense. If you stay in there, you'll be stuck in there until the attack is over. Are you sure you want to do this?"

Poseidon pinpointed his gaze on Aurora. "You two have an entire lifetime to be together. The Boulder will keep you safe, and there's enough food in there to last at least three weeks. There's no guarantee these bars will keep you safe." Training his eyes on Lewis, Poseidon pushed harder. "Your honeymoon shouldn't be a potential trip to the afterlife. You two could have a family."

"We decided on this well before today," Aurora said as she placed down her short rifle. "Without all of you, Lewis and I never would have met." She reached out for him. Lewis grabbed her hand. "You all have given us hope and a reason to live. That is something worth fighting for. This isn't going to be easy, but we're ready for it. Pierson, we'll have that family. And Dale ... we'll be right beside you when you tell the others that it's safe to come out."

Metal snapped and cracked in the not-so-far distance. Zeus leaned toward Poseidon and whispered something. Unforgiving heartbreak overrode Poseidon's cool demeanor. Waving Kevin and Hermes over, Zeus delivered the same hushed message, resulting in the same emotional reaction.

Hermes looked at Dale. "They've already made up their minds. Tell the others to lock the door to the Boulder."

Shouting from the farthest cage, Brandon chimed in. "What about you all? Aren't you going to hop in?"

Hermes looked at Zeus. "Unfortunately not," Zeus responded. Peeking over at the third cage, he nodded. "You're going up against an army. This isn't going to be easy. We're going to try to pull them away from here. Keep the radios on. We'll reach out to you when we can."

"We're going to do what?" Matt said in disbelief.

Kevin placed a hand on Matt's shoulder, put his mouth close to Matt's ear, and whispered, "These nihanem are too coordinated. Hades has to be nearby and attacking here because he knows we're here. If we leave, there's a chance he'll pull back his forces."

Matt angrily turned toward Kevin. "I can't just abandon these people. I know we haven't found Maddison yet, but Skylar is in the Boulder. We can fight them off."

"Not if Hades is directly controlling these things," Kevin retorted. "If Hades is here, everyone in this building is dead. We did what we could to protect these people. If you care about Skylar, leaving here will give her a chance at surviving this." Matt tried to fight back, but Kevin squeezed his shoulder. "Don't make me force you."

Stunned by Kevin's threat, Matt nodded.

Zeus looked at Dale before making eye contact with everyone else in the cages. "You are the last line of defense. Do not let a single one of these bastards through."

The caged fighters raised their weapons and cheered.

Dale glanced sadly at Lewis and Aurora, walked to the central cage with Brandon, and locked the cage's door behind him. "You had better come back to us, or so help me God, I'll find you and kill you myself," Dale stated, causing Zeus to softly chuckle.

Wishing them the best of luck, Zeus and his team exited the room through a side door. Matt lingered behind, not wanting to part from the pop-up community. Dale and Brandon had become the population's unofficial caretakers. Even in this final hour, they were the primary shield. Taking one last look at Lewis and Aurora embraced in each other's arms, Matt sighed and then turned to follow the others.

Quickly moving through a maze of maintenance passageways and stairwells, the quintet arrived at an old-looking steel door in the basement. Years of residing in the damp underbelly of the museum had taken its toll in the form of rust building up in the crevices of the door's metal trim. Neglected light bulbs cast a dying light that barely beat back the ravenous darkness. Tart, fermented odors hung in the stagnant air, tenderly violating Matt's nose.

Swearing at the sight of intermittent welding between the door and its metal frame, Zeus waved Kevin and Hermes over. "Get this thing open," he ordered.

They handed off their weapons to Poseidon and Matt and looked around for anything that could help them pry open the door. Mumbling to himself about the likelihood of finding a torch cutter down here, Kevin wandered into the darkness.

Matt looked down at Zeus' belt and studied the ornate details of the metal flashlight-looking item hanging from it. It was surrounded by swirling grooves with the image of a small skeletal hand stranded on a shield-shaped island.

Wanting to help, he put forth an idea. "What if we use that bar of yours like a hammer? Maybe we can crack the welds with it?"

Zeus, looking like someone had just killed his child in front of him, tightly grabbed the object at his side. "Even think about touching my chilt, and I won't hesitate to kill you."

Taken aback by the unwarranted aggression, Matt defended himself. "It was just an idea. That thing is always on you, but I've never seen you use it a single time. If it's broken, we might as well—"

Gathering the front of Matt's shirt in his hand, Zeus yanked him forward. "Might as well what, you flameless shit maggot? The fucking chilt isn't broken. Give me one good reason why I shouldn't knock you out right now," he growled.

"You'd have to carry him," Poseidon butted in.

With a huff, Zeus shoved Matt backward.

Matt nearly tripped over his own feet but caught himself by grabbing onto Poseidon. Fishing for sympathy, he eyed the somehow still decently put-together man. "What did I do?"

Without answering, Poseidon casually brushed Matt's sweaty hand off of his dress shirt.

"Found something that might work," Hermes said as he approached. He held a handful of screwdrivers in his left hand

and a hammer along with an LED light hanging on a headband in his right. He dangled the light in front of Zeus, who grabbed the headband and turned it on. With all but one screwdriver lying on the floor beside him, Hermes placed the tip of one against one of the welds.

TING TING TING!

The three watched in thick suspense as Hermes chiseled away.

CRACK!

Success! One weld had cracked. There were seven more to go. Moving to the welds at the top of the door, Hermes set to work. One by one, the welds gave way.

Matt didn't know how Zeus knew about this particular door or what lay behind it. But he also didn't want to make the man any angrier with him, so he decided it was safer to whisper his question to Poseidon. "So how did ..."

Cutting Matt off, Poseidon whispered back, "I founded this place."

Before Matt could counter the absurd claim, he noticed Zeus' glare. Remembering his recent threat, Matt decided to follow up with Poseidon at a later time.

Snap!

Tossing aside the broken handle, Hermes picked up another screwdriver and continued chiseling away at the seals on the door. Three more to go. Suddenly, a loud bang echoed against every crevice in the room, originating from deep within the basement.

Leaning back, Poseidon gave a concerning look to Zeus before peering past him. "Kratos! You alright over there?!" The sound of rattling and muffled voices vibrated through the artificial night.

Suddenly, the voices amplified. Ghoulish screeches and animalistic roars painted the dimly lit room in a new light. Hard footsteps hastily approached. "Get it open!" Kevin screamed. "Get the damn door open!"

Wide-eyed, Hermes set the tip of the screwdriver on the next weld. Poseidon slapped the tool from his hand and pushed Hermes aside. He twisted the handle and pulled as if his life depended on it. The metal creaked loudly,

Unsure whether to help or prepare to fight, Matt visibly bounced between both ideas. He heard the metal groan as it played a deadly game of tug-of-war with Poseidon.

The closer Kevin got to the team, the more bodies appeared beneath the dim lights behind him. Hermes put his hands around Poseidon's and fought to break the tie. Under their combined strength, the handle's attachment to the door waned. The two pulled as hard as they could on what felt closer to a dead fish. Behind, the horde quickly honed in on their location, looking like a lineup of bodies that had gone through wood chippers.

Groaning louder and louder, the door finally snapped open. Poseidon and Hermes fell to the dust- and grit-coated floor. Shining the LED light into the inky black hall, Zeus charged in, only managing to enter before Kevin by a hair. Hermes and Matt darted in after them. Attempting to buy them more time, Poseidon gripped the door handle and pulled the door shut. An arm reached through the threshold, narrowly swiping the air close enough to his face to see the blood-crusted lines of the nihanim's knuckles. Poseidon tugged harder until the handle ripped from the door. He stumbled backward, whipped the doorknob at the head of the emerging corpse, and sprinted toward the others.

Blended into a nightmare smoothie, the riotous noise from the nihanem echoed along the narrow tunnel. With Zeus using the only light available to guide the way, there was no way to tell how near the rotting mob was. Being a faster runner, Poseidon moved in front of Matt. Realizing he was now the caboose of the fleeing group, Matt impulsively looked behind himself. Immediately, he regretted it, tripping over his own feet and sprawling across the floor.

"*OOF!*" Matt grunted as he hit the strangely damp cement. His pipe sword took its own leave, skidding across the floor and out of reach. His fear-soaked legs quickly froze solid. Like an oncoming train missing its lamp, the blare grew until it felt like they were within reach.

Feeling something grab him, Matt let out a shrill scream. The force dragged him to his feet, and he was able to make out Kevin's face in the waning, indirect light.

"Not losing you that easy," Kevin joked through a forced smile. He shoved Matt forward as if to give him a running start.

Matt stumbled up to his sword and twisted down to grab it. Wrapping his fingers around the sword's hilt, Matt looked up.

Kevin stood like a statue, as if suddenly detached from re-ality. The screams of the undead echoed off the narrow walls, cloaking the horde's true number. Nihanem were right behind them, and they had to move.

"Kevin!" Matt yelled.

Despite the urgency, Kevin silently refused to budge. No longer concerned with the danger closing in behind him, his shoulders released their tension. Even through the darkness, Matt could see a strange sheen glaze over Kevin's eyes.

Matt's heart began to race. "Kevin, what are you ..."

Slowly, Kevin's mouth opened. Emerging slowly from it was the jagged edge of bone covered in dark ichor. As his jaw opened farther, a second bone ground along his bottom teeth. Overextended, a muffled crack announced his jaw's forfeit as it was forced open.

The nihanim attached to the arm tilted back, putting the full weight of Kevin's body on the limb. Like a meaty coat sleeve, the flesh of the living corpse's arm scrunched gradually down toward its elbow.

"Kevin ..." Matt muttered.

The nihanim tipped its arm down, and Kevin slid off, slapping the ground like a bag of sand. Pungent air gushed through a gaping hole in the undead killer's neck. With its jaw pushed open past the point of retrieval, the nihanim screamed silently at its next target.

"Kevin!" Matt screamed. Tears quickly welled up in his eyes. Rage overtook thought and swallowed his senses whole. It didn't matter if he had to face one or one thousand opponents. The fire inside Matt wanted to incinerate every shambling bastard in that tunnel.

Matt readied his sword. Sliding his foot back along the rough surface of the hallway's cement, he prepared himself for their arrival. As their outlines rose from the shadows and their slack faces came into focus, Matt let out a warrior's cry.

Then what felt like a cannonball took him from behind, smashing into the back of his head. Like a candle facing a tsunami, his consciousness was snuffed before he could blink.

Braced by a controlled tunnel of air, XI-24 hit the ground. He and Spike were dropped forty yards apart, assigned to the flanks of the operation while Chatter took the center. Wind-pushed emaciated fingers on dormant trees swatted at the metal invader. Barely hidden by the cover of night, the lonely kingdom dropship proudly heralded the oncoming fleet.

Understanding their assignments, the three Death-Touched advanced. Covered in lightweight, black-painted armor, they moved through the forests like ghosts. XI-24 cautiously crawled on the cold earth, careful to keep his implanted collar from getting caught on low-hanging branches. Reaching a clearing, moonlight revealed his scar-covered face. Before him, an encampment snuggled in a blanket of trees, disguised as a humble village

They had located the training camp of the insurrectionists.

XVII

CHARITY

With the iron gates sealing the entrance to the museum now open, Hades marched up the grand marble steps with more than a hundred of his shambling horrors. Tightly gripped in his right hand was Artemis' short sword. To his left and just a step behind, armed with her carbine and wearing a tight-fitting mercenary uniform from Artemis' facility, was Lindsey. Despite the chill of the autumn night air, she had elected to cut the black shirt to expose her midriff. Her tied-back ponytail swayed with each step.

Walking through the large entrance, a chorus of clicks, clacks, and squeaks from rubber soles against the dull gray, checkered tile heralded their arrival. Hades was greeted by discarded barricades and tipped-over, short metal poles connected by plump, red rope. He followed the toppled thread down the short hallway to the empty eyes of a double-seated booth encased in glass, which stared at the new guests.

On either side of the booth, ornate door frames highlighted the official museum entrances. A heavy metal gate prohibited their passage on the left, put in place from a cylinder high above the doorway; parallel tracks held it in place. Its sister gate, having been overwhelmed, stood violated and broken, with an opening in it big enough to allow one large person through at a time.

A dozen nihanem burst forward from behind Hades and gripped the broken, internal edges of the gate. Gray, rotting hands widened the hole to the sound of metallic popcorn. Arriving at the gate, Hades held up his hand and signaled Lindsey to stop. Despite their numbers, his controlled corpses still lacked their earlier effectiveness.

Observing the nihanem's pathetic motor skills, Hades shook his head and sighed. Once the hole was wide enough, the undead stepped aside. He took the lead and walked in first. The new room opened into a large, spacious chamber. Bodies of slain nihanem and host-less puddles of blood lay scattered on a floor peppered with bullet casings. The sounds of firearms and screams from the undead echoed from somewhere deeper in the museum.

In the center of the room was the information desk; it formed a twenty-foot-wide circle of fake granite topped with a smooth wood top. Lindsey jogged up to it and peeked over the tall counter. Random papers, including a detailed flier for an upcoming exhibit—"Thumbs: Are We Under or Over Them?"—lay in a loose pile on the desk below.

With a small hop, Lindsey planted her stomach on the counter and reached down. "Gotcha," she joyously cried out. She slid back onto her feet and turned around with a folded map in her hands. "This is just what we needed." Opening it up, her eyes widened. "This is ... *exactly* what we needed."

Joining Lindsey at her side and nudging a torn-off arm out of his way, Hades curiously inspected the glossy, colorful paper. Each wing of each floor was given its own colored slice. The names of current exhibits were printed in a bold white font within each area, and scribbled along the sides of the map were alternative room names in blue pen.

Noticing movement, Linsey moved the map aside. Like an injured goblin, a small nihanim hobbled around the desk until it found an opening. Gazing blankly at the papers on the counter, it reached over and clumsily grabbed two random fistfuls.

Running back around the desk to meet Hades, she was able to get a better look. Standing at roughly half of Lindsey's height stood a child in a green superhero shirt, holding up its fists.

Hades fingered through the papers. When Hades found what he was looking for, the child opened its tiny claws, and the remaining unwanted rubbish rained upon its body.

"That would have been cute," Lindsey mumbled to herself, "if half the kid's skull and teeth weren't showing." Short strands of matted, blond hair wildly stuck to their stained skull as if glued in place. As the child walked away and joined the rest of the horde spreading out over the perimeter, each step beneath their singular shoe reflected colorful lights off the tile.

"This one has been defiled as well," Hades said above the sound of crinkling as he turned over his own opened map.

Reaching over, Lindsey tapped on Hades' map. "We should start at the infirmary. Top floor. Where the telescope exhibit was at."

Before Hades could utter a word, Lindsey pocketed her map and quickly trudged off toward a hallway marked by a sign reading "EAST WING." Her footsteps clacked like bricks as she angrily moved away from him.

Hades closed his eyes. "Hold on."

Lindsey's advancement stopped. "If there's something else you'd rather do, you don't need me. I'll find you after he's dead."

"My nihanem are having difficulty moving forward." His eyebrows furrowed. "There's a barricade ... no ... a cage. Blocking a doorway. Well defended."

Lindsey walked back over to the rambling god. "Where is it? How do you even know this?"

Hades ignored her questions and carried on. "There's an image of a large yellow bird on a nearby wall. Multiple clear pods. Possibly for experimentation? The humans seem to have manufactured a living weapon." Opening his eyes, he turned his head toward Lindsey. "We cannot allow this project of theirs to come to fruition. This beast and any of its associated research must not survive. I believe our missions are now aligned. Your doctor has most likely found refuge behind the defense and is most likely part of this project."

Lindsey's soft chuckle quickly increased into laughter.

Chafed by her unwarranted joy, Hades narrowed his eyes. "You find this amusing?"

"I know where that is. No one is creating a *weaponized beast*," she said while wiping a tear from her eye. "It's the chick room. What are they going to do? Grab one of the puff balls and throw it at the zombies?"

Irked, Hades huffed like a bull. "Weapon or no weapon, we're still heading there. Since you're so acquainted with these halls"—Hades swept the air with an open hand—"lead the way."

Lindsey replied with a smirk and a curtsey. "Right this way."

The journey to the room of chicks was oddly pleasant. Curiosities and antiquities adorned rooms on hooks and pedestals. Tasking his rotting army to leisurely widen the fissures in the metal gates granted him time to peruse. The exception to this was the nearby Kingdoms of Egypt room. Hades ordered his nihanem to break through the gate with haste while every single sarcophagus in the room was destroyed. No sooner had the final stone coffin met its demise than Hades had rushed into the next room.

Hades jogged across the exhibit, still shuddering from the memories of his encasement brought about by the previous room. Feeling the room closing in on him, he rested his hands on his knees. Suffocating darkness filled his head and stiffened his body.

Thump, thump, thump.

Like a war horse, his heart sprinted onward.

Thump, Thump, Thump.

His fingers wrapped around the hilt of his sword and continued to tighten.

THUMP, THUMP, THUMP.

Hades didn't notice the small hand on his shoulder until he heard Lindsey's voice. "Everything alright?"

Placing his hand over hers, Hades waited until his breathing returned to normal before standing up fully. The moment of weakness began to pass, and he brushed off her hand. "Why wouldn't it be?" he growled. "We need to keep moving."

Hades continued forward. A moment later, he heard a muffled gunshot. Coming to a stop, he curiously peered to his left. A pair of pristine double doors smiled at him. The only designation on the doors was a square yellow sticker reading "Employees Only." As he approached them, a second muffled gunshot rang out from behind the doors.

The doors began to crack open, and from within, he heard the sounds of roars and high-pitched screams. Hooked by their call, he walked inside. Aside from a box here or a broom there, the windowless hallway he discovered was practically barren.

"Slow down!" Lindsey shouted.

Blasé to her request, Hades continued down the hollow, crooked spine of the museum. Lindsey's boots thumped on the floor as she ran to catch up. After numerous turns, he finally arrived at the source of the pandemonium. Beneath a placard labeled "Hatching Room" were two double doors. Chaos seeped through the thin metal with enough force to vibrate it. Like removing a bandage from a waterfall, Hades pushed open the door.

A section of the door exploded into splinters before him as a bullet ripped through it. Startled, he recoiled his arm back toward his body. Charging toward the source of the bullet and unable to stop, a large woman with exposed ribs collided with the open door and freed it from its hinges. She tumbled to the ground, but quickly scrambled to her feet and continued her course. A stocky nihanim soon stood before Hades and turned its back to him.

With tufts of hair from the back of the undead's head in his hand, Hades curled his fist and braced the dead weight against his forearm. Lifting the walking corpse standing before him from the ground like a shield, he hunched over and entered the fray. He closed his eyes and used the dead man's vision as his own.

Destroyed corpses littered the floor, some of whose skulls stopped at the jawline. Blood and bullet holes had transformed the feather-white walls into a canvas of war. Split between three areas, crowds of nihanem gathered in front of large cages, which formed a triangle of defense. Seemingly composed of various metal relics and modern-day objects welded together, the cages proved resilient to the rotting barrage. As Hades cautiously approached, he observed the entrenchment.

Creating the towers of the defensive, the two cages on either side of the room drew the ravenous dead toward them. At the farthest vertex, a larger cage blocked the exit. Sweat soaked and swearing, their inhabitants wearily fought. Flashes of fire burst toward the horde from muzzles inside. At the leftward defensive, a flesh-stripped arm pierced the bars and grasped at a man in a torn black blazer. Barely dodging its grasp, he swung at the arm with a foot-long blade made of a sharpened steel sign and a repurposed-wood hilt.

Stumbling backward, he positioned himself too close to another wall. Like a triggered trap, a spiked arm from one of Hades' modified nihanem plunged through an opening in the bars and into his side. His ear-splitting scream swept over the room.

Pulling the injured man off the bone spear, a female defender in a zipped-up jean jacket lowered her wounded comrade to the floor. He rested against the only safe wall in the cage, pressing a hand against his wounds. Even with the pressure, blood spilled between his fingers.

Despite the hungry hands and nightmarish screeching surrounding the pair, the woman teared up as she rested her forehead against his. He, too, shed tears as his face quickly drained. Wiping his cheek with her thumb and burrowing her fingers in his umber brown hair, she pressed her longing lips to his.

Laying his makeshift sword at his side, the man wrapped an arm around her. Even with the chaos around them, the only focus they had was on each other. Feeling his arm slide down her back, she kissed his cheek one last time before standing up. As he reopened his eyes and growled in her direction, she pulled the trigger.

Sprinting like a race dog, Lindsey dashed from the hallway and took cover behind one of the four large yellow pods in the room. Its thick glass dome, previously used to incubate chicken eggs and protect chicks from children, provided a safe view for the young gunner. Unable to ignore the contents of the pod while peering through, Lindsey couldn't help but frown upon the sight inside.

Lying on a bed of straw and surrounded by cracked open eggs was a single baby chick. Teeny feathers of sunlight yellow clothed its dainty body. Lindsey tapped on the glass, hoping to see those overly large eyes pop open. Nothing. She tapped harder. Her attempts were to no avail; the baby bird could not be awakened from its permanent sleep.

"Lindsey!" Hades barked at her from behind his undead shield, which now had its arms crossed in the shape of an "X."

Startled at hearing her name, she looked over at Hades.

"Kill the last guard on the left side. I'll take out the ones on the right. Stay low."

With a single nod, Lindsey acknowledged the assignment. She looked one last time at the baby bird, breathed in deeply, and let her sadness slowly carry the breath out. Aiming for a metal pillar, Lindsey kept as low as possible and ran until her shoulder smashed against the cold, colorful surface. Wires from a stripped terminal tickled her shoulders. She searched the other side of the room, but Hades was nowhere in sight.

Aiming her rifle toward her target, she softly cursed to herself. The dead were entirely in the way. She'd have to get closer, possibly even up to the bars themselves. Hoping to replicate Hades, Lindsey reached for a passing corpse in a tattered purple hoodie and blue jeans. She gripped the back of the hoodie and held on tight, attempting to make a personal shield of her own. Unwilling to stop, the nihanem continued onward and pulled her out from behind her cover.

RIP!

The fabric tore away from the rest of the garment, leaving her lying on her stomach in the middle of the room.

"Girl! What the fuck are you doing?! Get over here!" shouted a marshmallowy voice. Unsure if Hades had suddenly mustered up the ability of speech for his undead, Lindsey looked around in confusion. Hearing it again, she followed the voice.

Beckoning her to him from within the center cage was a burly man in a red tied-back bandana. She scrambled to her feet and darted through the horde, taking advantage of this seemingly impossible window of opportunity. She ducked and dodged imaginary attacks as she went. Following his directions, she met the man at the side of his cage. His raggedy, mahogany beard seemed to jumble about against his red and black plaid flannel as he expeditiously fidgeted with a lock.

"Get against the wall! Cover me, Brandon!" the man shouted. Gripping a handle, he shoved the cage door firmly forward, knocking back three huddled nihanem. Lindsey jumped inside. Metal clanged loudly as the door was hastily shut and relocked. Breathing heavily, the man turned toward the bewildered girl. "The emergency shelter order went out nearly forty minutes ago."

Making sure to stay out of reach from prying hands, the three inhabitants awkwardly shuffled about in the small space. Playing along, Lindsey spuriously acted as best as she could. Panic engorged her eyes and quickened her movements. "I ... I didn't hear it. Everything going on. Screaming. I freaked out! Couldn't move. Finally built up the courage and just ... ran ... as fast as I could here."

The husky fellow wrapped a single arm around her shoulders and pulled her in for a hug. Forced to breathe in the toxic stench rising like steam from his sweaty shirt, she wished she could be back among the sluggish decay of the walking dead. "You're lucky to still be alive! This is no place for a girl. Get to the shelter and give them a shout. Someone'll let you in."

"Dale, take her there," his leathery yet equally worn counterpart chimed in. Gray hair was readily visible beneath the black leaves of the overgrown bush on his head; he hadn't dyed his hair in some time. "I can hold this down." A sarcastic yet sweet smile formed on his creamy, hot-chocolate face. Lindsey sensed a warm grandpa feeling radiating from Brandon. "Bring back some ammunition and a milkshake for me, will you?"

Metal scraped together as Dale unlocked the back door. The rest of the cage rattled violently as the dead fought relentlessly to butcher those inside. Dale scraped the bottom of the barrel with a depleted chuckle. Creaking the gate open, he turned to Brandon. "It'll be a date."

A burst of rounds from Lindsey's rifle tore through Dale's body and shot out of his chest. Taken off guard, he turned his head to look behind him. Two more rounds fired off, sending the hefty man careening into the ajar door. The metal door flung open and clanked loudly as it collided with a wall.

"What the—" Brandon horrifically exclaimed. A new torrent of rounds ripped through his chest. Brandon tripped backward and hit the cage wall. Warm blood trailed behind him on the bars as he slid down. Before his ass hit the floor, cold hands gripped his clothing and held him up. Blood covered the inside of his mouth. "Wh—wh—why?"

Lindsey aimed the barrel of her rifle at the dying man's face. Before she could pull the trigger, two bony spikes burst from his chest. His eyes screamed in place of his lungs. Despite the roaring of the dead, Lindsey could still hear him choking. Just like a candle in a storm, the light within him soon blew out.

Lindsey looked over the dead man's shoulder into the hollow gaze of a blueish-skinned brunette woman with an inverted-bob haircut. The woman's cheeks tore as she emitted an eardrum-shattering screech, creating fleshy flaps that folded over and fell to her jawline. Retracting her arm, the old man slid the rest of the way to the floor with a solid thump, head slumped on his chest. After a brief moment, the bullet holes in his chest let out a sound like deflating tires. Slowly, Brandon lifted his head. He now shared the same empty stare as the dead woman.

The crowd in front of the cage parted. Hades walked up to the bars. The sword in his right hand and the front of his jacket were covered in gore. "Well done," he stated in a rare appraisement.

"Give me a moment, and I'll open the door." Letting her rifle hang from its strap on her shoulder, Lindsey knelt by Dale's body. She patted his pockets and soon found what she was looking for. Sidestepping the body, she gripped his left shoulder and tried turning him over. She grunted, struggling to even lift the behemoth.

Hades whisked his left hand, and Dale twitched to life. Pushing itself over, Dale's body soon lay face up, allowing Lindsey to access his chest pocket and retrieve a key.

Impatiently, Hades fidgeted with an object in his jacket's

bulging front chest pocket. Once he heard the squealing of rusty hinges, he retrieved his fingers from the pouch and zippered it closed. "Shall we continue?" he said sarcastically.

"After you," Lindsey said politely and waved him through.

The rebels barely put up a fight since they were accustomed to eluding the King's armies, not repelling them. Pulled from the assault by one of Spike's nihanem, XI-24 followed the spear-armed corpse away from the village. They'd set up a tactical command post within a short walking distance from the battlefield, and squads of Kingdom soldiers were now establishing a perimeter as they waited for the corpse callers to soften the enemy.

Above the sounds of dropships coming and going, he could hear Spike's raised voice in the distance. "Stay hidden," croaked Spike's nihanim as best it could with its slightly damaged vocal cords. Confused by the advice, XI-24 did as Spike asked.

"These people aren't rebels!" Spike argued. "I lived in this village. I saw my wife! Call off the—"

Alerting the public of its activation, the bomb injected into Spike's neck detonated with a bang. Headless in the blink of an eye. His disobedience had overridden years of enslaved service. Controlled by the metal collar, the explosion-fueled eruption of blood formed a fountain of red ink. Spike's corpse collapsed to the ground, earning laughs from a few nearby troops.

XVIII

HUMILITY

The very next room transported them to a reality of post-apocalyptic despair. Framed newspapers from the late 1940s through the 1980s covered a backdrop of toppled cities and blackened landscapes. Dusty clouds hovered like hungry seagulls around a mushroom of smoke and fire. The color of the stiff carpet covering the floor of the exhibit reminded Hades of charred flesh. Bodiless shadows printed on the carpet guided them along the winding path.

Trailing a few feet behind Hades, Lindsey paused at a display: "Bawking Crazy? Cockroaches: The Future Chicken." As if in position to fight, a confused-looking chicken faced an overly large cockroach. Lindsey cringed at the sight and the thought of consuming the ugly beetle.

Turning a corner, the room opened up, and they were greeted by the sight of a large, intimidating structure. A wall of stone spread the length of the wide space. As if a carver had taken a tool to its facade, two long crevices filled with closed steel shutters created the dopey face of a sleepy giant. Between them, a thick door of steel stood valiantly. Devoid of handles and marred with factory-produced scratches and small dents, it added to the formidable look of the structure.

"And this is what the humans chose to hide away in?" Hades scoffed.

Like sicked hounds, half a dozen corpses charged the faux bunker. Their nightmarish screams echoed off the walls. Flesh and bone smacked against the solid wall. Talon-like fingers scraped at the rough surface only to have their fingernails torn away.

Approaching a sign roughly four feet tall nailed to a square wooden post, Lindsey quickly skimmed over the expansive information upon it. "Don't think that's going to work."

A tinge of vexation spurred Hades' heart. "And what makes you say that?" he said while observing his nullified attempt to break through.

Lindsey's eyes jumped back to the top of the sign. "It says here that these walls are made of concrete. Two feet thick."

Hades released a drawn-out sign. "Anything else I should know about?"

"It's fully functional in case of a nuclear disaster, has a working radio station, and it's also the location of the employee lounge." Pursing her lips, she looked sideways at Hades as he stroked his temples with his left hand.

Like children recalled from a playground, the nihanem assault team looked back at Hades. Despite their blank expressions, Lindsey could have sworn they looked sad. Then they all at once returned to the horde.

"Can't believe I'm even saying this ..." Placing the tip of his sword on the ground and his right hand on top of it, Hades shot Lindsey a displeased look. "We could lay siege to this fortification. Assuming this is the only entrance to it, all we have to do is wait. If we're fortunate, they'll run out of resources within two or three—"

Click.

"Fuck off, ya putrid bastards!" popped a man's nasally voice.

Startled by the abrupt interruption, Hades looked left and right.

A young woman's voice butted in, muffled in the background. "Liam, get off the PA system! If we're quiet, they'll eventually go away."

The man's voice, now shrill, came back on. "The fact that they're here means the others are dead."

"Don't say that."

"It's true! They knew the risk, Skylar. And look on the screen. Right here ... No. To the left a bit more. The ugly one. The twat has a sword! The buggers can carry swords now!"

Lindsey spun in place, trying to find the source of the voices. Like an old married couple, the voices bickered. Meanwhile, Hades stood in place. His knuckles cracked as his fingers tightened on the hilt of the readied sword; his pale face soon glowed a ripe vermillion.

Hades shouted toward the bunker, ready to break through the cement walls himself. "Come out of hiding, you coward!"

"Can you hear me!?" Lindsey shouted. Having spotted the glint of glass in the upper corner of the room, she faced what she perceived to be a camera.

"Did ... Did one of them just talk?" said the man.

"Shhhhhut up, Liam! I couldn't hear," Skylar said.

Huffing to herself, Lindsey licked her lips. "CAN. YOU. HEAR. ME?"

Click.

Aside from the grumbling of Hades, not a single undead made a peep. *The ugly one?* Hades thought to himself. *That's really how they wanted to seal their fates? How dare these lower life forms insult me. Even if it takes a lifetime, the bunker will be breached.*

Click.

"Ya, we can hear you," Liam said. Feigned courage dripped from the speakers.

"Doctor Nosparchez is in there. Give him to us," Lindsey ordered.

"Alex? He's a sweetheart. What do you want with him?" asked Skylar.

"My business is my own." Imagining herself as Hades, Lindsey stood tall and shook loose the hair from her eyes. "You have two options! Option one: You can stay in there as long as you want, but eventually, you'll run out of food and starve to death." Hoping to push the envelope, Lindsey paused. "We can wait."

Despite being interrupted and sidelined by the human, Hades' curiosity had been piqued.

"Option two! You give us the doctor, and I let the rest of you live."

"That's not your call!" Hades growled.

Lindsey answered him with an upheld flat-palmed hand.

"If we hand him over ... can you promise to leave the museum alone? How can we even trust you?" Skylar's voice quivered with uneasiness.

"The building will be returned to you. It doesn't matter if you trust me or not. You have ten minutes to decide. After that"—Lindsey thrust a finger toward the camera—"the deal to spare you is off the table." She held her pose until she heard the speakers click off.

A strong hand gripped Lindsey's shoulder and spun her around. "We let them live!? I didn't gather an army to assault this fortress just to let the humans inside of it live!" Spittle flew from his curled mouth and landed on Lindsey's face.

Forming a sassy pose, Lindsey shot back. "Would you rather we wait here for weeks?"

He dug his nails into her shoulder, boring his gaze into hers. Shoving her shoulder away, he turned and walked to the other side of the room. Loitering dead quickly stepped out of his way.

Lindsey looked around for a clock, wishing she had marked the time. Spotting a watch on a business-like nihanim, she scooted over to it and grabbed its wrist. Seeing that it was an analog watch, she dropped the wrist. "Damn it," she whispered to herself as she went in search of a digital watch that she could read. Just as Lindsey found a working digital watch, she heard it: the sound of steel shutters.

Shunk!

The bunker shutters slid open, covering the sound of the activated PA system. Frantic pleading and shouting from various voices burst through the speaker system.

Suddenly, the familiar voice of Liam drowned out the internal chaos. "We'll take your offer. We're bringing him out."

Metal gears groaned from behind the door to the bunker as the thick locking mechanism released. What was heard over the speakers now spewed forth from the cracked, whining door. A single dirty gym shoe leapt out from behind the bunker door but retreated back inside. Like a wrecking ball, the voice closest to the door broke any remaining restraint Lindsey had.

Although it had been sanded down by age, his voice was unmistakable. It was Dr. Nosparchez's: "No, no, no. Please don't do this! Gabriel, I delivered you! David, I treated you last week. Please no!"

Unsure of what to expect, Hades made his way to the front of the horde. Two nihanem, ready to accept the offering, shuffled forward and stood on either side of the door. The dirty gym shoe appeared again. With skin like a soggy paper bag, a bug-eyed man in a dingy Hawaiian shirt and washed-out blue jeans stumbled forward. Dr. Nosparchez's short, tarnished-silver hair broadened like a dancer's skirt as he spun around and grabbed the door. Hands from inside pounded and tore at his desperate fingers. A stiff arm to the chest broke his grip, allowing the door to slam shut.

Hearing his name growled, the doctor flipped around. Grayish-blue hands grabbed his trembling arms. Despite the visibility of bone in their wounds, Dr. Nosparchez was unable to break the grip of his undead guards or halt their slow march.

Before him, Hades stood with an aura of superiority and malice.

Without warning, Lindsey's rifle roared in anger as hot lead turned his chest and skull to pulp. Bits of skin and bone fragments hitchhiked with passing bullets and landed amongst the rosy droplets painting the steel door.

Hades' eyes darted to his companion. The deafening thunder and quickly repeating flashes from Lindsey's raised rifle highlighted her wrath-twisted mask. The faces of onlooking bunker dwellers screamed silently behind the thick glass.

Lindsey held the bucking beast in her hands until the last round had been spent, and she kept pulling the trigger, hoping that her efforts would magically make another bullet appear. While the nihanem who diligently held the doctor had been hit multiple times, the unidentifiable remains of Doctor Nosparchez hung limply by his shoulders. Dark maroon, soppy hair fell into the bowl of red pulp that had replaced his once gentle face and wrinkled forehead. Bits of what looked like pink jello slid through the gore and down his exposed throat.

Finally accepting that her ammunition had run out, Lindsey let up her assault on the trigger. An eerie still swept through the room. Lindsey's broken, heavy breathing was the only sound. Lowering the gun's muzzle and her head, she brushed through the horde toward the exit.

Hades, dumbstruck, watched Lindsey until she disappeared around a corner. The nihanem holding the doctor released his arms, and his body fell with a heavy thud followed by a sloppy splat. Realizing that the PA system had never clicked off, his attention turned to the white faces behind the bunker's thick glass. "Consider yourselves fortunate. Our arrangement shall be honored."

This wasn't at all how he had wanted this to go. He hadn't made a deal even remotely like this in nearly three and a half thousand years. "Stay within your hole until the next cresting of your star. My soldiers and I will take our leave from this fortress. As long as you all stay within these walls, you will not be harmed. But hear me now. If even a single outsider finds refuge amongst you, our arrangement is forfeit."

Hades could barely hide his desire for the deal to be broken. Begrudgingly, he turned himself from his prey, causing the tail of his open leather jacket to sadly flap. Snarling to himself, he trudged after Lindsey.

Despite his pathway to her being more or less a line, finding Lindsey wasn't so easy. Slightly cheating and sifting through the visions of his walking dead, he eventually found her sitting in a different wing of the museum. He made his way through the building, keeping a nihanim's eye watching over her from a distance. Leaving his undead sheep in the main lobby, he continued the rest of the way alone.

Three exhibits in, down a tall and stretched hallway, Lindsey sat on a bench in the middle of the walkway. Approaching her, he could tell that the human looked different. She was bent over like a burnt wick, her vacant gaze lost amongst the grooves of the old tile floor. Her ponytail sat perched on her right shoulder. Like a sleeping dog, her rifle lay at her feet.

"Don't you dare overstep me again," Hades growled.

Ignorant of his threat, Lindsey's attention drifted into space.

Growing tired of what he perceived to be her insouciant defiance, Hades cracked his left-hand knuckles. He caught a glimpse of a painting down the hall, and echoes of hushed chatter filled his left ear. The soft touch of a ghost hand intertwined with his fingers. A warmth that he hadn't experienced since Aphrodite's death filled him and spurred a smile to the corners of his lips. Shaking the dying ember of Melissa's memory from his mind, Hades focused his attention back on Lindsey.

The first time Lindsey spoke, it was nothing more than a breeze. Her nose gargled as she drew air back through it. "I don't know what happened. The moment I heard his voice ..." Her eyes trailed off down the hall. "There were so many things I wanted to say to him. Since the day my mom died ... I dreamt of the day I would finally have my hands on him." She slowly entangled her finger in the bottom of her cropped shirt. "Wanted him to know what he'd done."

Like a sad puppy, Lindsey tilted her head up and looked at Hades. "It was like a bomb went off inside of me. Memories of my mom ..." After filling her lungs, she let out a lengthy sigh. "She was the last family member I had. Because of him, I had to watch her wither away." She shook her head. "He dated my mom before. Said that if we gave him the money, he would cover the rest. We sold everything just to get enough. Bastard took it and denied ever making that deal with her. She went through so much pain until her body finally couldn't take it anymore."

Hades watched the miserable girl stew in a red-hot cauldron of rage and suffering. As hard as he fought against it, he pitied her. Even worse, he related to her. Plopping down beside her on the bench, he unzipped his chest pocket and reached inside. "I was hoping to give this to you later."

Having already returned her gaze to the floor, Lindsey didn't get a glimpse of Hades' gift until it blocked her view. Hades held his closed hand between her face and the floor. Floating there, his fist looked massive. Then Hades uncurled his fingers, revealing a small, odd-shaped, yellow puffball.

At a glance, the object resembled a mold-conquered over-sized jellybean. Lindsey squinted and leaned in closer, curious as a squirrel. What first appeared to be overgrown spores turned out to be roughed-up, bristled feathers. As her finger moved in for a poke, the jellybean shook to life. The head of a small creature turned toward Lindsey, untucking its beak from beneath its tiny plump belly. Her face reflected off its beady, rotten-grape eyes. Standing tall on toothpick legs, it let out a joyous sound: "Peep!"

Fairy lights filled Lindsey's eyes as she gazed upon the baby chick. "There weren't any live ones in the exhibit. How did you find this?" she asked, remembering the pod she had taken cover behind and the single dead chick within lying still as if in a photograph. "You brought it back to life for me?"

Hades chuckled. "Not exactly." Using the back of his overturned hand, he lightly nudged Lindsey's hand.

Taking the cue, Lindsey cupped her hands and raised them to accept the disturbingly cute undead bird.

Hades studied Lindsey's face, searching for her reaction. Capturing what he had hoped for, he tilted his head away and allowed a tint of delight to cross his face. "It's not often that I've been able to say this, but I understand what's going through your mind."

"There's no way in hell that you do," Lindsey snapped. Grateful for the gift of the small bird, the cherry-faced Lindsey carefully laid her cupped hands onto her lap. "Over the last two months, I've watched as you've killed hundreds of people. Not a single one of them did a single thing to you. Let's say the world did something to you. What the fuck did the little girl at the hospital ever do? You kill just because you can. I killed Nosparchez because of what he did. I killed soldiers and other survivors to stay alive and rescue you." Her puffed-up chest rose and fell like a rooster's.

Hades angled his head down and closed his eyes. Breathing slowly, he reopened them and placed a hand on the distraught human's shoulder. "When I was a child, I, too, had suffered greatly from what you would call a doctor. What he did to me ... what he did to thousands of nameless others in the confines of enslavement, was beyond evil. For some time, I thought that he had been forced into performing unspeakable acts. Told myself I didn't remember my first time meeting him clearly." Hades solemnly lowered his head and then reached over to place his index finger near the chick in Lindsey's cupped hands. Happily chirping, the chick nestled against his finger.

"Over time, and with many rumors, I could no longer deny the truth. This ... monster ... wasn't forced into atrocities. He signed up for them. He ..." His face contorted wildly as if he was unsure which shape best conveyed his growing rage. "He invented the procedure." He struggled to contain himself, pushing his forearms against his knees and retracting his hands to lock his fingers together. "I knew he had to die." He turned his boiling eyes toward Lindsey. "Keeping that hidden away for years was almost as torturous as my everyday reality."

Lindsey struggled to come up with anything to say to this unusual and unforeseen openness. Not wanting the unnerving quietness to continue, she cleared her throat. "What did you do?"

"Me and the rest of my kind who were unfortunate enough to be captured became critical yet expendable weapons for a kingdom. During a mission, a brief opportunity presented itself to escape. Another Cursed and I ran into the forest, hoping the trees would aid us." Pulling in the corner of his bottom lip, Hades chewed on it softly. "I was the only one to survive."

"I never knew ... was this during World War Two?" Lindsey said.

"World War what?" Hades shook his head. "No ... No. This was on Deotram."

Perplexed, Lindsey mouthed "Deotram" to herself, hoping the movement would bring clarity to the alien word.

"Weeks went by where I just hid," Hades continued.

"Maybe it was anger, or possibly the lingering taste of spirits, but I eventually built up the courage to return to my previous prison. It wasn't easy, but the *Void* must have smiled upon me that day. Before the first alarm went off, I was able to free a quarter of my brothers and sisters."

"After that alarm, it was a bloodbath. Instead of finding Cursed awaiting freedom, we only found headless corpses in cages. I ordered survivors to retreat and shelter at an external rendezvous point. Not a single one wavered. We slaughtered every last non-Cursed at that facility." Hades looked toward a painting on the wall. Vibrant flowers, seemingly pushed together, formed a marvelous cityscape. Swirls of black ichor created a whirlpool night sky. "Except two. The doctor and a Blessed."

Tucking its legs beneath its body, the chick sat somberly in Lindsey's palms.

"We put him through his own procedure. Collar and all. He begged us to activate the bomb. Instead, we sliced off flesh from his body."

The chick began to emit a strange, yet cute, growling sound.

"One cut for every brother and sister he hurt. We didn't let him die until every last atrocity was accounted for."

Lindsey gently stroked the back of the small bird's head with her thumb. "And what of the other person?"

Hades slyly smiled. "We needed a healer. It didn't take much convincing to get them to join us."

"Why are you telling me this?" Soft pinfeathers kissed Lindsey's skin each time the nihanim in her hand moved.

Hades' eyes, previously focused on the drowning darkness in the painting, crossed the threshold and buried them in the petals of the vibrant bouquet towers. "That was my first, truly personal kill. The people I was forced to kill before him were as numerous as the stars. I thought I could treat his death like any of the others." He lingered on a golden dahlia before snapping free and meeting Lindsey's mixed gaze. "I was wrong. It was freeing and terrifying. What I had craved for so long should have been easy. But personal never is. Killing a soldier in battle when threatened with your own death for noncompliance is like breathing air. Killing a target you know ... a target you loathe ... it breaks you."

"I'm not broken. He deserved it. I'm fine," Lindsey growled. "You've practically killed this entire city for the hell of it."

"Your tears say otherwise."

Touching her own face, Lindsey pulled back wet fingers, the tips reflecting in the lights above. She quickly wiped her face with the back of her hand and faced away from Hades.

"And it hasn't been for the hell of it. I lost someone long ago. I can use the *Essence* stored within my army to bring them back. Each created nihanim brings me closer to her. The amount of *Essence* required for the resurrection ritual has nearly been reached. By tomorrow, my army will be large enough for it to succeed. I owe that to you, Lindsey."

Warm peeps from the chick formed the duct tape wrapping around her cracking heart. "Happy to have helped," she said wistfully through a forced smile. The chick happily chirped and flapped its baby wings.

Lifting himself from the bench, Hades looked down at Lindsey. "Let's head back."

Conditioned shackles melted in the inferno enclosed within XI-24's chest. While he planned the most effective warpath, he ordered his nihanem to gather at his location. He gazed down at the body of Spike's self-executed nihanem. Spike's life had been thrown away quicker than a malfunctioning rifle, and it pained XI-24 even further to know that his friend wished to keep him concealed.

Hearing a leaf crunch behind him, XI-24 lunged backward like a striking snake with a single lethal fang. The blade of his knife stopped just before the point of tasting blood and then was recalled. Hunched over so the flesh of its torn-open neck draped downwards like moth-eaten banners, one of Chatter's nihanem held up a closed fist to its mouth. Keeping quiet, XI-24 and a number of his gathered nihanem followed the silenced corpse.

Winding through the streets of the village, Chatter's nihanim approached a quaint home. XI-24 pushed open the blood-splattered door and entered.

Sitting at the head of a rough wooden table, Chatter motioned his apprentice to take a seat. "Keep your nihanem in the town." Before XI-24 could speak, the tenured Death-Touched cut him off. "Keep them active, but avoid the inhabitants. There's a chance we can bring Spike back, but we don't have much time."

XIX

LAST CALL

Matt awoke to the sound of shattering glass, his back on a hard floor. Feeling like he had visited every college party in the world in a single night, his head throbbed. He pushed himself up into a sitting position. Stainless steel cabinet doors and countertops fought for breathing space in the cramped room. What smelled like concentrated dung garnished with a lemon slice shocked his senses. Gripping a handle above, he lifted himself up, only for a pan filled with congealed grease and pungent brown mush to come crashing down on him. Matt wiped off what he could beneath his soured face and stood up without the help of any support.

Hearing a familiar popping sound, he peered through a congested kitchen line and saw Zeus outside the room. The man sat alone at an elegant walnut-topped bar, surrounded by high-proof companions. Broken bottles lay beneath a cracked mirror, highlighting a vintage wood cash register. Morning light fingered its way in through mostly closed, lavish, emerald-colored curtains at the far end of the room.

Weaving between tables well above his pay grade, Matt walked across the shined oak floor. He leaned on the bar with his hand, groggily looking at Zeus. Already a fifth of the way done with the freshly opened bottle, the man looked miserable. Even more so with the lilac hue cradling his puffy eyes.

"What happened? Last I remember, we were in that tunnel or whatever. Kevin was with me."

"Zeus knocked you out," Poseidon said while he sat slumped at a table near the kitchen entrance. Matt hadn't noticed him sitting there. "He even carried your ass out."

That didn't make any sense. They were being chased. Why would Zeus do that? "Thought you were joking about it. Didn't know you'd actually follow through with it," Matt jabbed at Zeus.

Placing the nearly drained bottle down, Zeus spoke up, "Saved your life. Show a little more gratitude." His voice was a low growl.

Ticked off by Zeus' pompous remark, Matt lashed back, "Show you more gratitude? Kevin was right behind me. You didn't knock me out to save my life. You took a damn cheap shot at me!"

Leaping from his stool, Zeus stood eye to eye with Matt. Inhaling his breath was enough to fail a breathalyzer test. "If you weren't such a klutz, he wouldn't have needed to be behind you, and he'd still be ALIVE!"

Globs of Zeus' spittle speckled Matt's anger-flushed face. "What do you mean he'd still be alive? He ... he was right behind me. That's impossible." Looking back at Poseidon for even a hint of deceit, Matt found only the somber face of a man who couldn't even bear to look him in the eye. Mumbled words slipped off Matt's tongue and faded into the abyss. If he searched the building, he'd surely find Kevin somewhere in it, gorging himself on anything that wouldn't get him sick or planning the next course of action. There was no way Zeus could be telling the truth.

Plopping back onto his stool, Zeus snatched his half-emptied bottle and tipped it back.

Gazing through a wall, Matt's mind flashed through his last few days with Kevin. Pausing on the memory of a silhouette of Kevin in the light-starved hallway, dark thoughts crawled forward. "Do ... Do you think he became one of those things ... one of those nihanem?"

Moving behind the bar counter, Poseidon spoke to Matt without looking at him. "From what Zeus saw, I doubt it. Too much damage to his neck." He lifted a blue bottle of tequila tucked away behind a wall of bottles, removed the spout attachment, and dropped it on the counter. "Although, the possibility is always there."

Practically resting on his bottle, Zeus mumbled into it. "The fall of Deotram. The deaths of Aphrodite, Apollo, Asclepius, now Kratos ..." Zeus looked at his haggard reflection in the broken mirror. His image was split into disconnected pieces. "And we're no closer to finding Artemis."

Swallowing a generous mouthful of agave, Poseidon gently grabbed Zeus' bottle and dragged it out of his hand. He took a swig for himself and put it out of the drunk man's reach. "We'll get her back. I promise." Poseidon noisily collected the remainder of the bottles congregating around Zeus, moving back and forth between the bar counter and bar shelf. "When we find Hades, we'll take him out so this doesn't happen a *fourth* time."

Startled by how quickly Zeus stood up, Matt popped up and whacked his hip against the unforgiving side of a stationary stool.

Furious, Zeus unloaded on Poseidon. "So he can learn our strategy?! Do you think he'll just gloss over the fact that we can't even hold a candle to our former selves?! All I can do now is hold a phone and slow down how fast it drains! What are you going to do? Throw a water bottle at him?!"

Wishing he was anywhere else but here, Matt stood motionless.

Poseidon threw himself against the counter opposite Zeus and yelled in his face. "It was a fuckin rumor! The warlord was killed and then miraculously was spotted attacking another post a few days later?! They all look the same! If we kill him, he's not coming back."

Zeus tried to get a word in, but the now steaming Poseidon cut him off. "No! We tried your way last time. Put him in that damn stasis pod like *you* wanted." His arms spread out wide like an eagle ready to swoop in for the kill. "Now look at where we are! You couldn't control Nyx, and you can't control Hades. The Royal Hand isn't a thing anymore. We're equals. Get fuckin used to it!"

Seeing movement in the broken mirror, Matt followed the reflection. Hermes stood in a doorway roughly twenty feet from the kitchen entrance. With the look on his face, he had either discovered the cure for cancer, or this restaurant was about to receive a wave of ravenous customers. Meeting each other's gaze, both Hermes and Matt soon had the same awkward expression.

Locked in a heated verbal sparring match, Zeus and Poseidon were no longer mentally part of this world. Embers, long since buried by civility, melted the bonds of their relationship and spewed forth oceans of repressed hatred. Watching Hermes cautiously approach, Matt internally begged for him not to upset them further.

Hermes waited patiently for a moment of calm, resting his arms on the bar counter roughly a yard behind Zeus. Thick, tinted-glass shards exploded on the edge of the bar counter as dark liquor splashed against the wood cabinet below. The gut-punching smell of sweet rum overrode the odors creeping out of the rotten kitchen. Poseidon now held the jagged end of a bottle less than half a foot from Zeus' left eye.

Figuring there wouldn't be a better time than now, Hermes verbally jumped in. "I think I know where Artemis is!"

Lowering the bottle—and Matt's anxiety—Poseidon sternly commented back, "You think you know where she is?"

"If you remember, back on Deotram, *Essence* was concentrated enough to sometimes be visible." Hermes quickly pointed at the gap in the closed curtains. "I was surveying the area when I noticed it. *Essence*. Flowing, visible *Essence*."

"Do you think it's him?" Zeus asked.

"Unless a tear recently opened in the *Veil*, Hades is the only one with a high enough capacity for *Essence* in this city."

While Hermes went over his findings, Matt approached the window. Without disturbing the curtains, he peeked outside. There were crashed cars, smashed windows, and one facade poorly concealing its charred insides. Considering it was the apocalypse, the street looked completely normal. Matt imagined himself driving the expensive-looking red car parked down the street. Finally, he noticed what Hermes had mentioned. Like a mirage created under the thumb of an overbearing sun, the air shimmered.

Matt studied the street again. Maybe it was the headache, but he hadn't noticed the movement before. Instead of staying in place, the various shimmers moved in the same direction. As if a paint-coated needle had been dipped into a river, the mirages were laced with a blue tinge. Matt watched the ghostly river move down the street, expecting it to flow around a building. Instead, the river of *Essence* simply phased through the obstructing brick wall. Feeling a nudge to his arm, Matt turned his head and found Zeus standing next to him.

The man shoved a half-empty open box of dry pasta into Matt's hand, leaning over to get a look out the window. "It's not ideal, but eat up," he said while trying not to slur any of his words.

"What's going on?"

"We're going after Hades. After you eat, find something to use as a weapon."

"When you knocked me out, you didn't happen to grab my sword, did you?" He already knew the answer, but thought it was worth asking anyway.

Zeus rolled his eyes and grumbled to himself as he walked away.

Almost human shrieks and screams hurled into the cold night sky, piercing the closed shutters. Moonlight filtered through cracks around the room. XI-24 could only see the tops of gore-darkened heads and the occasional reflective eye. Laced with Spike's blood, Chatter's dagger rested in the center of a ring lined with living corpses.

Summoning Essence *from his present nihanem,* Chatter pulled faint streams of blue energy to himself. He then directed it toward his weapon on the floor, and a shallow cyclone formed around the tainted blade. Like starving animals, the spiraling ribbons of light dove onto the dagger. A shape took form from the miniature storm, morphing into something humanoid. Quickly losing its blue glow, a color-drained body lay before the jury.

Chatter walked to the center of the circle, knelt, and offered a hand to the bone-white specter.

As the new guest gingerly rose from the floor, XI-24 saw its face and gasped. "Spike!?" he shouted. He rushed over and wrapped his arms around his naked friend.

"You probably have questions. Unfortunately, they'll have to go unanswered," Chatter said slowly. Approaching with a set of clothes, a gore-throated nihanim pushed its gift into Spike's hands. "Your wife is safe. She's hiding at the edge of the forest. This nihanim here will take you to her. Do not use your abilities unless absolutely necessary." Chatter placed a firm hand on Spike's shoulder. "Go now," he ordered.

DILIGENCE

Outside a wide circle of inward-facing nihanem, Hades stood with both hands held forward like the talons of a striking hawk. Delicate trails of blue smoke flowed from each nihanim and traveled toward the center of the circle. Fluorescent aqua streams of condensed *Essence* poured through the thick brick walls of Artemis' facility, sweeping away the individual nihanem contributions and whirling into a shallow, ethereal spiral around the ancient blood-stained piece from Hades' clothing.

Two thousand years had Hades waited for this moment. Endless years of regret and isolation. Thrown into a new age without his full strength. But against all odds, he had succeeded. The ritual had begun.

Pushing his concentration to its limits, Hades tightened the eye of the circling whirlpool of *Essence*. Without Aphrodite's body, all Hades had to anchor her soul to this side of the *Veil* was the small cloth containing her blood. Due to the extent of time that had passed, using even a small remnant of her was like lighting a candle in an endless dense forest and hoping the light makes it to the other side.

Laughter broke out behind him. "Performance troubles?" Artemis mocked. She was kneeling on the ground roughly fifteen feet away. Weakened from her forced fasting, she was helpless against the multiple nihanem that twisted her arms painfully behind her back and gripped her neck. Cold steel pressed against her temple.

"Give the word, and this bitch'll stop talking," Lindsey said. Pulling back her rifle, she quickly jabbed the tip of her barrel into Artemis' head.

Swearing loudly, Hades eased his hold on *Essence*. No longer driven by his will, the whirlpool of energy dissipated. "She's leverage." He walked over to the cloth on the ground. Artemis' sword, nestled in the embrace of an open-bottomed leather holster, bounced against his leg. Crossing his arms and resting the dimple of his chin against a tightened fist, he stared intently at the stained fabric. "At the very least, she'll be a source of nourishment later on."

Eager to vent her frustrations, Lindsey could almost hear the barrel whine as she pulled it away from the prisoner's head.

Never before has the ritual gone this far and faltered, Hades thought. *By no means is the* Veil *on this planet thin, but the anchor and the exorbitant amount of* Essence *supplied to it should have overcome that.* His eyes skimmed along the floor with increasing intensity. He had done everything right. Aphrodite should have been resurrected. All this time, all this effort—wasted. His effort, he realized, wasn't enough. Every vessel on this planet could be turned and tapped, and the result would be the same. His only chance to bring her back had died in the street of that primitive city. His team, the ones that supposedly put the old world behind them, had stolen his only chance.

"Just do this planet a favor and kill yourself," spat Artemis.

Like sparks to gunpowder, Artemis' words ignited his pent-up frustrations and fears. Shoving a nihanim aside, Hades barreled toward his captive and swung a dizzying right hook at her head. Her corpse restraints struggled to keep Artemis upright as Hades unleashed his rage, but they held tight, nonetheless. He pulled his sword from its holster, dug his fingers into her tangled hair, and tugged her head up.

The sword's razor edge rested on Artemis' neck. Battered, she looked up at Hades through a puffy slit. Blood poured from a gash above her shut-eye, flowed down the edge of her nose, and dripped into her mouth. "You ... are exactly the monster ... she thought you were."

Bending down to meet her eye to eye, Hades stared into the depths of her soul. "I have a better idea for what to do with you." As soon as he stepped aside, the nihanem clutching Artemis lurched forward. Pulled along like a fresh kill, her legs degradingly dragged behind her. When they reached the center of the dead circle, the procession came to a halt. Breaking up the monotony of the concrete floor beneath the goddess' head, Hades' stained cloth smiled up at its visitor.

"Copy, Lindsey," erupted a staticky voice from a two-way radio clipped to Lindsey's belt. Removing it, she glanced at Hades and brought it to her lips. She spoke quietly into it, and seeing that Hades had control of the room, she quickly excused herself and walked out into a hallway.

Back on the outside of the circle, Hades prepared himself. Lindsey soon joined him. He held his hands at his sides like a candelabra, calling to the confined *Essence* within each of his creations. Thousands upon thousands of phantasmal strings, reaching out like tentacles, wrapped themselves around his fingers and concentrated into a visible blue aura in the palms of his hands.

Feeling the approach of his summoned *Essence*, Hades balled his hands into fists. He pushed with all his might, fighting to redirect the flow toward Artemis and the anchor. Exhausted from his first attempt, rage was all he had left to draw strength from. Each arm was an immovable mountain that stood between him and his love.

Gradually, Hades forced his fists forward. Beneath the

burdensome weight, his tearing muscles begged for clemency. He had lost Aphrodite once before, and he couldn't bear the weight of losing her again. Filling his lungs with musty air, he let out a roar.

Supported by bulging, vein-wrapped arms, his asphyxiated fingers sprung open from their eggs of flesh and bone. Like race hounds behind a dropped gate, the *Essence* contained in his hands flew forward. The incoming streams of *Essence* adjusted course, chasing their standard-bearer.

What had begun as dancing ribbons around Artemis quickly transformed into an unforgiving rampage of crystal dragons. Fearless, the nihanem ring held their positions. Artemis attempted to flee, twisting and bucking to no avail. As the eye of the storm tightened, so did her vigor.

Praying that the addition of a living Deotrite vessel would turn the odds in his favor, Hades strengthened his focus. Mere inches from Artemis, fastidious tongues licked at the air. *Take, damn you!* Hades blared within his mind. The stockpile supplying the ritual would not last forever. If the anchor and the body weren't accepted soon, he knew, there might not be enough left for the final step.

Eyes closed, Hades stormed through his thoughts, flipping them over like scandalous tables in a temple. *Why isn't it taking? Has this planet altered Artemis? Is there not enough of Aphrodite's blood on the cloth for the* Essence *to make a connection between the physical anchor and her spirit in the* Void? *No ..."*

Hades opened his eyes.

Scampering into the circle, one of the guarding altered-nihanem approached Artemis. It crouched, its decrepit flush facade close enough for Artemis to make out each individual collapsed vein. Awkwardly, the creature picked up the cloth. Digging a sharpened bone into Artemis' forearm, it dragged the spike across until blood readily fled through the breach.

Laying the ancient cloth over the wound, the nihanim clamped its hand around her arm to keep the anchor in place.

The circling *Essence* dove upon the sacrifice like wolves. Thousands of glowing streams entered her body, seamlessly boring into Artemis like parasites. Lurching to the side, Artemis clenched her teeth, but her corpse shackles held her in place. Her eyes locked on Hades; something seemed to be on the tip of her tongue, but she couldn't release the words. Her stomach began to spasm, and bile soon escaped from between her teeth.

Holding position, Hades watched as the ritual violated his former captor. Performing the final step at the right time was imperative. Too soon, and the link might not be strong enough to break through the *Veil* and bring Aphrodite back. Too late, and the volatile life source of the *Void* would burn up Artemis. It had to be perfect.

Artemis spewed forth another volley of vacant vomit. Tears ran down her face as she struggled to take in air between regurgitations. Steaming sick dripped from her drenched, unfortunate hair. As she raised her head, her eyes glowed an eerie blue like ghostly lanterns piercing the midnight fog on an unseen ship.

Having spotted the signal, Hades began gradually moving his hands together. Sliding the back of one hand into the palm of the other, he formed them into a devilish crown. With all streams now tethered, moving his hands in any direction was like wading through setting concrete. Hades breathed deep and prepared himself.

On Deotram, the *Veil* was as thick as the morning dew. Interacting with the *Void* was effortless. In contrast, the *Veil* on Earth was as impenetrable as a wall of diamond. Never before had he gathered this much power for a single resurrection. Grunting, Hades forced his hands up. *Essence* coursed through Artemis like water through a broken dam. She cried out and threw her head back.

Confident about the pending success of his mission, he allowed memories of his last night spent with Aphrodite the day before she died to settle in. Wanting fingers slithered along her scalp. Craving flesh, the snakes latched onto tufts of hair and pulled her head backward. With Aphrodite's neck exposed, bared teeth gently dug into her carotid artery. Overcome by pain, a moan escaped her lips. Cradling Hades' head just above her breast, she rotated her hips in a wider circle.

Leather straps groaned as they rubbed on the kline's wooden frame. With each euphoric rotation, elegant woolen blankets caressed her legs. Light from a nearby flickering oil lamp cast dancing shadows on the plaster walls of the small room. Faint smells of perfumes and her favorite flowers filled the air.

Feeling the approach of Elysium, Aphrodite dug her nails into Hades' lion-ravaged back. She ground into him, pounding closer to the banks of the White Island. Crawling ashore, calming winds warmed her throughout. She released Hades from her bosom, and her golden hair massaged her shoulders and tickled his flush face. Breathless, Hades laid his head against the cold wall and closed his eyes.

Pain like a red-hot nail pierced Hades from behind, effectively pulling him out of the memory. Opening his eyes, he saw the tip of a blade poking out from his chest. Like dogs into the night, his hold on the streams of *Essence* slipped through his fingers. The incoming streams quickly disappeared, taking with them the whirlpool.

In a more excruciating move than the initial penetration, the blade was ripped from his body. Hot blood spilled down his stomach. No longer able to support the weight of his own hands, his arms fell to his sides. *We were so close,* he thought. Taking one step forward, his knee buckled out from under him, and he slammed his shoulder and head on the floor.

Fuzzy support beams under the steel sky danced overhead. Eclipsing the incandescent stars, a concealing hood darkened Hades' view. The figure lowered down to Hades, and details under the hood began to emerge. Stoic lips deadened the soft features on the hood's charcoal face. Eyes of glossed-over ivory coldly peeked out from behind their cotton cover.

"Nyx," Hades coughed out.

Pressing her heel into Hades' chest, Nyx pinned the gravely wounded man to the ground. "Took you long enough," she said in a feathery voice. "Can't believe you made a girl wait." Extending an arm toward Artemis, Nyx recalled the strings of *Essence*.

Just as a bone spear made contact with her sleeve, Nyx dissolved into shadow. Like the morning sun, a pillar of darkness rose from the ground forty feet away. Solidifying, Nyx continued to hold the reins. She smiled, serenaded by the chorus of nihanem, and carried on with her task.

Having returned from her conversation in the hallway, Lindsey was greeted by the surprising change of events. Clattering on the floor, Lindsey's radio angrily squawked. "Hades!" she shouted, racing across the room and dropping to her knees. Despite applying pressure to his wound, warm blood leaked through the crevices of her pressed palm.

"Nyx is hijacking the ritual," Hades weakly stated. "We need to stop her."

"If you die, there's no point in saving it." Frantically, Lindsey's eyes searched the room. Every single available nihanem was preoccupied with Nyx, with more coming in from other areas of the facility. "Make one of your zombies come here."

Disregarding the human's concern, Hades quickly earned Lindsey's scorn. "Are you really this stupid?" Lindsey raised her voice further. "All of this is to bring someone back from the dead. For what? To trade places with them?" She applied more pressure to the wound; Hades grunted beneath her. "If you care so much about them, why bring them back just to leave them? You can be as stubborn as you want. I'm not letting you die."

Removing her hands from his chest, she picked up one of his hands and placed it around her neck. Blood from her drenched hands ran down her limbs. "Use me. Even if it kills me. Use me."

Furrowing his eyebrows, Hades tightened his fingers around her throat.

Tears ran down Lindsey's cheeks. Closing her eyes, she prepared herself for the misery she was about to undergo. Having watched so many die in this manner, she knew the brief hell that awaited her.

Hades loosened his grip and slid his hand up until it lay against her cheek. Tears from her eyes mixed with the blood on his hand. The uneasy rumbling of aethereal thunder from Artemis' direction drowned out his words. Then, unwavering arms wrapped around Lindsey, causing her eyes to burst open. Against her will, the arms tore her from Hades. Through woeful screams and pleas, she begged Hades to stop. As two nihanem dragged her into a hallway, a third closed a heavy door behind them, cutting off her cries from the violent room.

Sorely raising his hand, Hades soon touched cold flesh. Dark ichor oozed out of the dead man's eyes and wounds. The corpse wouldn't yield much, but it would stem the bleeding. Like a teddy bear in a vacuum-sealed bag, the blue flesh tightened, making ribs protrude and cheekbones surface. Bled dry, the dead man collapsed to the side.

Following the ferocious mass of bodies unleashing themselves on Nyx, it was clear to Hades by the trail of downed corpses that the new contender was winning. Eager for revenge, Hades retrieved his sword. For the moment, the ritual could wait. Once his dear old friend had been dealt with, Aphrodite's reclamation from the *Void* could resume.

He looked to the center of the room to make sure Artemis was still secure. What he saw instead drove him further into a rage. Cut to pieces, his three guards restraining his prisoner lay in ruin. Now kneeling beside her was the culprit. Cradling Artemis in his arms and lifting her from the floor was the face of his first betrayer.

"Dragon," Hades growled..

Kneeling among captured civilians, XI-24 held his hands up. The officer had lined everyone up in front of the forest, believing the wild animals could easily take care of the evidence. Glancing over at Chatter, his mentor's demeanor was far too calm for what the situation warranted. Pulling a soul back through the Veil was something heard of only in legends. Was he so proud of himself that he believed he could resurrect himself if he were to be cut down today?

Kingdom soldiers readied their rifles. If he was fast enough, he could turn some of the civilians as they were executed and shield himself. He was literally knee-deep in ammunition. Silver armored troops shoved past the line of soldiers. Red trim decorated them from head to toe.

"Shit," XI-24 whispered to himself. Rifles he could deal with, but with fire-touched at this range, he couldn't turn the deceased fast enough. Even if he did manage to escape, there was still the matter of the bomb in his neck.

Lifting off the ground fifty strides away, a drop ship violently exploded, sending out a shockwave. Burning shrapnel landed amongst the feet of the stunned troops. Sprinting from their hiding places, Chatter's few remaining nihanem charged the soldiers. The nihanem barely reached their targets before they were quickly reduced to tatters or incinerated husks. Those that saw through the diversion unloaded into the crowd. Unwilling to leave the death of the Corpse Callers to fate, their handlers tapped on their bomb activation buttons, only to find them unresponsive.

Forcefully spun around, XI-24 was then yanked off his knees by Chatter. Bullets whizzed past their ears as they sprinted toward the forest. As civilians fell, Chatter looked back to raise a few corpses to join in the fight. They were almost there.

Then a blast from a Scorcher hit the ground behind them, throwing them off their feet.

XI-24's entire body ached from the blast. But he had to keep moving. Rolling over, he reached for his friend.

Down a leg, Chatter laid on the ground in anguish.

Dragging himself over, XI-24 knew what had to be done and readied himself for the pain. "Use me to fix yourself up a bit. I can take it. We'll get out of here," XI-24 nervously insisted.

Allowing for the assist, Chatter put his arm around the young man's neck. "You'll thank me later for this," vowed the old man. Chatter pulled XI-24 down to him, placing his hand against his pupil's head.

Memories and secrets poured into XI-24's mind. Blinded by the mental traffic, he was helpless against Chatter's blade as it dug at an angle beneath his collar. Excruciating pain rippled down his spine. Finding what he needed, the blade's point flicked out the bomb and released him from the memory fusion.

Slyly smiling, and to the astonishment of his apprentice, Chatter ran the blade across his own throat.

With soldiers entering the forest behind him, XI-24 had to choose between two terrible paths. He could force Chatter to regenerate, leaving them both weak and vulnerable, or he could take his friend's blood and escape alone. Clenching his fist, he glared at his friend's mutilated leg. They could never make it out alive together, and they both knew it. With tears in his eyes, he hugged his dying friend and called for the old man's blood to heal his wound.

Looking into his friend's shriveled eyes one last time, he abandoned Chatter and retreated into the forest. All around him, trees exploded and splintered from the barrage of bullets and fire. With new knowledge in his head and a brighter hatred in his heart, he knew what he had to do. No matter what it took, he'd resurrect his friends—or, at the very least, avenge them.

XXI

RISE OF ANCIENTS

Matt, Zeus, Poseidon, and Hermes watched the scene unfold from behind pillars and crates. Armed with two pipe swords, a cleaver, and a compact silver handgun, the team still felt unprepared.

Glancing at the firearm, Matt wished it was in his hands instead of Poseidon's. *Note to self*, Matt thought, *when the staff carries knives, the boss' desk hides a gun.*

Blue energy freely flowed into the room below them through thick walls. Practically halfway up to his knees in the ghostly lake, Hades stood face-to-face with at least a few dozen of his nihanem. Subduing the bastard and killing the ghouls was going to be damn near impossible—assuming there weren't more nihanem lingering out of sight. Held hostage in the center of it all was Maddison.

Despite the kitchen tool's stubbiness and lack of range, the cleaver Matt wielded felt more like a great sword the hotter he became. The only thing standing between him and the monster hurting his wife was a guardrail and a few feet to the ground floor. In less than ten seconds, he could be halfway through hacking away at Hades. Feeling a hand on his shoulder, Matt fiercely glanced at Zeus.

"Keep a cool head. One wrong move by any of us and we jeopardize not only our lives but Artemis' as well," Zeus whispered.

Matt looked back at Maddison. That was going to be easier said than done.

Drying up like a spilled cocktail in Las Vegas, the thick mist that had previously washed over the room evaporated. Standing over Hades, who was now bleeding on the ground, was a figure Matt had seen before. He didn't need them to turn around; he didn't even need to hear their voice. The same feeling of dread he had received each time he saw them sent shivers down his spine. The onlooker, the phantom in the hallway, it was ...

"Nyx?" Slickened by shock, the name slipped off Hermes' tongue.

Sharing the same look of disbelief, the three men hiding with Matt struggled to find a proper place for their jaws. Poseidon lowered his gun. Zeus, just as lost as the others, looked to his team for direction. Her appearance changed everything. Plans A through Z no longer applied. Hades was a known threat, but Nyx ... Nyx wasn't even on the board. Looking toward Matt for ideas, Zeus instead found a vacancy. With his second leg already over the rail, Matt plunged into the fray.

Matt landed hard on his feet, pain radiating from his arches and up into his ankles. Falling back onto his ass and rolling onto his back, he did his best not to crack his head against the cement. Adrenaline propelled him upward through the pain. He clambered to his feet and sprinted toward Maddison.

Looking to intercept the bold attacker, the living dead broke ranks and abandoned their circle. Seeing his window to free Maddison from her three captors, Matt rushed over and swung at the closest one. Each strike had to be calculated, or he risked wounding Maddison. Hacking through the neck was the only way to take out the shambling horror.

Putrid gore splattered on his face and shirt. Ducking a deadly right hook from a spike-armed ghoul, he felt the dead man's forearm grind against his head as it passed over him. Using his opponent as support, Matt kicked the second nihanim just above the left hip, causing it to stumble backward. Having entirely forgotten about the third captor opposite Maddison, he looked over just in time to see the rotting fiend collapse under the rising sword of Zeus.

By the time Matt removed the head of his own nihanim, the rest of the team was on the floor engaged with Hades' army. Nearby, Poseidon bludgeoned the corpse puppets with his pistol's gorgeous handle, having already run out of ammunition.

Turning Maddison over, Matt cradled her head in the crook of his left arm. He flipped the cleaver around in his right hand and gently brushed vomit-clumped hair off of her face. The last time he held her like this was on the worn-out couch in the living room. Pressing two fingers against her throat, he prayed for a pulse. "C'mon, baby. I'm right here."

No pulse. His greatest fears rushed to the forefront of his mind and battered the back of his eyes. "No no no no no ..." Matt whimpered. Desperately, he tested multiple areas around her neck. What good were any of those First Aid classes he had taken to try to become more hirable if he couldn't find a pulse when it actually mattered?

Halting his jumping fingers, Matt moved them back to their previous position. Holding steady, he needed to make sure that what he felt was real. Silence strangled the room. No longer functional, his ears relinquished their ability to listen and gifted it to his fingers. Time seemed to stop. Maddison used to tell him that some moments can last forever, but the best ones never seem long enough. Each time, he would just kiss her head and roll his eyes. He wished he had believed her sooner.

"M—Matthew?"

Her voice was like a gentle summer breeze on the opposite

end of a tunnel: faint yet beautiful. Awestruck, Matt looked down at Maddison. She weakly turned her head to face him. As her eyelids cracked open, blue light erupted from behind them. Islands of vintage silver swam in fluorescent ponds of turquoise. Removing his dumbfounded fingers from her throat, he touched his palm to her cheek.

"Told you not to come for me," Maddison said in a voice as thin as oil.

"When I married you, it was for better or for worse." Doing all he could to keep himself together, Matt forced a smile. "Last I checked, we never signed divorce papers."

"You always were an idiot," Maddison said while resting her forehead against his chest. "I love you."

He had dreamed of the day she would say those three words to him again. Now, the day had finally come. Matt moistened his lips. "I lo—"

"No condition to fight," Maddison said, cutting Matt off. "If I die, I can't die knowing I took you with me. Run ... What are you doing?"

Knowing he'd rather watch Maddison walk out the door again than watch her die, he slipped his right arm beneath her legs. "Always did say that I was a bad listener." He stood up with her cradled in his arms. She felt lighter than she had on their wedding day. "We're getting out of here together."

No more than thirty feet away, a sturdy metal door had been left ajar, beckoning Matt with promises of escape. But when he stepped forward, pain radiated from his ankles. Attempting to move quickly was not an option.

"Oof!" Matt flew off his feet and landed hard on his shoulder. Losing his grip on the cleaver, the kitchen staple clattered to the ground and slid out of reach. Too weak to brace herself, Maddison tumbled to the ground. Her head cracked loudly on the cement, and her body fell still in a crumpled heap on the floor.

Towering over Matt, having weighed at least two hundred and forty pounds pre-death, a man in bite-marked black slacks and a torn-open, navy blue shirt emptily gazed down upon him. A silver star badge, somehow still pinned to the shirt, proudly displayed the deceased man's name: "YOUNG." The only hair on his hazelnut head was a pencil-thin, black beard circling his mouth, creating a miniature racetrack for lice and bacteria. Still holstered on his side was a standard issue handgun, holding out its metaphorical hand to the world.

Matt lunged for the pistol, but before he could get the clasp undone, Officer Young pounced. Distracted by the immense weight and ferocity of the public servant attempting to kill him, Matt struggled to free the firearm.

Finding hold, dead nails dug into Matt's arm and ripped away four elongated patches of skin. Roaring in pain, Matt abandoned the clasp and fought to get Officer Young off. He held the nihanim by the neck, hoping to take getting bitten out of the equation, but the move did nothing to stop the battering and tearing of the creature's relentless arms.

Like a laptop after milk bypasses its keys, Officer Young suddenly went slack. His weight was immense. *Is his strategy to simply crush me to death?* Matt thought. Young's bloated face silently hung like a broken marionette. Sensing his foe had undergone a second death, he gradually slid out from underneath him.

Matt circled Young and realized that the creature's back had been deeply cut from hip to neck. Looking around for his team, he spotted Hermes defending Matt's location with a pipe sword.

Maybe we do have a real chance of pulling off this rescue, Matt thought.

Through the chaos, Hades emerged. No longer in a pool of his own blood, he marched directly toward Matt. Hades' fatal chest wound had nearly healed, the last vestiges framed by his open leather jacket. Long onyx hair partially covered his deathly pale face. Despite only carrying a short sword, he seemed to wield all the rage of the Underworld.

Flipping over onto his hands and knees, Matt sorely crawled to Maddison. She sat on her heels, supporting herself on one arm. As if awakening from a night of heavy drinking under apathetic lights, she groggily swayed in place while covering her eyes.

Before Matt could reach her, mist swirled up beside her. Solidifying, an elongated stalactite grew from it and plummeted toward Maddison's back.

"Look out!" he screamed.

Too much distance had been put between the estranged lovers, and all Matt could do was watch the now-solidified sword skewer the unaware woman.

Shooting her hand up and twisting her body, Maddison caught Nyx's wrist. The tip of the biting sword snapped at her back, narrowly missing her flesh.

"Stabbing me in the back?" Maddison said in a disapproving tone. "Aren't we over this already, Nyx?" Boosting her lower knee forward, she took the witch off guard.

Having succumbed to Maddison's attack, Nyx lost her balance and was flung over her thwarted kill. Maddison tore the sword from Nyx's hand, released her foe, and sent the witch crashing to the ground. Vaporizing before impact, Nyx's body became dark smoke and quickly slithered through the air until it splashed down a few feet away. Materializing in a crouched position, Nyx eyed her suddenly formidable opponent.

"Lost your touch, old friend," Maddison said in a much softer tone.

Even though under the thick hood, Nyx's head noticeably tilted in response to Maddison's snide remark.

Maddison adjusted the weapon in her hand. "Did you know that the dead can see through the *Veil*? On a planet of endless fireflies, I never imagined that you would be the most disappointing."

"Grab her and go!" Zeus screamed, cutting a rotting woman's head in half just below her eyes. The woman's body collapsed into Zeus. Knocking the woman out of his way, he ran to place himself between Matt and Hades.

Holding out his hand, Matt beckoned Maddison to come with him. To his surprise, she remained steadfast. Looking into her eyes, Matt realized that the emerald halos that he had fallen in love with had been replaced with alien cerulean crystals.

"Get her out of here!" Zeus demanded.

Like an electrical charge sluggishly traveling along the strands of steel wool, Maddison's toasted cinnamon hair burned from its base, transforming into delicate strands of gold as if touched by Midas. No longer carrying their loving shimmer, the new eyes that looked at Matt seemed embittered.

Dread loomed perniciously over Matt's heart. Stitch by stitch, the haphazard mending of his heart began to give way. Maddison stood right before him. If the mission of finding her had been a success, then why did it feel like he wasn't fast enough?

Unrecognizable, Maddison turned her head to face Nyx. "What you did to our family ... what you made them do to Hades ... is unforgivable."

Essence, like a spectral pyroclastic flow, spread out in all directions from Maddison. Stepping backward, Nyx slowly began to fade away. Vines of glass leapt from the unholy rolling cloud and wrapped around the fleeing witch, halting her retreat.

"Did you really expect to tap the forbidden tree and gorge yourself?" seethed Maddison. "Famine was forced by your hand." Holding up an invisible chalice in her left hand, Maddison swirled its contents. "By my decree, your lips shall remain a desert," she firmly declared while swiftly bringing her hand to her opposite shoulder.

What had previously turned to lead smoke melted back into place on Nyx. Grounded and experiencing an emotion that she hadn't felt in two millennia, the cloaked woman did the only thing she could. "Fuck you, Aphrodite!" she spat, turning tail and running. Blocking her escape, three nihanem formed a wall.

Matt watched as Maddison walked toward Nyx. Elegance guided each of her steps. The Maddison that he knew had a grace to her, but this new stature was beyond that.

Sounds of sparking metal and cleaved bone blustered nearby. Handling a blade, the god of thunder was unmatched. His sword was the brush, and his foe the canvas. But while Zeus had the finesse, Hades had the support. Attacked from all sides, Zeus locked himself in a defensive dance.

Spitting blood, Zeus put enough distance between himself and Hades to survey the battlefield. Even a stranger could tell that more than just Artemis' appearance had changed. "Hades, what did you do?!"

"What you interrupted so many years ago," Hades growled. "Artemis finally served a purpose."

Contemplating his foe's words, Zeus soon became owl-eyed. Fear-struck, he turned to Matt. "It was a resurrection! That's not Artemis! Abandon the—"

Blood sprayed the nearby nihanem as Hades cut a line across Zeus' chest with his blade. Zeus toppled backward.

Thoughts raced through Matt's mind. *A resurrection? Maddison was right in front of me. How could it not be her? When she looked at me ...* Ice slithered into his veins. Maddison's eyes might have changed, but that shouldn't have changed the way she looked at him.

She was in his arms. After they had fallen the first time, he had felt off about her. Whatever that monster had done to her, it took effect during that brief moment. Zeus had shouted to abandon the rescue. The man wasn't the type to abandon anything unless it was absolutely necessary.

"Kevin ..." Matt whispered to himself. Zeus had abandoned Kevin in that hall because he knew Kevin was dead. *Dead ... Maddison is dead.*

She had been in his arms. So close to freedom. So close to safety. Damned from the start. Now, he would never have the chance to say goodbye. Matt wanted to cry, wanted to let every ounce of his tears wash away the pain, but his eyes wouldn't allow it. As if the sky had been painted with blood, a maroon haze filled Matt's vision.

Hades stood over Zeus. He kicked the sword from the defeated man's hand while nihanem readily dove to restrain the wounded god.

Everything started with him, Matt thought. From what he had picked up from the rest of the team, Maddison had ended their relationship to protect him from something. That something had to be Hades, and Matt was damn sure Hades would pay the price for it.

Kicking up grit from the floor, Matt sprinted toward the god of death. Ducking beneath the lunges and strikes of the undead army, he reached the executioner standing above Zeus. Lowering his shoulder, he attempted to put his full weight into Hades' stomach.

Hades turned his body to dodge and watched the rage-driven man hit the ground.

Recovering, Matt was just quick enough to see Hades' short sword swing down to split his peasant crown. Shoving forward, he caught the hilt and deflected it to the left. Then he grabbed Hades' jacket, balled his right fist, and cracked the demon across the face.

Recoiling from the strike, Hades managed to snag Matt's disheveled hair. Forced down, Matt's face met Hades' knee.

White light blinded his vision. Clones of the Corpse King spun about each other. Moving as one, the visions charged forward. Matt jumped back just enough to evade the taste of the metal tongue and prepared himself for a quick counterstrike.

What felt like a bean bag chair left out too long in the rain collided into Matt from behind. Breath-stealing fire ripped through his stomach. He wanted to scream, but the excruciating pain silenced him. Supported by his ribs resting on Hades' blade, Matt saw his reflection in pools of madness. So sure of success, he never even considered his own mortality.

Through their deadly connection, Matt could feel the muscles tensing behind the hilt of the blade. Zeus remained pinned and ready for execution. Over Hades' shoulder, the brilliant hair on Maddison's commandeered body flowed like a summer breeze. Poseidon and Hermes were locked in their own battles. There was no way out of this.

Forced from its burrow in Matt's gut, Hades dragged his sword laterally to Matt's left. Like a sheet of water holding together just before its surface tension is broken, his skin bulged before the sword ripped through. Slipping down his side, the half-crescent strip of his torn shirt began the descent of the whole. He collapsed to the floor, blood spewing and spurting from the gaping wound.

Lying on a bed of his own blood, Matt's sight of the ceiling began to sway. As if painted with alcohol, his wound began to burn, and his eyelids became drunk. Just over the darkness, creeping in from all sides, he could make out Zeus' beaten face as he was lifted from the floor into a final kneeling position.

Embers birthed into an odyssey. Pulling any remaining strength he had left, Matt cried out in agony. Delicate trails of smoke rose toward the rafters. Looking for their source, he realized they were billowing up from beneath his blood-drenched shirt.

Despite the medical anomaly and the torment it inflicted,

Matt found that he was able to sit up. While a tad wobbly, he tried to stand. Pain spiked in his side, and he fell to the ground. Clenching his teeth as the burning in his side spread to his eyes, Matt pushed through the pain and clambered to his feet.

Caged by bone, the rage within roared in Matt's throat. He hobbled toward his nemesis, leaned into a punch, and connected his fist with the back of Hades' head. Not allowing the chance of a reaction, Matt then kicked in Hades' leg, bringing the god to his knee.

Spinning on the ground, Hades swung the sword in a wide arc. Matt allowed the blade to pass just below his chin before sending a right hook to the man's eye. Gripping his foe's armed hand with his left, Matt wrapped his other hand around Hades' throat.

"Matt! No!" Zeus wailed as he bucked about on the ground.

Locking eyes with Matt, Hades looked even more sinister than he imagined.

"Miss me, Dragon?" Hades snarled. Wrapping his own fingers around Matt's choking hand, Hades began to call to the blood coursing within it.

Matt's entire body felt like it had entered a vacuum. Feeling blood pushing on the back of his eyes, he refused to concede. Blood began to run down his face from his eyes. He dug the tips of his fingers into the god of death's throat, the friction between their union sparking something deep within Matt. Beneath his palm, the pocket felt like an inferno. Ignoring the blistering heat, he tightened his grip.

Hades struggled to break free. He roared in a fit of agony and rage. Disengaging from their targets, the remaining nihanem charged toward the conjoined pair. Fire lashed out between Matt's fingers, originating from his palm as a flash before becoming a roaring flame. Like air pushing through cracks in a sinking ship, smoke escaped between Hades' teeth.

Feeding on a trickle of air and a stockpile of regret, the

flames escaping Matt's hand turned a dark shade of blue. Reflections of flames danced within Hades' blackening eyes. Illuminated, Matt could see every scar covering the demon's face. No longer able to scream, Hades' strength to fight began to wane. Trickles of blood flowed from Hades' eyes moments before flames visibly filled his mouth. Artemis' sword fell from the god's hand and clattered against the cement.

"OOF!" Strongly forced off Hades, Matt flew through the air. He rolled on the ground and managed to drag a hand on the floor and turn himself toward the attack. Looking more like Cerberus than an angel, Maddison stood between Matt and Hades' crumpled corpse. Tears ran down her now-pale skin. Like puppets with cut strings, the remaining nihanem lay motionless on the floor, their bodies in various states of dismemberment.

"Fool!" Although filled with rage, Maddison's new voice was angelic. Circling her legs, a hurricane of energy grew in ferocity. "You fucking fool!"

Sensing an incoming attack, Matt braced himself. Swinging her arm wide, Maddison lashed out with condensed blue *Essence*. Taking the full brunt of the luminescent strike to his chest, Poseidon's attack from behind failed as he flew back and clipped a pole with his shoulder. Rolling to a stop on the dusty floor and no longer conscious, Matt's cleaver slid out of his limp hand.

"Hermes, get him out of here!" Zeus shouted as he struggled to stand. Obliging, the bruised man ran to his fallen comrade. Looking over to where Nyx had been, all Zeus could see was a pool of blood and a trail leading away from it toward an open door. "Aphrodite, if that even really is you ... What did you do to Nyx?"

The goddess of beauty inhabiting Maddison's body gazed toward the pool of blood. "Less than she deserves." Reaching behind her, she drew tentacles of *Essence*, shot them over

Hades, and wrapped them around Artemis' sword. Recalled like a severed cord, the tendrils rushed back toward Aphrodite. She snatched the sword from the air and positioned the weapon at her side.

Meeting her eyes, an overwhelming sense of passion came over Matt. Even though Matt knew the woman before him was no longer the woman he had fallen in love with, he still yearned for her. With each step, his woes lifted and were replaced with a pillow of solace. Approaching carefully, he unwillingly drank from the poisoned cup.

A wounded Zeus pulled Matt backward, snapping him from the trance. With Zeus now in front of Matt, he and Maddison became the new contenders.

Lowering his weapon, Zeus softened his posture. "Don't do this. Just let him go."

"Stand aside."

"He didn't know," Zeus protested.

"He. Killed. Him."

"Aphrodite, please," Zeus begged.

Tenderly molded, Aphrodite's face formed a scowl. "That name died with me, as should have the rest of yours."

Making sure Hermes and Poseidon were safely out of the room, Zeus looked back at his resurrected friend. "You know why we took them. They had meaning then, and they still do now," he argued.

"Aphrodite. That name was fitting ... for a time. And that time has come to an end."

Behind Zeus, Matt looked over his previously burning hands, unaware of his brief ensnarement by Aphrodite. Whatever had happened between him and Hades hadn't left a mark on him. From the heat alone, his skin should have been peeled off. But his hands were still very much intact. Suddenly, Matt's mind was willingly forced in another direction. He raised his eyes toward Aphrodite, who radiated euphoria.

Nearby, Zeus struggled to keep himself from falling under her trance. Averting his gaze from Aphrodite, he squeezed the hilt of his sword to the point of pain.

"Oh, I am well beyond the need for eye contact," Aphrodite sneered.

Zeus' sword clinked loudly on the cement, his hand no longer willing to hold it. Electricity jumped between his fingers. Seeing the return of his ability, he looked up at Aphrodite. "Please ... the ritual ... broke the *Veil* ..."

Aphrodite brushed off his plea. "Protecting this world is no longer my concern. Nyx orchestrated everything that has happened: from my death to the tear in the *Veil*. If you had just let Hades take that city and resurrect me then, the *Veil* would still be intact, and Nyx would have been in that stasis pod instead. You allowed her to escape and betrayed Hades yet again. *You* couldn't protect the team. Killing Nyx is my only concern. You, more than anyone else, should understand that a man should never do a woman's job."

"We can still fix this!" Screaming to keep his sanity, Zeus' knees hit the cement and he fell upon his hands.

Extending her arm, Aphrodite placed the tip of her sword beneath Zeus' chin and lifted it up. "So incessant," she cooed, gazing into his eyes. "If you claim our names still hold meaning and I must continue to use mine ..." The goddess looked back at Hades' body. Peering into his charred eye sockets, a sweet smile blossomed. "Then my desire is for the one he gave me." Her smile faded into a scowl. "Call me Persephone."

EPILOGUE

In a tucked-away apartment on the South-East side of the city, a nihanim in a gray sweater stood like a statue beside a broken glass jar. A pile of headless and mutilated corpses, originating from the corner but having since fallen over, dominated the floor space. Their state of rot left bones exposed and the few faces unrecognizable.

Walls once beautiful and green were now peeled and molded from the trapped moisture. A single body, stripped of clothing and eaten by decay, lay in a bathtub full of crusted-over, congealed blood. Bursting to life, the human soup began to boil, spooking a rat balancing on the ceramic edge of the tub. Unbalanced by the bubbles, the floating corpse slipped beneath the surface.

Hands of liquid red flesh shot up from the depths and, in a desperate search, slapped at the walls of the tub. Finding hold on the side, one hand gripped the edge while the other plunked back down. The upper half of a man breached the surface like a shark. Walking a fine line between choking and gasping, the man struggled to pull air into his still-forming lungs.

As breathing became easier, a majority of the blood clinging to him was slowly absorbed. A deathly pale skin materialized in patches and soon spread like an infection over his entire body. Thousands of miniature maroon tendrils sprouted from the top of his head, growing long and falling down over his face. The tendrils quickly darkened into a starless night black. A slit in the eyelids formed, allowing him to open up his eyes and expose ghostly blue pupils.

Groaning in his gravelly voice from the painful rebirth, Hades bent his head and peered out through an opening in the curtain of hair. Expecting an awkward assist, he held up his open hand. Gray Sweater tightly gripped his hand and pulled him to a standing position. Naked and covered only in a thin film of runny blood, he looked at the pile of bodies before him.

Pulling a towel off of a nearby hanger, Hades patted his hair and face dry. He might have fallen, but Aphrodite lived once again. Peering through a dust-coated mirror, he examined his body. Where there had once been horrid scars, pristine flesh had taken their place.

Expecting the worst, Hades waved his hand toward the gray-sweatered nihanim, ordering it to retrieve clothing. He leaned on the faux marble bathroom sink and examined the specks of summer blue warming his hoarfrost irises. Would Aphrodite still love him after all this time? He had failed to protect her back in Herculaneum. Staying there was supposed to bring a time of unwinding from affairs, not the unwinding and severing of her thread.

Chewing on the corner of his lower lip, Hades pondered further. Most of his treacherous team had been there at her resurrection. Would they openly accept her? Due to the lives consumed for the sake of the ritual, would she be seen as a monster in need of slaying?

Pulled from his thoughts by a knock on the door, Hades pushed off the sink, fully expecting the nihanim to return with a single item—or nothing altogether. Instead, he was greeted by a full set of folded clothing in its hands: clean, dark blue jeans, three different colors and styles of shirts, and a single pair of black socks serving as the pile's crown.

The nihanim instinctively stepped aside to grant an unobstructed view when Hades noticed the top of someone's head behind Gray Sweater. Clutching a pair of boots in one hand

and a belt in the other was a nihanim of a young woman dressed in office attire; her crooked, bruised nose vainly attempted to distract from the rest of her face. Drawn, toasted-almond curtains exposed a row of broken and bent-backward teeth. Her lower jaw hung awkwardly on the right side. Placing down the clothing on a table in the living room, the two nihanem went in search of more towels.

Hades looked over the decorations and then stood in the apartment's bedroom. Although weakened by the blood rebirth, he now felt different from the prior day. His *Essence* now flowed freely as if by the removal of an asphyxiating tourniquet. With only the minor display by his soldiers since his rebirth, he was certain he had been blessed. His ability had returned to full strength.

"Well, this is an interesting turn," Hades said to himself with a sinister smile.

GLOSSARY

Essence
Supernatural energy radiating from the *Void* and absorbed by those touched by the *Void*.

Nihanim, plural **Nihanem**
A corpse controlled by a Death-Touched.

The Void
A demonic dimension that is parallel to our own. The veil between the two can sometimes be thin or cracked. Souls of the departed cross over and exist within it.

MATT AND HADES

WILL RETURN

FOG

The fog hung thick in the air as the sound of rustling leaves played in the wind. It was an early autumn morning, and the forest was filled with the songs of birds just waking. Ashlynn groggily slumped down the trail after a night in tents with friends, clothes still grimy from yesterday's hike.

Air from a cool breeze slipped through new tears in her jeans and kissed her cinnamon skin. Begging for rest, her aching feet cried out. Ignoring the plea, the young woman trudged onward down the path toward her pillowy bed, awaiting her at home, but how far that was, she could not recall. Despite the long walk ahead, the jostling of treats in her purple backpack quelled the worries of her rumbling stomach.

Before she knew it, the newly risen sun was already plummeting behind the tree line. Ashlynn observed the quickly darkening path before her. Torn between continuing her walk through the suffocating darkness beneath the trees or waiting until morning, she looked to the stars for answers. *If only I hadn't asked Christine to take my tent back with her*, she thought to herself.

As she looked through the opening in the trees above her, the branches gave her an idea. Her childhood training in the Wilderness Club was about to pay off. With a smile, she quickly climbed a tree and scanned the area for a desirable location. In the near distance, she observed a calm brook beside a small clearing; her campsite had been found.

Along her way to the clearing, Ashlynn found a sturdy stick to use as a support beam. After she arrived at her destination, she gathered various branches and set to work. Under the light of the moon, she constructed a shelter just as she had countless times before as a child.

Finished, she threw in her pack and crawled in. Her sleeping bag was soon out and spread across the shelter floor. She laid down and listened to the relaxing sounds from the brook. Its water gently splashed against rocks, adding to the serenity of the forest. As if laying in the gentle stream, sleep washed over her tired body.

CRACK!

Tearing Ashlynn from her sleep, the cracking of sticks could be heard outside the shelter. Crawling from her sleeping bag, Ashlynn slowly repositioned herself within the shelter and took a peek out. Spotting the source of the noise, she was filled with relief: a lonely deer drinking from the brook. Excitedly, yet quietly, she retrieved her camera from her bag.

Crouched within the shelter, she aimed her camera for the perfect shot. Just as the camera flashed, blood suddenly spewed from the deer's side. Although only visible for a second, she swore that she saw a blood-smeared face looking right at her from beside the deer.

Ashlynn covered her mouth and froze, all too aware that she was too late in attempting to muffle her own peep. Praying that her eyes had betrayed her, she gazed into the darkness. Confirming her fears, a figure moved toward her and into the moonlight.

Gnarled horns perched upon an elongated head appeared first. The taupe salamander-smooth skin of its upper torso gave way to the dingy layer of fur that covered the lower half of its hunched, lean body. With each hungry breath, the beast emitted a low, rumbling growl.

Fully bathed in moonlight, the creature rose up and stood upon its hooved hind legs. Bloody clumps of deer fur clung to claws at the end of human-like arms. Eyes black as charcoal surveyed the area in the terrified woman's direction.

Ashlynn slowly retreated deeper into her shelter, hoping the creature would just go away. Curled up in the back of her shelter, she could hear the beast sniffing the air just a few feet away. Beads of cold sweat formed as her heart beat louder and louder. As if her prayers had been answered, the creature returned to the deer.

Minutes turned into a millennium as the deer was devoured. Sounds of tearing flesh with the occasional snapping of bone filled the emptiness of the quiet forest. Not even the wind dared disturb the feast.

Finished with its kill, the creature turned to leave. As Ashlynn adjusted herself, a twig from her shelter wall scratched her arm. She let out a startled cry. Holding her breath, she listened for any telltale signs of the beast's location.

Silence.

Suddenly, claws appeared and wrapped themselves around a branch at the entrance of the shelter. As the predator lowered its head to look in, Ashlynn grabbed her bag and used it as a shield to burst through the back of the shelter. Leaping out of her fallen construction, she ran into the forest.

Scattered trees turned into a dark labyrinth of pine and oak. Despite her speed, the creature could be heard not far behind. Ashlynn wanted to look back, but knew she could stumble and become its next victim.

Piercing the darkness, a dim light shone through the trees. Desperately, she ran towards it. Once she was out of the forest, she could find refuge in the arms of civilization. She broke through the trees, only to discover a single lamp post providing light for a wooden billboard that displayed a map of the trails.

Terror constricted her heart as the beast gripped her backpack and pulled her to the ground. Towering over the woman, the beast raised an arm and brandished its dagger-like claws.

Ashlynn slipped from her backpack and tried to dodge. Razor-sharp nails tore through her shirt, drawing blood. Ashlynn clambered to her feet and ran without any sense of direction.

Not willing to give up, she spotted a tree with low-hanging branches. *I might not be able to outrun this thing, but I can definitely out-climb it.* She confidently thought to herself. Jumping high, she grabbed onto the closest branch. Galvanized by her will to live and drunk on adrenaline, she latched onto the first branch and lifted herself upon it. Bringing her leg up, she rested her knee against the rough bark and reached up for the next branch. Pain shot through her hanging leg as the beast dug its nails into her calf. Ashlynn let out a high-pitched wail. With her hanging leg, she managed to kick the creature, gaining her freedom and losing her shoe in the process.

Demons seemed to surround her as she climbed up the tree. Every twig that caught on her clothing was another murderous talon. The sounds of the creature's grunts only came closer the higher she went. Fighting through the pain of her injured leg, she moved faster.

Covered in sweat, each branch became slicker than the last. As she tightened her fingers around a branch, a sharp pain entered her palm. Instinctively, her hand released its grip. That's when she felt it. A claw wrapped around her ankle and yanked her downward. Unable to maintain a solid grip, the woman began her descent.

Sounds of snapping twigs and bone-shattering collisions against sturdy branches violated her senses. Finally reaching the bottom, the ground seemed to shake with the force of her impact. Bloody and battered, the woman gasped for breath. Excruciating pain radiated from her chest due to a collapsed lung.

Helpless, she watched as the monster leapt from the tree and landed with a resolute thud beside her. Standing tall and silhouetted by moonlight, the horned beast resembled the King of Hell.

Blood filled her sight as the first blow was struck. Ashlynn tried to crawl away but was dragged back. Helpless against the attacks tearing through her, she was at the mercy of the beast. Each slice through her flesh was more agonizing than the last. After an eternity, the beast howled as it noticed the bushy tail of a squirrel and ran after it.

The attack was over, but the damage had been done. Tears ran down her face in a steady stream. Unable to wipe the tears away and torn to ribbons, her arms lay lifeless beside her.

Feeling increasingly faint, an icy cold permeated Ashlynn to her bones as blood formed a spot around her, mocking her attempt at life. Shallow breaths brought with them the heavy taste of iron.

The sun started to rise above the tree line as her last breath was released. The fog was thick in the air as the sound of rustling leaves played in the wind. It was an early autumn morning, and the forest was filled with the songs of birds just waking.

ABOUT ATMOSPHERE PRESS

Atmosphere Press is an independent, full-service publisher for excellent books in all genres and for all audiences. Learn more about what we do at atmospherepress.com.

We encourage you to check out some of Atmosphere's latest releases, which are available at Amazon.com and via order from your local bookstore:

Icarus Never Flew 'Round Here, by Matt Edwards

COMFREY, WYOMING: Maiden Voyage, by Daphne Birkmeyer

The Chimera Wolf, by P.A. Power

Umbilical, by Jane Kay

The Two-Blood Lion, by Nick Westfield

Shogun of the Heavens: The Fall of Immortals, by I.D.G. Curry

Hot Air Rising, by Matthew Taylor

30 Summers, by A.S. Randall

Delilah Recovered, by Amelia Estelle Dellos

A Prophecy in Ash, by Julie Zantopoulos

The Killer Half, by JB Blake

Ocean Lessons, by Karen Lethlean

Unrealized Fantasies, by Marilyn Whitehorse

The Mayari Chronicles: Initium, by Karen McClain

Squeeze Plays, by Jeffrey Marshall

JADA: Just Another Dead Animal, by James Morris

Hart Street and Main: Metamorphosis, by Tabitha Sprunger

Karma One, by Colleen Hollis

Ndalla's World, by Beth Franz

Adonai, by Arman Isayan

The Journey, by Khozem Poonawala

Stolen Lives, by Dee Arianne Rockwood

ABOUT THE AUTHOR

ALLEN G. REBOT is a lover of whiskey, wine, and well written words. Born in the quaint town of Chicago, he attended
the only school within a day's horse ride, Northeastern Illinois
University, to receive his first degree. To break free from the
thriving local beaver trade, he ventured to the distant school
of Colorado Technical University for his MBA in Human Re-
source Management. In 2022 he married the love of his life,
and now enjoys hiding love notes to his beautiful wife around
the house and within his writing.